Exposed

The Education of Sarah Brown

MICHELE E. GWYNN

An M.E. Gwynn Publication

Contents

Acknowledgements

It takes a great deal of support to complete any project, and I've been fortunate to have such a wonderful group of friends and family cheering me on. First, thank you so much to my whip-cracking muse, fellow author Jami Brumfield (*The Winters Saga, Lone Wolf Rising and Vampire Princess Rising; PBI Case Files, Dating a Werewolf Series*) for brainstorming with me, and always asking me how the book was going, basically guilting me into writing a few more chapters. It's because of Jami's encouragement that this story made it all the way to "The End." Thank you, my friend!

I'd also like to thank my beta readers for offering their unfiltered, honest opinions of the book so I could make sure it was the best possible telling of this tale. Thanks to my mom for not grouching about all the late nights I stayed up writing into the wee hours. Big thank you to my fabulous language editors, Silke Beischl, my brother, Bill Michael, and R. Tagliavacche. If any of the phrases say anything completely off the wall from what I explained in the book, it's their fault!

None of us gets anywhere without help, and I'm ever thankful for the amazing group of people in my life who encourage, assist, collaborate, and cheer for me. With that said, I'd be terribly remiss not to thank you, for choosing my book to add to your reading list. Thank you, and happy reading!

Checkpoint, Berlin Novels

Exposed: The Education of Sarah Brown
The Evolution of Elsa Kreiss
The Redemption of Joseph Heinz
Checkpoint Novella
The Making of Herman Faust
A Checkpoint Prequel
Welcome to the Checkpoint, Berlin Detective Series, your passport to a
world of dark passions, international crime, and ever-present danger.

Description

A Dream Vacation Turns into a Nightmare...
"You think someone took him, don't you?" Understanding dawned on Elsa, and then she realized that her brother may have been abducted. Tears flooded her green eyes again, smearing mascara down her cheeks. "Sarah. Oh, mein Got! What am I going to do?"
"You're going to hold it together because Anno needs you. And until we know there's something to worry about, we should keep cool heads, okay? Keep it together, Elsa." Sarah took her by the hand and led the way back to the living room where she calmly talked Elsa through calling the police again. It took about thirty minutes for the detectives to come back. KriminalKommissar Heinz, in particular, did not seem pleased. *But that might just be his normal countenance.* Sarah gave them the information on what they found and pointed out that Anno's phone was still in the apartment. They both looked at the washcloth, sniffed it, and immediately pulled out gloves and a plastic bag to put the cloth into.
"You should've shown us this before, Fraulein Kreiss." Heinz gave Elsa a stern look. Elsa's face registered the slight in his address, but before she could reply, her friend spoke up.
"She didn't know this when you first came. I'm the one who found it."
Sarah stood and faced the detective.

"And who are you? How did you know where to find this?" He started treating Sarah like a suspect and she was not the least bit pleased with his attitude.

"I'm Sarah Brown, friend of Elsa and Anno. I didn't know where to find it. I simply did what most rational people would do and looked around his room. Elsa was with me, and we found it together. You should have done this the first time you were here!" Sarah's temper blazed to the surface.

Prologue

*B*erlin, Germany
Fall, 2013

He was beautiful. Absolutely the embodiment of divine creation with his golden curls, blue eyes, and the promise of perfect cheekbones beneath a touch of what people refer to as lingering baby fat. It wasn't fat, per se, but the roundness of youth on the boy's face that would fade away in another year or so. At fourteen, he was angelic. Striking. One could almost see the bones stretching and growing like a young sapling that would one day be a mighty oak tree. For now, they lacked the musculature of a grown man. The limbs were long and the back straight. His blue eyes sparkled when he laughed and were fringed with thick, dark-blond lashes. His cheeks were painted naturally with two spots of color, and his lips, as they spread across his face with a hearty laugh, were lush and full. Even his teeth were pearly white. Perfection.

The sight of him took the man's breath away.

The boy was tossing a ball to a young woman with red hair. She was older, a sister. Just as lovely and striking, but not so much as the boy. The man watched as the two played a game of catch in the park. He had come to this park every day in the last two weeks since he first sighted the glorious creature. On the third day, they returned with a Frisbee and a picnic lunch. He followed them that day as he did today. They left, and the man trailed them, walking far enough behind not to be noticed, casually swinging his cane as if enjoying an afternoon stroll.

They lived in an old, faded yellow apartment building with too many units to discover which one was theirs. He waited. Two hours later, she left carrying a black duffel bag over her shoulder. He followed her for four blocks where she took the stairs down to the tube and hopped into a car that took them deep into the industrial center of the city. Tourists didn't frequent this side of Berlin. Here, native Berliners came out to party at the clubs and to indulge themselves in the bars. Then there were the others who blended into the hip party crowd, but then slipped down back-alley staircases to a world most didn't know existed. That's where she went now without hesitation.

He waited, then followed. The staircase led to a steel door painted black. The logo at eye level was three large letters—XXX—painted red. Above those in bright neon yellow were the words 'Club Sexo.' He went inside and was greeted by a glass-enclosed ticket booth which contained a shirtless, dark-haired man wearing a leather collar decorated with metal studs sitting behind the counter. To the left was a door, but it was closed.

"You have an appointment?" he asked.

"No. No, I don't." The man stood there, looking at the list of club rules hanging on the wall behind the host inside the ticket booth.

"You have to have an appointment." Shirtless pointed at the rules behind him. Sure enough, that was rule number one.

"How do I make an appointment?" the man asked.

Shirtless gave an assessing glance to the man in the suit. He noted the gentleman dressed well; seemed distinguished, even, with his groomed white goatee and hair accented by dark eyebrows above cold blue eyes. His accent wasn't quite German; more like Dutch. Still, he looked much like the caliber of men who came and went nightly.

"You go online to this website." He handed him a business card through the dip under the glass window. "Pick who you wish to see, whatever your particular thing is. All our dommes have bios that describe their specialties. We take all major credit cards, and you pay up front online before walking through that door. The charge shows up as CX3 LLC to protect your privacy. Once your appointment is made, you'll receive a confirmation email or text, your choice, and you just show up. Oh, and no refunds."

"Thank you." The man took the card and put it in his inside breast pocket. He tipped his hat and left.

He made his way back to the UBahn in the quickly falling temperature and found the tube heading back toward the side of town where he was staying. Once back in his room, he shed his suit jacket and pulled the card out of his pocket. He set down his cap and cane next to the jacket. Sitting on the edge of his bed, he pulled out his mobile and surfed the internet for the website on the card.

The splash page asked him if he was over eighteen and to press 'Continue' to indicate he was, and that he accepted the rules for the site. He chuckled to himself. Beyond the firewall was an 'About Us' section and an icon for 'Our Talent.' He tapped that key. Several images popped up of women in various bondage costumes looking alternately fierce and sexy. He found them amusing. Scrolling through, one image stood out. A red-haired woman in red lace bra and panties wearing thigh high red leather boots. She had a red leather riding crop in her hands and appeared to be smacking it on her palm suggestively. Mistress Elsa, it read.

He tapped the image and her bio sprang up. *Mistress Elsa is an experienced Domme in the art of bondage for beginners to professional submissives to include extreme roping. Mistress Elsa will bind you, beat you, and/or humiliate you. Your pain is her pleasure. Make your appointment today.*

The man smiled. He changed screens to NOTES and typed. Message saved, he put the card into his wallet and tossed it onto the bedside table. He thought about the boy and young woman. His thoughts went to dark places. Feeling edgy, he stood, picking up his jacket, swinging it over his shoulders, and sliding his arms in.

He grabbed his cap and cane. Walking toward the door, he checked his breast pocket for his room key card. Satisfied it was there, he left.

Out on the street, he turned right and headed toward the tube station. A ten-minute ride south and he was stepping onto the platform. He pulled his coat tighter around him. The night air was cool in September. Up the stairs and onto the street the wind met him head on. This was not a decent side of town. This was a slightly seedier area of Berlin right on the edge of the best tourist spots. Here, prostitutes plied their trade. Women from Eastern Europe ended up trapped in this lifestyle after being brought in by sex traffickers. Most were strung out on drugs. They looked dirty, ragged, and pathetic, old before their time, and used up. The man walked past these women in their platform heels and short bargain basement skirts as they called out to him.

One block beyond he came upon a few young hustlers. Three of them. One was a tall, lean black boy with a shaved head. His shoulders were broad and his arms muscular. *Not him.* The second one had dark hair and a feminine stance. He smoked a cigarette while talking and gesturing wildly with his hands. *Italian. No good. And too many facial piercings.* The third one was more clean-cut with short blond hair. His jaw was squared, and he had a dimple in his chin. This one hadn't quite yet filled out. His limbs were slim and well-formed, and he wasn't overly tall, either. He appeared to be about seventeen, maybe eighteen. *He would do.*

The man walked over and asked the blond male for a cigarette. The other two hustlers gave him the once-over, noting the quality cut of his clothing, their expressions envious. They waved at their friend and moved off, leaving him alone with the man.

Berlin, Germany
Nighttime

The temperature dropped as soon as the sun went down. Anthony de Luca walked around downtown, trying to capture the nightlife of the city on camera. The images would be part of an article he'd been contracted to write for an online tour guide about Berlin. He was being paid for the job, compensated for his hotel and expenditures, and they promised to promote his guidebooks. He was famous for unearthing the unusual about any city he photographed along with the normal tourist sites. With that in mind, he found himself on a side of town that wasn't quite the best. Still, it was all part of Berlin.

For fun, he'd photographed a few street walkers trying to lure in some business. They were bold, approaching cars as they slowed down to ogle the local 'talent.'

As he aimed and clicked the shutter, he noticed a distinguished looking man walking quickly out of a back alley with a young blond man following behind. The blond walked fast and shouted at the man in the cap. He was speaking in rapid German, so Anthony had no idea what he was saying, but he seemed pissed.

The blond reached out and grabbed the gentleman's arm and tugged. That was when Anthony noticed the cane in the older man's other hand. That cane came around and connected with the blond's head—hard.

Shocked, Anthony aimed his camera again, and began shooting picture after picture. The older man continued to strike the younger one on the head, back, shoulders, and legs just outside the alley. Bleeding now, the blond raised his arms to fend off the blows while trying to land a couple of weak punches. He wasn't strong enough to defend himself against the older man.

Two men came running, one black and the other white with dark hair, and chased off the older man. Anthony kept shooting.

As he half-limped, half-ran away, the older gentleman looked around him. His eyes landed on Anthony standing across the street with the camera in his hands. The man's panicked look changed to one of dark anger.

"Shit!" Anthony turned and ran back toward the city center. He didn't wait around to see whether the older man would follow him.

The man did attempt to follow, but Anthony was soon swallowed up into the crowd, gone.

The old gentleman stopped to catch his breath. He wasn't worried that the blond hustler would report him to the police for not paying for play. He hadn't intended not to pay him but discovered too late that he'd left his wallet in his room on the bedside table. No other way to deal with that situation since the deed was done, but someone else might report him to the police. Someone else with an expensive camera, who was not a prostitute trying to protect himself. Someone who was most likely legitimate. Someone who now had his image on film committing a crime.

He'd have to leave Germany sooner than he planned. He'd have to leave that night; go before he could set up a meeting with Mistress Elsa. A sigh escaped his thin lips.

As he pondered the situation, a Volkswagon with a familiar blue stripe and the word, *POLIZEI*, across the doors drove by, slowing down. The driver, a cop with hard, dark eyes and graying hair at his temples peered out, watching. Next to him, his partner, a woman, checked the road ahead, scanning the sidewalks. The man offered a brief smile and gave a slight nod of his head before continuing down the street at a leisurely pace. The police car made its way another block down before turning right and disappearing out of sight.

The man exhaled, whipping a handkerchief out of his coat pocket and mopping his forehead. It was a close call, one he intended not to repeat. He hailed a taxi. A quick trip back to his hotel had him packed and off to Tegel within the hour. He had no time to spare. If the man with the camera had reported him to the *Polizei*, his image would be on an all-points bulletin shortly, and he'd be unable to get out of the country and back home. He'd find another way to gain what he wanted.

Chapter 1

The flight was long—twelve hours and forty minutes long to be exact—and that didn't include getting to the airport two and half hours early for an international flight. *Thank God for being able to afford first class*, thought Sarah. *Otherwise, I might never have gotten any sleep.* This was her very first transatlantic flight, first any kind of flight. Despite the stress of the past several weeks, she was enjoying herself, even relaxing finally.

As the Boeing 747 flew her to a new chapter in her life, she reflected over the last five years. Her mother, Mary, developed breast cancer, a condition she blamed on her husband's animal lust, something she grew to believe, more as the years passed. She called such lust a sin against God outside the need for procreation. After her daughter, Sarah Ann Brown, was born, her mother found more reasons and ways to avoid intimacy with Ed Brown, eventually driving him to seeking sex elsewhere. Unfortunately, for Mary, this also led to Ed finding love and eventually leaving her. Still, Mary would not grant him a divorce. Instead, she maintained all the financial security of marriage without the benefit of a loving partner. Her fundamentalist mentality grew along with her bitterness, which she heaped upon her only child, Sarah.

For her part, the young blonde-haired, brown-eyed girl kept to herself, having few friends due to the embarrassment of having a mother who preached at them about their sinful ways. When others around her began dating, Sarah spent her time in the local library, reading. Anything to avoid being dragged off to the Church of Christ alongside her mother. It was there; she'd discovered romance novels. That was Sarah's only introduction to relationships, and when she'd turned eighteen and could check out books from the adult section, her only education about sex.

After Mary's diagnosis, she declined further, wrapping herself in scripture, and berating Sarah when her jeans were too tight, her skin showed below her neck, or when a young man happened to smile upon her while out.

"Cover yourself! I did not raise a slut to be a whore for Satan," she would rant. This level of fanaticism seemed to increase after chemotherapy robbed Mary of her hair and what was left of her health.

A home-health nurse was hired by Ed to take care of his estranged wife, and only out of love for his daughter. He knew the burden the girl carried upon her young shoulders after he left. Guilt ate him up even as he selfishly stayed away, living with his new girlfriend, and starting a new family. Meanwhile, Sarah graduated high school in her hometown of Helotes, Texas, and while friends and classmates went on to college, she remained behind, going to work at the library she'd come to love and see as a haven from the ugliness that was her life.

Her days were spent working, and her nights, caring for her mother, who'd reached stage four in her cancer. Each morning, Sarah would rise, dress for the day, and then bathe her mother, dressing her, feeding her, and making sure she took her morning medication before Vangie arrived to take over her care for the day. Most days, her mother went off on a tangent, spewing bible verses, and reminding Sarah to remain chaste and pure. She still felt a little guilty over her relief when, after prolonged illness, Mary lost her ability to speak.

The silence was a blessing.

As her mother spent more time sleeping, Sarah stayed longer at the library after hours. Vangie knew the girl needed the break. It was there, within the quiet walls of the building, after her co-workers left for the day, that she would pick out a new book, and curl up into one of the overstuffed chairs. It was also there that she first explored her sexuality. Lost in the tale of a Duke seducing the daughter of an Earl, she'd first felt desire. The book went into detail on how he touched the woman's breasts, caressed her nipples, and reaching further down, slid his fingers deep within. Having never experienced more than a stolen, wet kiss from a boy, Sarah had no reference point for comparison.

Knowing she was alone, she'd continued to read, but allowed her own fingers to skim her body, and touch all the places the duke touched Henrietta. The sensations were pleasant, but it wasn't until she'd reached her core, sliding her hand inside her jeans, and letting her fingertips rub her most sensitive spot, that she first felt the tingles. As she read on, she rubbed harder, until a wave of passion sent her over the edge. After enjoying her first orgasm, there was no going back, no putting the genie back in the bottle. She wanted more. Sarah knew she would wither away and die inside if she didn't escape the living hell that was her life. She knew she needed to get out into the world and discover herself.

She had prayed to God for an answer. That answer came three weeks ago when Mary Brown finally passed away peacefully in the night. Sarah awoke on that Monday morning, dressing for work as usual, and then entering her mother's room to get her prepared for the day before Vangie arrived. That was when she'd noticed her mother lying there, eyes closed, not breathing.

Instead of sorrow, she'd felt only intense relief. Numbness followed.

Over the next several weeks, she'd planned a funeral and discovered that Mary had a rather large life insurance policy, one that named her only daughter as beneficiary. Sarah felt the first prickling of tears as she realized her mother had shown her in the only way she really knew how that she cared. With the money necessary to settle debts, she still had plenty left over in which to break free of the tiny Texas town where she'd felt trapped for so long.

She made plans, shopping to replace her drab, utilitarian wardrobe with modern, sexy clothes including a few lacy undergarments from Victoria's Secret. She purchased a Louie Vuitton luggage set, and then sat down in front of the world globe her father had given her for her desk. With new hope in her heart, she spun it, letting it go and then stopping it abruptly with one finger. This was her first destination.

A trip was planned for Europe, one that would take her first to Barcelona, and then to Berlin. From there, wherever a train took her. Sarah wanted to experience it all, freedom, love, sex. It was past time. She was a twenty-three-year-old virgin, and it was time to put that into the past. She booked her fare, and hopped a flight out of San Antonio to Atlanta, Hartsfield Airport. There, she boarded her flight to Spain, and she spared no expense.

First class accommodation featured reclining seats that let her stretch out. She slept for at least four hours, fitfully, on the overnight flight from Atlanta to Barcelona. Somewhere around halfway through the journey, Sarah awakened from a disturbing dream, one in which she was trying to leave her house, but every time she walked out the front door, she ended up back inside. And her mother was yelling from her sickbed, *"You're never going to leave me! I'm not letting you go."*

Rattled, she looked around at her fellow passengers. An older woman sat across the aisle to her left. She'd fallen asleep partially reclined with a book on her lap. She was snoring loudly, her mouth hanging open. Next to the snorer was a man who was most likely her husband. He lay turned toward the side of the plane with his backside pointing toward his wife. As Sarah watched, the man farted. Sarah stifled a giggle. *So much for first class!*

Her eyes wandered to her right. The seat next to her was not occupied. But the next one over was filled with a rather large woman. She sort-of oozed into the unoccupied seat. The woman was wearing a bright print muumuu-style dress in fuchsias and orange tones. Her eyes were covered with one of those sleeping masks. She snored lightly with both hands resting on her protruding belly.

Across that aisle lay a man, sound asleep. He was long, indicating his height. He'd kicked off his shoes—an expensive looking pair of brown leather loafers. He was wearing a dark blue suit with a lighter blue button-down shirt. The suit jacket lay on the empty seat next to him along with a briefcase. Further perusal revealed a handsome face in repose. He had a strong jawline, dark brows, long black eyelashes, and dark brown wavy hair. His lips were full and slightly parted. Sarah wondered at the color of his eyes.

Her gaze wandered back down over the rise and fall of his chest. It was wide and strong. He looked fit, like he worked out regularly. His hands, at rest at his sides, were tanned with well-manicured fingernails. Her mind instantly began fantasizing about who he was, whether he was single, or if he had a wife or lover waiting for him wherever he was traveling. Her eyes returned to his lips. They looked soft, inviting, yet firm. She wondered what it would feel like to be kissed by a sexy, grown man with nice lips. Her lids drooped as her thoughts turned inward as she tried to guess at the color of his eyes.

"Can I get you anything?"

Sarah jerked, startled. "What?"

A smiling flight attendant stood behind her cart of drinks. "Sorry. Didn't mean to wake you. Would you like some juice or a soft drink?"

Sarah shook her head no.

The flight attendant looked at the old woman and man and moved on.

Removing the blanket, Sarah stood, heading toward the lavatory. Minutes later, arriving back at her seat, she noticed the cabin lights were on, and the man had awakened. He was sitting up, sleepy-eyed, but still very handsome. He looked at her and slowly smiled as if they'd shared something intimate. His eyes were green.

Amsterdam

April 2014

It had been seven months since the redeye flight out of Tegal, and still he couldn't stop thinking about the angel he'd left behind in Berlin. It had been a long time since his soul craved someone so much; not since his Paul was a little boy. *It's really too bad that they have to grow up,* he thought. Paul, with his blue eyes and dark curls framing his cherubic face, ignited a fire inside that threatened to consume him. But having Paul, so sweet and trusting, and so easily led, quenched that fire with his innocence. The tears that fell from those big blue eyes were like rain on the hottest day, and so he'd caused a storm as often as he could get away with it, never minding that he damned himself with each infraction, every assault upon the boy. But Paul grew—into a man filled with rage. His hatred was an ugly thing despite the fact that Paul was still every bit as beautiful fully grown as he'd been while just a boy. Men, however, just wouldn't do. He did still love Paul, very much, although the lifestyle he'd chosen—irresponsible and incorrigible—was not one of which he approved. *Women! Nothing but women and more women. Women are simply cattle, good for nothing except for making money!* His business relied on using women, and it relied on the very type of men he eschewed—men like Paul.

There'd been many young boys in the interim, but none that possessed his mind, body, and soul the way in which Paul had, until the angel of Berlin. *I must have him, but how?*

He picked up his mobile and searched through his contacts. Picking the one he needed, he hit the CALL button.

"I'm not available now, but you know what to do." BEEP. The voicemail began to record.

"It's me. I know you don't want to hear from me, but I have a business proposition for you. Call me back." The man ended the call and stared out the window of his office overlooking the famed Red-Light District in Amsterdam.

On the street below, customers and tourists mixed. You could always tell the difference because the tourists stopped to gawk while the regulars walked with purpose to their chosen destinations. On the corner, the two famous old whores, twins Lulu and Merry Vandane, were signing autographs and taking pictures with the gawkers. He remembered when he first began his business running a brothel. He knew next to nothing about the ins and outs of such, but he knew men wanted women, and they would pay good money for no-fuss sex. He tried charming the two old Hoerens to come work for him, knowing their fame and the fact that they were twins would draw customers. They wouldn't budge. *The bitches,* he thought. They'd played hardball with him, demanding seventy percent of their own take, leaving not much for him, but as they pointed out, just having their names on the list would bring in men eager to sample Amsterdam's legalized prostitutes, so when their dance card was full, the other working gals could take the overflow. The gambit worked and he'd made a lot of money for the two years Lulu and Merry had worked for him before going into business for themselves, and eventually retiring after fifty years servicing every Tom, Dick, and Harry that wandered into their doorway. They'd written a few books and put out a documentary film, and now they were considered one of Amsterdam's treasures. Tourists came to meet them and take 'selfies' with the very type of women they would spit on anywhere else in the world. He both hated and grudgingly admired them.

A knock on the door interrupted his thoughts.

"Enter," he said with a growl.

"Sorry to bother you, but Yeline is garnering complaints again. She refused two customers this morning." Daniel, the effeminate young man who was his secretary, stood with his hands folded in front of him, head down, his glasses threatening to slide off his slender nose.

"Yeline," he said with distaste. Yeline was a Ukrainian import who often forgot her place. He paid her well and still she caused him problems.

"What for this time," he demanded.

"She claims the first one smelled like fish, and the other had bad teeth and severe body odor." Daniel wanted to laugh but knew better. His boss could be nice when he wanted to be, but his mean streak was legendary.

"She's a whore! What does she care how they smell? They come in, fuck, and leave within fifteen minutes. Surely, she can hold her breath that long?"

The young man stood quietly and waited for an order.

"You tell Yeline that if she turns away another paying customer, I'll not only not pay her, but I won't send her grandmother any more of her wages, either, and the old bitch can freeze come winter. Further, if she does this again, I will personally ensure that every dockhand and unbathed fishmonger gets a free pass to her room."

The man's anger was palpable. The secretary turned to leave, intending to immediately deliver the message; the sooner the better for Yeline. He hated seeing the girls get into trouble, and Yeline had always been nice to him. He was stopped at the door by a hand on his shoulder. He froze. His boss could move fast for an older man with a cane.

"Is everything set for tonight's show at The Dungeon?" The Dungeon was one of his boss's many sex clubs. It catered to those who liked a little pain and domination--or a lot--in their sex lives.

Relieved that was all he wanted, Daniel turned his head and replied, "Yes. All the lighting and stage props have been set up. Thomas is overseeing the final details, but he said there is nothing to worry about. Your guests will get an amazing showing."

He patted the young man's shoulder. "Good, good. Now go and tell Yeline what I've said and tell her this is her final warning. Any more of her bitching and it's back to that shithole mining town she came from."

Daniel walked out, shuddering. Deportation was the last thing Yeline would want, but compliance with his boss's rules was just as bad more often than not. The poor girl was stuck, what with his boss keeping her passport locked away with the others. That was how he controlled these women. Sure, his business was legal, but the means by which he employed many of the women was not. The government regulations were lax, and inspectors could be bought off cheaply. It was the illegal and ugly side of a publicly legal business. As long as the government received their tax payments, they were happy not to look too closely.

Back in the office, the man looked impatiently at his phone. Paul wouldn't call him back. He knew this, but he also had business to attend to that night. *Tomorrow would be soon enough to pay the recalcitrant pup a visit.* He picked up his overcoat and cane, preparing to leave. He had guests to entertain this evening and there was still much to do. As he walked out of the office, the two employees left behind released a collective sigh of relief.

Chapter 2

Barcelona was gorgeous! Sarah had barely flagged down a taxi to take her to her hotel before she began to look around at everything like an excited teenager. The sun was shining in the morning sky. People were going about their day, looking very stylish while doing so. She noted that Europeans dressed far better than Americans. So far, she hadn't seen one man exposing his underwear while wearing baggy pants or one woman dressed less than 'to the nines.' Back home, it was normal to see women wearing sweatpants, hair undone, and without makeup while out. Here, the women presented well; very chic.

The cab pulled up in front of the Hotel Claris. The five-star structure was in the middle of town next to the Passeig de Gràcia, which featured an abundance of shops for tourists.

Sarah pulled out her wallet. "Por favor, ¿cuánto?"

"Dieciséis euro, setenta, señorita." The cab driver tipped his hat respectfully after Sarah handed over the fare with tip.

"Que disfrute su estancia," he said, smiling at the crazy American girl who had just over-tipped him. *(Enjoy your stay.)*

"Gracias, señor."

A bellhop approached, taking Sarah's luggage and placing it on a trolley. "Bienvenida."

"Hola." Sarah smiled as they walked into the lobby and approached the front desk. She checked in, handing over her passport for inspection. She was given the key to a room on the fourth floor.

Riding up the elevator, the young Spanish bellhop tried to engage her in conversation, but it quickly went south as he realized her Spanish was limited and his English, non-existent. He looked to be all of eighteen—a very young-looking eighteen. Sarah thought he was quite cute and would be handsome once he grew up, but for now, he appeared far too young for her taste. She craved a man with maturity and sophistication, someone who could take-charge, and knew his way around the female body. This boy looked as if he hadn't even experienced his first kiss yet.

They exited the lift and turned right, walking down the hall. Her room was midway down on the right. Inside, the modern décor welcomed her. Wood floors, contemporary furnishings, and every amenity greeted her tired but excited eyes.

She tipped the bellboy, thanking him in her meager Spanish. He smiled awkwardly at her, then turned to leave her alone in her room.

Sarah sat down on the edge of the bed and lay back, falling onto the thick duvet. *Whatever will I do first?* Her stomach grumbled.

"Guess that answers that!" Laughing, she got up and began to unpack a few items. Once she'd hung her clothes to get the wrinkles out, she picked up her toiletries and headed off to the bathroom for a quick hot shower. An hour later, Sarah was refreshed, dressed in jeans, colorful cork-heeled sandals and a bright peach tank top. She was ready to find the nearest restaurant. It was nearly lunch time. Room key and purse in hand, she walked out into the corridor and down to the lifts.

In the lobby, she approached the front desk and addressed the female clerk, who stood smiling at her in her uniform of white blouse and blue skirt and blazer.

"Excuse me. Can you recommend a good place to eat close by?"

"Sí, sí. My cousin owns a very good place. You will like it. You just go two blocks down and turn right at the second street. It will be on the left. It is called La Mediterránea."

"Gracias." Sarah thanked the girl and turned to leave.

"Tell them Maryella sent you, okay?"

"Okay, I will. Thanks."

Two men entering the hotel paused to ogle Sarah as she walked by, admiring the sway of her hips in her new jeans. Unaware of the attention, she walked through the lobby doors and out into the bright sunshine. The sound of cars driving by and people talking as they moved along the sidewalks greeted her ears. She headed in the direction indicated by Maryella. Her stomach grumbled again. *Okay, okay. We're going!*

The heat of the day enveloped her as she stepped out into the fresh air. All around, new sights caught Sarah's eye. She found herself looking at everything, trying to soak it all in. She stopped now and again to peer into storefront windows and admire their wares. Around her, people passed going about their day, either to work or just enjoying leisure time. All were dressed beautifully, adorned in ways that complimented the architectural feel of this small portion of Barcelona. A smile bloomed on her lips. For the first time in a long time, Sarah felt free, and even happy.

∗ ∗ ∗

Anthony fished around in his pockets for his keys. Locating them, he locked the door to his room in the pensión and hoisted his camera bag over his shoulder. The day was hot, bright, and all around him, shapes, colors, and textures begged to be photographed. Two weeks in

Spain had provided a wealth of material for his next book on travel, but it had begun to get a little lonely. The women of Spain were beautiful, but his poor Spanish hadn't helped him score any time with any single, sexy señoritas. He was both horny and hungry, and since his limited grasp of the language focused on ordering food and inquiring about prices, he knew it would be another day by himself with only good food to comfort him by day, and his hand to alleviate his ever-present lust at night. He opened the door to his rental vehicle and tossed his camera bag in the backseat. He unrolled the windows to let the heat out of the car, then put it in drive and maneuvered onto the road.

Back in New York City, Anthony de Luca was a respected photographer, whose five books on global travel had set him up for life. He focused on places off the beaten path and always included information about the locals, their history, folklore, and odds and ends that are just not found in most travel books. De Luca's descriptions were broken down into simple lay terms and then brought to life by vivid pictorials. Traveling also afforded Anthony many other photographic opportunities that, although he didn't necessarily need the money, still lined his pockets further and increased his fame in the field. He was known to be quite the Casanova as well, leaving a trail of warm beds in his wake that quickly cooled as he generally never visited the same bed twice. He loved women, but that may have been the problem; he loved them too much, and they came far too easily for him. Anthony's looks were only exceeded by his charm. His buff body was well-sculpted from his love of running and weightlifting, but the true allure was to be found in his big brown eyes and slow smile that ended in two deep dimples. A girl could drown in those dimples and not lift a finger to save herself. Many had done just that and suffered heartbreak and sexual withdrawal after the affairs ended abruptly.

At the age of thirty-one, Anthony considered himself a confirmed bachelor, not ready to settle down and commit to one woman; not when the world had so many to sample. Besides, he hadn't yet met the woman who could hold his attention for more than a week, and in his view, most were just as much of a bed-hopper as he was. They just didn't admit to it.

Traffic was congested and the pace in town was slow-going. He didn't mind since it gave him time to get a good look at the buildings with their mix of architecture. He noted Moorish, Roman, early Gothic, all of which when put together were part of the beauty that was Barcelona. Nearing an intersection, Anthony's wandering eye caught the sway of blue-jeaned hips walking ahead on his right. His gaze traveled up to her long, blonde hair. He watched as she looked left, right, up, and all around. *A tourist*, he thought. She turned right at the intersection and then skipped across the cobbled street to the restaurant on the other side. The jiggling of her breasts as she moved caused an answering twinge in his pants. *Damnit!* He made a split decision to grab a bite at that restaurant and maybe, if luck was on his side, he'd have her for dessert. A quick turn of the wheel to the right brought him into the side street and as luck would have it, there was a space available in which to park.

He'd eaten at La Mediterránea the other day. The food was pretty good, and the atmosphere nice. He'd even taken a couple of pictures inside and one outside, but it wasn't the food that had Anthony getting out of his car and walking across the street this time. It was her—the pretty blonde woman with the nice ass and bouncing breasts. *Maybe she's English-speaking. Please, God, let her be English or American. Even Canadian! Hopefully single too.* Either way, a deeper hunger than food drove him physically to follow this woman.

Sarah waited to be seated after giving her name at the hostess' desk. There were two couples ahead of her and the restaurant appeared to be very busy. The scents of garlic, cumin, and other spices filled the air. Her stomach grumbled again. She sat down on the bench and looked around. Palms and bright flowering plants were arranged neatly in the small lobby. Bamboo fans spun over the heads of the diners and wait staff wearing black pants or skirts topped by white shirts, moved in and out of the crowd, delivering plates of delicious-looking food with efficiency. She couldn't wait to get a plate of her own!

"Smells good, doesn't it?"

Sarah turned her head and locked eyes with a very handsome man. "Pardon," she asked.

"The food," said Anthony. "It smells good." That slow, lady-killing smile spread across his face, ending in two deep dimples. "You're American?"

Sarah sucked in a breath, having felt as if the wind had been knocked out of her. "Yes."

Anthony knew he was the cause of her stunned expression, having seen it on countless female faces over the years. He first discovered the devastating effects of that smile as a child. It had gotten him out of more trouble than he could say, but as a man, it had gotten him into trouble more often than he cared to admit.

"Hi, I'm Anthony de Luca." He reached out offering his hand.

Sarah placed hers in his big, strong one and felt warmth spread up her arm and into her cheeks. Blushing, she replied, "Sarah. I'm Sarah Brown."

"Where are you from, Sarah Brown?" Leaving the smile on his face, Anthony noted her almond-shaped brown eyes, pert nose, soft, full lips. He let his eyes wander down her neck to her breasts, and lower in one of those quick sweeps men do that lets a woman know she's been assessed, but without being creepy about it.

Sarah watched his eyes skim down her body and felt everywhere his gaze landed. Heat spread throughout her stomach, replacing her hunger for food with a hunger far more primal. "I'm from Helotes, near San Antonio."

"Texas, huh?"

"Sarah, your table is ready," the hostess interrupted.

"Oh! S-sorry. I have to...well...are you here alone?" Sarah stuttered as she stood up to follow the hostess.

"I am." Anthony waited, knowing she was about to issue an invitation to join her.

"Well, I'm dining alone, and you're dining alone. Maybe we can dine together?"

Anthony stood up and looked at the hostess. In his limited Spanish he asked her if they could add another place setting to Sarah's table.

The hostess nodded and asked them, again, to follow her. "I'd be delighted," he replied. He offered his arm and Sarah placed her hand through the crook of his elbow. Together, they followed the hostess to their table.

Anthony was feeling optimistic about the day. A stray thought occurred; *I never even requested a table when I walked in!* He pulled Sarah's chair out for her before sitting himself. The hostess placed menus in front of them and informed them in her broken English that their waiter would be right with them.

Sarah glanced at the menu, but her thoughts were on the gorgeous man seated across from her. *Just look at those eyelashes! Gosh, a girl could melt like a stick of butter just looking into those beautiful eyes.* It hadn't escaped her notice that he was covered in muscles, either.

The attraction she felt was immediate, making her feel both anxious and excited. Sarah wanted to know more about him. Something about his name seemed familiar, but nothing came immediately to mind. "What do you do, Anthony?"

Anthony smiled. "I'm a photographer."

"You are? What kinds of pictures do you take?" Sarah leaned forward with her elbows on the table, causing her breasts to squeeze together, exposing her cleavage to his view.

Anthony's crotch perceived this action quicker than his brain could receive the image from his eyes. Blood pooled low in his groin and he took in a slow, steadying breath. It really had been too long since he last slid between the warm thighs of a beautiful woman. He felt like a schoolboy. "I take travel photos, mostly. I've written a few books on travel with illustrations, but I also do some commercial work for various businesses."

Leaning onto the table closer to her, Anthony stared deep into her eyes, determined to make her feel his vibe and to gauge her response. She was lovely. The blush on her cheeks told him she was definitely feeling the heat he was putting out there. "And what do you do, Sarah from Texas?"

Her lips parted to reply, but were so dry, she had to lick them twice before she could speak. "I'm a librarian, that is, I work at my local library back home."

Anthony watched her pink tongue make two passes over her lower lip before she spoke. *Little Anthony* twitched as his imagination flew to thoughts of her tongue performing that same maneuver in a more intimate setting. *God! Never again will I go two weeks without sex. This is ridiculous. A fucking librarian has me panting like a dog at her feet for treats. A fucking librarian! Fucking hot librarian. I wonder if it's true about librarians. I wonder...*

"And what do you do as a librarian?" Anthony reached across the table to touch the gold bracelet on Sarah's wrist. He seemed to be touching it in an absent-minded manner, but the sparks skittering all over her skin said it was deliberate. She didn't mind.

"I file, mostly. You know, check books out, check them back in, maintain files. That kind of stuff. It's very boring." Her thoughts wandered to all the nights she'd spent in the special reference section, curled up with an erotic novel, indulging herself in a room that had been full of random people only hours earlier. Now, someone real was touching her, not some figment of her imagination made up from a description in a book, and she was feeling more sure that by tonight, he would be touching her everywhere. Maybe sooner. The opportunity she'd hoped for had arrived, packaged inside a gorgeous, kind, flirtatious American man.

"Hola. Soy Javier. What will you like to order?" A tall, young Spanish boy, around the age of nineteen, interrupted the conversation with an exuberant smile. He seemed completely unaware of the heat passing between the two Americans.

"Oh! I haven't decided yet. I barely glanced over the menu." Sarah quickly picked it up and scanned the contents. It was written in Spanish, and she couldn't quite decipher the dishes.

"Allow me?" Anthony threaded his fingers through Sarah's, holding her hand. She smiled and nodded her consent. Turning to the waiter, he gave their order in his limited Spanish. "The lady will try the Rustido a la Catalana, and I'll have the Paella. To drink, we'll have the house Sangria, and two waters as well, please?"

"Mucho gusto, señor." Javier took their menus and left to put in the order.

"What am I eating today?" she asked.

Anthony bit his tongue to keep from answering inappropriately. "It's a very tender veal roast cooked in white wine, rum, and it has a side of cut, cooked red potatoes and vegetables. I had it here the other day. It was very good."

"White wine, rum, and Sangria. Are you trying to get me drunk, Anthony?" Sarah attempted a flirtatious tease.

Anthony chuckled, charmed by her question. "No, of course not. I just want you to enjoy a great meal, relax, and have fun." He caressed her palm with his thumb. Warm tendrils of sensuous languor spread throughout her body. *Who needs alcohol when he makes me feel drunk with one touch?*

"So, what brings you to Barcelona, Sarah?"

"Vacation. My first, actually." The waiter arrived back with a carafe of Sangria and a pitcher of ice water. He filled the water glasses and took his leave. Anthony reached for the carafe and poured the fruity red wine into Sarah's empty glass, then filled his own.

"Are you visiting relatives or friends here?" he asked.

"Neither. I don't know anyone here." Sarah glanced down shyly. She sipped her Sangria, feeling the cool liquid slide down her throat and soothe her nerves. This gorgeous man had her on edge. It was a good edge, but an edge, nonetheless. She looked up at him, taking in the natural wave of his dark brown hair. It was so thick. Her fingers itched to run through it and see if it was as soft as it appeared.

"You just took off to Spain on your own? That's pretty ballsy! I'm surprised your family didn't try and stop you. It's not entirely safe for a woman alone, you know?"

Something changed in Sarah's eyes. She suddenly seemed both sad and distant at the same time. "I don't have much family anymore. My dad has been with his new family for a while now, and my mother passed recently."

Sarah's vulnerability touched Anthony, arousing a protective urge within him. The feeling surprised him. He still wanted to fuck her, but that feeling softened with her admission. He wanted to see the smile return to her eyes, and he didn't want anyone else to be the cause of that except him.

"I'm sorry, Sarah."

Sarah felt Anthony's free hand touch the side of her face. His rough fingertips caressed her cheek before tucking a stray strand of hair behind her ear. He dropped his hand down to hold hers, now clasping both in his comforting grip. Her face burned from his touch, and she couldn't help but smile.

"Thanks. It's okay, really. She'd been sick for a long time; cancer. It was expected."

"Still, it hurts either way, expected or not. So, you decided to just take some time for yourself?" He had to add 'gutsy' to his assessment of her.

"Yeah. I've always wanted to travel but couldn't leave. I took care of her. But now, I can go anywhere, do anything, and there's so much I want to do." Sarah looked deep into Anthony's eyes with her last statement.

Anthony understood. She needed someone, wanted someone at that moment, and he was happy to oblige.

Dinner passed in pleasant conversation and intense flirting. The candle on their table burned low, but the fire inside them roared to life. Anthony paid the check and together, they walked out of La Mediterránea. He offered a ride back to her hotel. She accepted, both knowing full well where this would lead. The hotel was only a few blocks away and the ride was short. Sarah felt shyness sweep over her but fought it long enough to ask Anthony if he wanted to come up.

Anthony said nothing but drove straight into the parking garage. He placed the hotel's ticket in the windshield, then got out and walked around to the passenger side. He opened the door for Sarah, offering his hand in an uncommon gesture of courtesy. It wasn't that he lacked manners, but most of the women he bedded down with didn't bring out this need to be chivalrous. He kissed her hand as she placed it in his. The smile that earned him was worth the effort. He closed her door, then quickly grabbed his camera bag out of the backseat. Once the car was locked up for what he felt would be the rest of the day into the night, he took her hand again and together they walked toward the lobby.

It was the longest elevator ride of her life. Sarah was caught between extreme excitement over finally losing her virginity and extreme nerves. She liked Anthony. He was nice, educated, well-mannered, and sexy as hell. She was glad she'd ended up at La Mediterránea. She was also glad she'd put herself on birth control a month before her vacation. Still, she should have asked about condoms. She wanted to experience sex, but she didn't want to suffer irreversible consequences. She knew there was a convenience shop in the lobby so if he didn't have any on him, maybe they sold them. It would have to be addressed either way.

They exited the elevator and walked down the hall to her room. Anthony placed his arm loosely around her waist and his hand slid to the small of her back, caressing in intimate circles as she dug the key out of her purse and struggled to get it in the slot. His hand was distracting, and it took Sarah three tries before she got the green light to open the door. He tried not to laugh at her obvious anxiety. Inside, she flipped on the light and set her things down on the dresser. Anthony placed his bag on one of the chairs and turned to her.

"Would you like something to drink?" she asked. "I only have bottled water. Sorry."

"That's fine. I'm not picky." Anthony watched as she fumbled with the cap, noticed the slight tremble in her hand as she poured a glass for him and one for her. He smiled to himself. *She isn't used to this.* He found that he couldn't wait to make her tremble for other reasons.

"Here." Sarah handed him his glass and then she sat on the foot of the bed. Taking a long drink, she gulped it down and plunged headlong into her speech.

"Anthony, I really need to ask you if you have...well, do you carry ...um, condoms?" Her eyes peeked up at him on the last word of that sentence.

"Yes." He smiled, both dimples coming out to play. It did crazy things to her insides.

"...because I don't usually do this sort of thing..."

He stopped her. "I know. I know you're not that kind of girl. I can see that clear as day, but hey, you're on vacation. We're both consenting adults, and it's okay. I'm not going to hurt you, Sarah. Hell, exactly the opposite. I'm going to make you feel so good." He dropped down before her, his hands parting her knees so he could get closer. "I'm going to touch you everywhere, kiss you everywhere." Anthony's lips lightly touched hers but skipped off like the wings of a butterfly to skim along her jaw, down her neck and back up to her ear. "I'm going to taste every inch of your beautiful body." His tongue flicked out, catching her earlobe and sucking it in. He nibbled for just a moment before returning to Sarah's lips.

"Oh!" It came out as a sigh, but Sarah couldn't manage more than that. Hands cradled her face and masculine lips claimed hers in a searing kiss. It was gentle and commanding all at once. He sought deeper contact and swept the inside of her mouth with his tongue. He felt her respond, parrying her tongue with his own. The duel had begun. Tongues thrust, parried, tasted, caressed, as lips glided across each other. Sarah felt Anthony suck in her lower lip and skim it with his teeth before giving a playful nip. She could feel the scratchiness of his facial stubble against her own softer skin. The roughness of it in contrast to his smooth lips seemed to start a fire deep down inside. Flames licked every spot his hands touched. A persistent ache built in her lower belly. The heavy, swollen surge of heat between her thighs made her wrap her arms around his waist and pull him closer.

Anthony pulled back and quickly pulled his T-shirt up over his head, tossing it onto the floor. Sarah gazed at the perfection that was his chest and arms. Tanned and muscular, all she could think of was being held by those arms. Dropping her gaze lower, she licked her lips in anticipation of exploring his rippling abs. A light dusting of hair sprinkled along his belly button, running down below the waist of his cargo shorts. As she continued to stare, he kicked off his hiking boots, then reached down to remove each sock. She locked eyes with him while he stood and unbuttoned and unzipped his shorts. They dropped, leaving him standing in only a pair of dark blue boxer-brief-style running shorts. He had a huge erection that strained to be freed from its cotton confinement.

It seemed like time slowed down as he hooked his thumbs under the elastic waistband and tugged them down. Sarah's eyes widened at what his striptease revealed. She gulped, both anxious and fascinated. It was big and bobbing freely pointing in her direction as if to say, "I want you!" Granted, it was the first one she'd ever seen up close and personal, but it was truly a sight to see. She reached out to take it in her hand. Anthony shuddered and his head fell back. Feeling powerful, she caressed it lightly, loving the velvety feel of his turgid skin on her palms. It was hot, rigid, and oddly bumpy around the head, but smooth as marble along the shaft. She leaned in, intending only to kiss it lightly, but once her lips rested on the crown, Anthony groaned, and the sound aroused a need inside her to please him as she'd often read about in her erotic books. Her tongue flicked out, catching the tiny drop of moisture oozing from the tip. It was a little salty, but the scent of sex affected her so that she licked again, running her tongue along the underside, down to the base and back up again. Without hesitation, she opened her lips and took him inside her mouth, sliding back until her lips nearly touched his torso. She felt him shudder, felt his hands slide into her hair and cradle her head.

"Yes!" he said. "God, yes!" Anthony pumped his hips, thrusting. Sarah repeated the sucking-sliding motion of her mouth and tongue, circling the tip with small flicks. She had no idea what she was doing, only imagining how she would want him to pleasure her with his mouth and performing those moves on him. Her hand reached beneath and cupped his testicles. They were large and tight, barely covered in hair. She massaged them gently, sucking on his shaft, taking him in deeply.

"Jesus, Sarah!" Anthony's thoughts fogged over. He was at the mercy of her hot, wet, and eager mouth. If she kept this up, he wouldn't hold out long. Regretfully, he pulled her head back.

"Stop. I won't last if you keep doing that, baby."

"Did I do something wrong?" Sarah didn't know if she'd somehow messed up or what. Confused, she stared at him.

"No." Smiling, Anthony pulled her to her feet. "No, sweetheart. You did everything so right, but now, it's your turn." Kissing her deeply and tasting himself upon her lips, he lifted the edge of her top, pulling it up and over her head. He quickly unbuttoned and unzipped her jeans, pulling them down and helping her kick them off. She stood before him in red panties and bra edged in lace to match. He slid his hands up her sides, around her back, and expertly unhooked that bra. It fell off her shoulders and she unconsciously reached up to hold the cups in place. Anthony gently took her hands away, observing the small bit of satin and lace slip off her perfectly shaped breasts. Her nipples peaked, tiny rose-colored nipples that begged to be sucked. His hands cupped them, feeling their weight. He leaned in, wrapping his arms around her back and lifting her off her feet. Climbing onto the bed, he laid her down in the center.

Sarah felt overwhelmed. She watched as this Greek God of a man treated her with a gentleness she didn't expect. She was glad. It suddenly struck that he would soon be inside her, and all her fantasies had not prepared her for the reality. She was a little afraid and a lot turned on. Her mind might be anxious, but her body was restless, unconsciously lifting her hips to meet his. She reached to draw him to her, but he grasped her wrists and pulled them above her head, pinning them down.

"Patience, baby. We'll get to that, but right now it's my turn to taste you."

The implication of his words caused a wave of heat to wash over her. She was so wet, so ready that she didn't know if she would be able to wait. He held her wrists with one hand while he kissed her deeply. He robbed her of breath with each sweep of his tongue. His free hand ran up her ribs to capture her breast. Strong fingers squeezed and caressed. He rolled her hard nipple between his fingertips, thumb rubbing across the peak keeping time with every thrust of his tongue. Sarah arched her back and moaned into Anthony's mouth. He replied by leaving her lips to trail hot, wet kisses down her neck, over her chest, and finally replacing his fingers on her breast with his mouth. He sucked hard, nipped the puckered skin with his teeth, then laved the pert nub with lips and tongue. Sarah was so achy and swollen that she longed for him to satisfy that untouched part of her. Again, she ground her hips up, rubbing her satin-covered mound against his hardness. Anthony swiveled, his hips showing restraint as he only barely allowed himself to caress between Sarah's legs. He tried not to smile, knowing her frustration, but wanting to drive her crazy with desire. His lips moved to attend to her other sweet nub where he showed equal attention, making her writhe. He felt her body tremble beneath his and fought the urge to rip off her panties and plunge balls-deep inside what he was sure would be the tightest, sweetest, snuggest fit he ever experienced.

"Please, Anthony," Sarah begged.

"Please what, baby?" Anthony's hands slid down over her arms, releasing her wrists. His mouth traveled lower, kissing and licking her stomach. He held her hips as his nose tickled along the top of her red lace panties. The aroma of sex rising off her in sensual tendrils clouded his senses. He grabbed at the scrap of lace with his teeth, pulling the panties down. His hands helped, slipping them over Sarah's thighs, past her knees as his lips rained kisses over her smooth skin. He yanked them over her feet and dropped them unceremoniously to the floor. Circling her ankles with his strong hands, Anthony spread her legs wide. His eyes beheld the feast of naked beauty before him. She was bare of any hair. Drops of moisture beaded along her nether lips, glistening like dew on a spring morning. Leaning down, Anthony ran his fingertips up and down her thighs, beginning at the outside and moving to her inner thighs.

He watched Sarah's eyes darken in their intensity and flutter closed. Her lips parted and she breathed in short pants. The sight of her open, aroused, and ready for him, caused him to tighten painfully, but he held on to the last of his control and reached his hands beneath her lovely derriere, lifting her to his mouth. He plunged his tongue deep into her wetness and felt her shudder as he had longed to make her shudder earlier. She tasted like sex, woman, and strawberries. *Incredible!* Anthony lapped at her, feeling her thighs tighten around his ears. He flicked her hard nub, and then placed one hand over her stomach, feeling her abdominal muscles spasm and tighten each time his tongue tweaked that sensitive spot.

"Ohhh! Anthony, please, please, please!" In answer, he sucked hard, licking harder, and inserted two fingers inside her tight opening. Caressing her inner walls, he rolled his tongue in a way he knew pleased the ladies.

Sarah felt tension coil. Her whole body was like a taught rope stretched to its limits. She was about to snap. She reached down and grasped his soft hair in her fingers, tugging while thrusting her hips against his magical mouth. Waves built, rising higher until she exploded. Anthony felt her tummy tighten and rhythmically licked her, swallowing her sweetness while alternately sucking her orgasm into himself, tasting all that was good about this lovely woman.

Panting heavily, Sarah lay still. Her body still felt needy. Anthony leaned over the side of the bed, fumbling in the back pocket of his shorts to pull a condom out of his wallet. He came back up, sitting on his knees between her lax thighs. He ripped the package open with his teeth, placed the condom over his erection and rolled it down. She watched him the entire time, lips parted, legs spread.

Anthony leaned on one hand over her and used the other to guide himself to her opening. He began sliding inside, discovering she was tighter than he imagined.

He placed both elbows on either side of her head and bent down to kiss her. "Relax, baby."

"Anthony…" Sarah started to warn him about her virginity but was cut off by his lips claiming hers. She felt stretched with every inch of ground he gained, and she tried to do as he bid and relax. It would all be over within a moment.

"Sweet Jesus, you feel so good," he whispered against her lips. He suddenly thrust deep, breaking through a barrier he was not aware was there until he felt it rip. "What the hell?" Anthony pushed up onto his hands and looked down at Sarah's face. His wide eyes mirrored hers. "You're a virgin?"

Sarah bit her lower lip, one small tear escaping her eye as the last of the discomfort ebbed away. "Yes. I'm sorry I didn't tell you sooner."

The sight of that tear, and her obvious discomfort moved Anthony. He'd never been anyone's first before. He made a point of avoiding virgins, preferring women with experience. He didn't like the complications that a virgin brought to the equation. They usually got clingy fast, expecting far more than he was willing to give. But amid her confusion and discomfort was a strange hint of bravery. This rare woman, who'd just lost her mother, and had traveled halfway around the world, had chosen him, bastard that he was, to be her first. He damn well would make it as good for her as he could, despite the fact that he'd just bore down into her like a clumsy fuck.

"Shhh. It's okay." Anthony gently kissed her lips once, twice, and again. He caressed her face, while dropping kisses over her cheeks, her eyes, tasting that one tear before returning to her lips.

Sarah felt warmth spread over her at his gentleness. He was embedded deep within her but remained unmoving. His fingers began to massage her scalp as his kisses deepened. It felt good. His tongue teased hers and she lifted her hips a little. Anthony felt her begin to respond again. He pulled back a few inches, praying for control to make this good for her. As he pulled away, Sarah felt a loss and pushed her hips forward. He pulled back again and began slowly thrusting in and out, swiveling a little. Heat filtered through her thighs, relaxing her body and filling her with a new, aching need. She matched his thrusts, getting bolder. Her arms snaked around his broad shoulders and her lips sought out his jaw, neck, and chest. She liked the taste of his skin. She loved the catch in his breathing when she did something that felt good for him.

The pain she first felt when he burst through her virgin skin was now replaced by an amazing feeling of being filled to the brim. It was a hundred times better than anything she'd ever read about. Each time he pulled back and thrust deep; she drifted higher. Each time his hot shaft stroked her tight, slick walls, she lost her mind a little more. *This feels so good. Oh, God!* Sarah wrapped her legs around his lower back. Anthony slid one hand beneath her bottom and thrust even deeper.

Fuck me, he thought. *I'm not going to last much longer.* Sarah sank her fingernails into his back, arching and rubbing her breasts against his chest. Anthony's mouth angled down and caught a nipple, sucking hard. The pleasure-pain combined with his thrusting inside her brought that familiar tension back. Her walls tightened, straining, rubbing, and grinding against him. He continued sucking her nipple with his mouth, pumping harder and harder.

"Anthony! Oh my God!" Sarah climaxed, her whole body shuddering from deep within.

Anthony felt her tighten around him and he couldn't hold back any longer. With one last, deep thrust, he went over the edge, rearing his head back, and arching his body. The pleasure was intense, wracking him several times before he collapsed on top of her.

They lay entwined, panting.

Sarah smiled like a Cheshire cat. She was happy. She had finally had sex, good sex! Well, she didn't have anything with which to compare. This was what she'd always wanted—a nice, sexy, incredible man to gently initiate her body into the ways of love. He was still buried inside her, albeit much smaller now. Still, she cherished the connection and hoped he wouldn't be in any hurry to move just yet.

Anthony lay thinking. *A virgin. Son of a bitch. Now what? What does she want? Do I even care right now? Fuck me. That was great! She's so sweet, so damn sexy.* Lethargy wrapped around his body and dragged him toward sleep. He fought it, knowing he couldn't just pass out on top of her. Finally, he lifted his head and looked at her.

"Hey, you okay?" He said, dropping a kiss on her lips.

Sarah smiled. "Yeah, I'm fine."

"You sure? Can I get you anything?" He started to pull away, but she wrapped her arms and legs around him, anchoring him down.

"Wait," she whispered.

"What? What's wrong?" Anthony felt a twinge of anxiety.

"I'm not ready yet," she sighed.

"Ready for what?" A perplexed look settled on his face.

"I'm not ready for you to pull out of me just yet. I like this feeling of you inside me." She whispered the last, turning her face away in embarrassment.

Anthony smiled that slow smile that melted her insides. The twinkle in his eyes was only matched by the relief he felt that it wasn't something he'd done wrong making her demand that he not move but something he'd done right. He liked being inside her too. That part of his anatomy twitched with approval, not completely dead.

He stayed still and watched her face. She shyly peeked back at him and saw him smiling down at her. It was hard not to be stunned by that smile. Sarah lifted her head and softly kissed his lips. Several soft kisses later, he pulled out.

"Sorry, baby. I have to go take this thing off. It gets uncomfortable after a while." He kissed her again to show his regret for pulling out and got off the bed, heading to the bathroom.

Sarah stretched her muscles. She waited for him to come out so she could then clean up. When he walked out, she soaked in the sight of his nakedness. He was such a beautiful man. She got up and grabbed the towel left on the chair that she'd used to dry off earlier after her shower and wrapped it around herself as she walked to the bathroom.

Anthony playfully swatted at her ass as she walked by. Sarah giggled, trying to side-step him. In the bathroom, she dropped the towel and looked at herself in the mirror. Her hair was mussed, her lips looked bee-stung, and her body was chafed red here and there from lips, teeth, tongue, and stubble. She peed quickly, then wiped. There was a little blood on the paper, and she felt raw. She decided to run a quick shower and wash off. The hot water eased the stiffness in muscles she never knew she had. She lathered and rinsed, then dried off. Looking around for her robe, she realized she'd left it in her suitcase. *Oh, well. He's already seen me completely naked, so what's the difference?*

She turned off the bathroom light and opened the door. Walking back to bed, she noticed that Anthony had turned off the light in the bedroom. Daylight was waning as she climbed in beside him. He pulled the comforter up over her and tucked it around her body. She laid her head on his shoulder, snuggling close. It felt good to be curled up next to his warmth. He kissed her forehead.

"Feel better?" he asked.

"Um hmm," she replied, sleepy.

"Good. Get some sleep. You're going to need it." He chuckled, the sound rumbling deep in his chest, tickling her cheek where it lay.

"I am? Why?" Sarah yawned.

"Because we're not done, yet, Miss Brown. Not by a long shot."

Sarah raised an eyebrow, surprised. "You mean that's not all there is to it?" Knowing full well it wasn't but feeling giddy.

"No, ma'am. There's so much more." Anthony's lips found hers and he kissed her until she was breathless. "Now go to sleep." He tucked her head back into the crook of his shoulder and wrapped his arm around her waist.

Sarah lay there in the darkening room, smiling until she drifted off into an exhausted, travel-weary, and *newly-initiated into the world of sex* sleep

Chapter 3

"Hey, I'm going to take a quick shower. Wanna join me?" Morning dawned and Anthony rose before the sun in a cheerful mood.

Sarah stared at his devilish grin through gritty eyes and smiled back. "I'll join you in a minute. Go ahead and start without me."

Anthony went into the shower. Sarah lay abed, trying to figure out how she would relieve her bladder while he was in there. She'd never peed in front of anyone before. It was just awkward despite their intimacy the night before. It was all wonderful, but some things remained sacred. Urgency trumped propriety and she leaped out of bed, feeling stiff in all sorts of places. She ran into the bathroom and sat down on the toilet. Immediately her bladder let loose. He seemed not to notice or was, at least, politely ignoring her. Maybe he couldn't really hear over the sound of the water. Either way, she wiped quickly and flushed.

"You coming in or what, baby?"

Laughing, she stepped inside and got under the spray. Anthony helped her lather her hair, then worked his way down her body, massaging her back, arms, and legs, but going gently when he reached around to wash the most intimate part of her. Sarah suddenly felt a little shy. It was one thing to have sex, but quite another to let a man wash her like this. His fingers were gentle and expedient. He brought his hands back up and massaged her scalp as she stood in front of him.

"That feels so good." She sighed. He turned her under the spray again and began to rinse her off. Grabbing the conditioner on the shelf, he squeezed some into the palm of his hand and worked it through her tresses.

"I love your hair. It's so gorgeous." Anthony ran his hands down Sarah's back. He stood there watching his own fingers caress and rub her fantastic ass. She giggled, and the feminine sound made him smile.

She turned around, grabbed the soap, and began washing him the way he had washed her. She hesitated only a little when her hands reached his penis, but she overcame the weird feeling and lathered it, making sure to reach lower and roll his testicles around, manipulating them in her sudsy fingers. He groaned. To her amazement, he grew erect. Under the heat of the warm spray, they indulged themselves.

Sarah was very happy. Not only was he a wonderful lover, but he was a patient teacher. Anthony pulled away from their kiss and turned off the water.

Together, they dried each other off, brushed their teeth, and got dressed.

"Anthony, I'm starving!" Her stomach rumbled. She felt like she hadn't eaten in days.

Laughing, he pulled on a fresh pair of underwear and shorts that he always carried in his bag. "Well, let's feed you, then. You've more than earned an Olympic-sized breakfast."

"There's a café in the hotel. I think I get a Continental breakfast with my stay here."

"Whenever you're ready. How long are you staying here, anyway?"

Sarah looked at him. "Five days, then I'm traveling to Berlin."

"Berlin? Why Berlin?" He pulled on his socks and boots, admiring the sight of her in light blue panties and bra as she put on her makeup.

"I don't know. I'm visiting there, then taking a train to England. I just wanted to see a little bit of everything, you know?" She didn't tell him about her initial plans to visit and explore the infamous Berlin underground sex clubs. At this moment, it was the furthest thing from her mind. All she could think of was him and the powerful attraction she felt every time she looked into his eyes and saw him smile. He was her first, something very special in a woman's life. Today, she just wanted to get to know as much about him as she could. She knew better than to think it could ever be anything more than a vacation fling—at least her head knew that—but her heart was beating happy little beats just being with him. *Enjoy the moment, Sarah. It will be gone too soon.*

"Huh." Anthony eyed her.

"Well. I've been to Berlin recently and taken the trains across Germany, so maybe over breakfast I can tell you all about it, help you out so you know what to expect."

Sarah smiled, finishing up her light makeup. She combed out her hair and pulled the courtesy blow dryer from the drawer in the vanity. Anthony watched her flip her head down and blow out her long, blonde hair. He'd never watched a woman get herself ready before despite the multitudes of women he'd been with. It was fascinating and damn sexy. *She* was fascinating and sexy.

With her hair dry, pulled up loosely on the sides with jeweled clips, and her blue and white floral sundress sliding over her curves, Sarah stepped into a pair of canvas flats. Together, they left the room to eat. It was going to be a beautiful day spent in the company of her first amazing lover. She refused to think about leaving him here in Barcelona. Heck, he might not even want to see her beyond today, so she was determined to make the most of it. But secretly, she hoped he'd spend all five days with her.

Breakfast passed in a whirl of conversation and flirting. Anthony told her everything he knew about Berlin; the best places to visit, to eat, even how to successfully get her train tickets from one of the many automated kiosks so she wouldn't have to wait in line. "You have to check out Fassbender and Rausch in the Gendarmenmarkt. It's on Charlottenstrasse. It's the best-smelling place on Earth, seriously! When you walk in, there's just candies, chocolates of every kind, everywhere. When I was there, there was a giant chocolate teddy bear in the display window. I felt like a kid in a candy store!" Anthony's eyes were lit up with such joy describing the German chocolatier, that Sarah laughed.

"You *were* a kid in a candy store, obviously!" She clapped her hands together, laughing, and waited for him to continue.

"Upstairs, they have this amazing restaurant. You can sit at a table by the window which goes all the way from the main street around to the side street. From there, you can watch everyone come and go. There's an awesome building across the street. Great architecture."

"It sounds like Willy Wonka." Sarah sipped her coffee, staring at Anthony's face. She wanted to remember every detail of this amazing, sexy, and gentle man.

"It's way better. Well, there are no Oompa Loompas as far as I could tell, but you can sure satisfy your sweet tooth there! And that was one of my fave movies as a kid, the original one with Gene Wilder, not that Johnny Depp remake crap."

"What do you have against Johnny Depp" Sarah teased.

"Oh, come on. He's a pretty boy!"

Sarah couldn't stop laughing. "So are you."

Anthony did that slow, melting smile that flipped Sarah's insides like a troupe of acrobats. "And you like it." He sipped his coffee without taking his eyes from hers.

Sarah blushed, having been thoroughly dumbstruck once again by his dimples. Anthony watched pink tinge her cheeks, loving the way she could still be easily embarrassed even after last night, and this morning.

"You ready to head out and see some sights, princess?" Sarah melted just a little bit more at the term of endearment. It was way better than 'baby' which she was sure he probably called every woman he bedded when he couldn't remember their names. Calling her 'princess' seemed special. She didn't know if it was or if it was just part of his easy charm, but she wanted to hold on to this moment, keep it like a treasure in a box that she could take out some day in the future and reminisce over this time when this wonderful man made her feel this way.

"Whenever you are." She started to get up. Anthony rose quicker, offering his hand to her, and together they left. He was determined to show her a great time, take her around to all the sights he'd already photographed. He'd make love to her again, all kinds of ways and maybe in a few unique places, and tomorrow, he would leave for home. He thought about telling her that he was set to head back to New York the next day, but he didn't want to bring her down or spoil the day, or the night for that matter. Four days after tomorrow, Sarah would be leaving for Berlin, and he would never see her again. *Why does that suck so much?* He thought. *No attachments, de Luca. Sure, you were her first, but she's still just another woman like all the rest. Just go enjoy the day, and tomorrow, no regrets.*

Barcelona offered so much in the way of culture, architecture, shopping, and more. They visited Gothic churches, markets, and shops. Anthony took pictures of her everywhere they went, sometimes including himself in the shots. They laughed and had fun. He made her write down her email address so he could download the images and send them to her. She added her mailing address and cell number, insisting he might need it. After four hours of exploring the city, Anthony suggested they find a café and grab some lunch.

"There's a good place near the marina that has amazing seafood. What do you say?" Anthony held Sarah's hand as they walked back to his rental car.

"Sounds good." Sarah was game for anything, especially if it included Anthony. She looked over and found him watching her. He stopped and tugged her hand, pulling her close. Sarah willingly allowed herself to be drawn into a deep, sensuous kiss. His tongue swept the inside of her mouth, teasing, and taunting. His arms wrapped around her waist, hands gripping, caressing. She felt him harden against her, and her own body responded with heat and moisture pooling low in her belly. Sarah buried her fingers in the soft waviness of his hair, kissing him passionately as they stood against the side of the car. Finally, Anthony pulled away, leaving her breathless and wanting more.

"If we don't stop, I'm going to be eating you for lunch!" Anthony held on to her hips, rubbing his erection against the juncture of her thighs.

"That sounds good too" she purred.

"Get in the car, you nymphomaniac!" He turned her toward the passenger side and swatted her ass. He climbed into the driver's seat after closing her door. Anthony reached over and pulled her seat belt around her, securing it. He kissed her again, unable to help himself. He liked seeing her on fire for him. The sexy look in her eyes made him want to strip off all her clothes and lick every inch of her, and he knew she'd let him. Worse, he knew what she was wearing beneath that skimpy sundress since he'd watched her get ready that morning. While he'd watched, he knew he would be taking those little bits of lacy blue scraps off of her later.

Sarah was high on life. Staring into Anthony's eyes as he drew away from their kiss, she let her mind wander to all the wonderfully wicked things he had done to her that morning, and that she had done to him. Her thoughts were reflected in her eyes, causing Anthony no end of sweet pain.

In a low, deep voice, he told her, "Lady, I'm so going to fuck you later. And in case you're wondering where I'll start, it's going to be tongue-deep, licking you until you cum all over my face!" Sarah turned red, but her body caught fire.

Trying to hide her blushing cheeks, Sarah half-scoffed. "Promises, promises!"

He laughed as he reached across to touch her still flaming face.

Anthony started the car, put it into gear and pulled out onto the road, heading toward the Passeig de Colom. They spent the car ride listening to music, laughing, and with Anthony's hand upon her thigh.

Chapter 4

Amsterdam, The Netherlands

Amsterdam was finally warming up, though the nights were still cool. Summers were short in Holland, and Paul Christiansen was ready to enjoy every moment, knowing all too soon the chilling temperatures would return, ruining his fun. He loved the outdoors. The freedom he associated with summertime was priceless in his mind. No walls, no darkness, and no bone-chilling cold. It was the only time of year he didn't have nightmares—at least, not so many. The sunshine worked its magic all around him, stirring up his creative juices. Color seeped into his soul. It was during summer he could paint canvases with inspiring hues and subjects rather than dark, depressing, and tragically nightmarish imagery. Paul also looked forward to the influx of female tourists wearing itty-bitty sundresses, seeking brief but intense affairs. He was happy to provide these fantasy seekers with unfettered exploits of every kind. Paul would happily lose himself between the legs of a willing woman and for just a little while forget the early years and the monster that haunted his dreams. For those hot moments when he was in control, lost to ecstacy, hearing their moans and sighs, he could drown out the raw screams that still raked his soul and dragged him from fitful sleep in the middle of cold winter nights. His summer exploits often found themselves translated through broad and bold brushstrokes onto massive canvases that littered his loft.

They reminded him of blissful moments. For that alone, he considered them his treasures.

Two lovely ladies walked by the café where Paul sat sipping a glass of Merlot. He slipped his sunglasses down the tip of his model-straight nose with his middle finger. The women eyed him as they passed by, smiling when they saw the wicked gleam in his bright blue eyes. He winked at the blonde. She giggled and blew him a kiss. They looked Parisian. He liked Parisian women; no inhibitions. Standing, he threw a few bills down to pay for his drink and took off after them. He couldn't decide which one he'd rather have, so he figured *why not both?*

Adjusting the lapels of his gray sports coat and smoothing back his black hair, he caught up to them. Putting his arms around their shoulders, he began his practiced pitch. As expected, they were both charmed by his easy manner. Being both tall and overly handsome never did hurt his cause. Wasting no time, Paul threw down the gauntlet.

"What do you say, ladies? I'll show you around the city, and we'll dine on good food, drink the best wine, and then, we'll make love," he said, eyeing the lovely woman on his right. A similar line had worked for Javier Bardem in *Vicky Cristina Barcelona*. He gave a smolderingly suggestive look to the other. "Or will the Gods bless me and you both grant me the enchantment of your lovely bodies? I would be happy to rise to the challenge and pleasure you two sexy ladies for hours."

Both women laughed as if unimpressed, but they put their arms through his offered ones and set off together. Paul knew women, and he was confident that he would persuade these beautiful tourists to grace his bed that evening. *They like to pretend they're not here to get laid, but they are definitely here to get laid.* Everything about them screamed '*take me,*' from their hairstyles and makeup to their short skirts and tight jeans; the way they moved, flirted, retreated, then advanced again. They wanted it, but they wanted to fool themselves into thinking it was not their idea. They needed some kind of mental scapegoat to get through the Puritanical guilt ingrained into their psyches by their families, society, the church. If that meant he must be the bad guy, the seducer, the one to blame for charming them into bed, then so be it. What does it matter if everyone gets what they want? Sometimes, though, it became tedious. Sometimes it felt as if he were on a strict diet, eating the same food all the time, over and over again. It would be nice to sample something new, someone new; someone not so jaded. '*What am I thinking,*' he chided himself, '*I'd just corrupt her. Hell, I'd enjoy corrupting her.*' Paul laughed to himself and then turned his attention back to the two tasty French pastries at his sides. He would definitely not be dining alone tonight.

His phone vibrated in his coat pocket for the third time in the last hour. He knew who it was and refused to answer, refused to be drawn into the pit. The fact that he'd changed his phone number twice, and still this did not seem to deter the unwanted phone calls made Paul angry. He knew he would need to have words with his mother again about respecting his privacy and not giving out his number to anyone, with emphasis on '*anyone*'. The only reason she even had it was because she was older now with deteriorating health issues. Paul still felt the loyalty of a son to his mother despite his internal grudge against her. If anything happened to her, if she needed him, he would be there, but this did not extend to any other family members, especially the one calling now. Quite the opposite. The vibration stopped and Paul shook off the awful feelings that he immediately associated with this intrusion into his day.

"What do you think, Paul?" The blonde French woman seemed to be waiting for him to speak. Somehow, he'd missed whatever it was she said, so he covered by throwing her a wink and asking a very personal question. She giggled and they moved on. His mood restored once again; Paul allowed himself to become immersed in their charms.

Under the umbrella of their smiles, flirtation, and innate softness, he felt safe and warm. Nothing bad could happen while in the company of a beautiful woman, and when multiplied by two, he was certain Utopia beckoned.

Chapter 5

Sarah was in mind-blowing ecstasy. It was wonderful. Amazing.

A few more strokes and they both flew over the edge. Together, they collapsed onto the sweat-soaked bed, panting. Anthony enjoyed the feeling of this sweet young woman in his arms as he memorized the curves of her body and the taste of her skin. Her smile was already etched in his mind. Even so, he was scheduled to fly home tomorrow, and he didn't know how to tell her; then decided he wouldn't. She was young and looking for adventure. He was older and had been there, done that. It was probably arrogant of him to even think she would consider more when she was clearly just now sampling life. Plus, he wasn't ready to settle down. *So, what's the point of trying to drag this out? What will we do, exchange numbers? No. That would just be a waste of time.* Better that he just go back to his hotel, pack, and then leave. This would be their goodbye; one without words. He touched her face and turned her toward him. Gently, he kissed her already kiss-swollen lips. He knew he'd miss this sweet, open and brave young woman, and each time their lips met, he was telling her just how amazing he thought her to be.

This feels like goodbye, thought Sarah. She looked at Anthony. His eyes, those sexy, sweet brown eyes looked at her with something...affection? Love? *No! It can't be that. We've only known each other for barely two days.* Whatever it was, it made her feel all gooey inside. For the millionth time, she felt grateful that this was the man who was her first. One last kiss and they curled up in each other's arms allowing the post-coital lethargy to drag them under. When Sarah awoke next, Anthony was gone.

Sarah looked around the room. The sunlight slanted through the cracks between the heavy hotel curtains, telling her it was already late morning. "Anthony?" No reply. She looked on the floor and toward the chair where he'd laid out his clothes last night. They were gone, and so was the duffel bag he carried around. She got up and checked the desk and dresser to see if he'd left a note. None was found. She reached for her cell phone to call him and realized she didn't have his number. He'd never given it to her. The only thing she knew was where he was staying. She went to the nightstand to use the hotel's phone. It was a local call, after all. She picked up the receiver and realized she didn't know the name of the Pensión where he was staying, only knew where it was located since he'd driven her by there to pick some things up yesterday. That didn't really help.

She headed to the bathroom. *Maybe he went to get some breakfast,* she thought. Sarah showered, dressed, put on makeup and waited. An hour and a half had gone by, and Anthony had not returned. Grabbing her purse, she walked out the door, making her way down to the lobby to grab some breakfast. If he came back, she'd see him passing the café to get to the elevators.

The café was crowded. Sarah found a seat and ordered eggs and toast with orange juice. The juice was brought over immediately, and she sipped it while her eyes scanned the sidewalk up and down the street. Ten minutes later, the waitress brought her breakfast. It was difficult to both eat and be on the lookout for Anthony. Her food grew cold before she could finish it. Downing the last of her juice, Sarah stood and took her ticket to the counter. She paid her bill and took off in the direction of his hotel. She didn't like this; this feeling that he would just leave without saying a word. She was working herself up into a solid anger, practicing what she would say when she got to his room. *How dare you just leave? If you don't want to see me anymore, just say so, but to just up and leave, no note, nothing...that's just rude!*

Three blocks down, one left turn, over another street, and then turning right, Sarah found herself at the hotel—*a Spanish version of an American bed and breakfast.* She walked around to his door and knocked. No answer. Sarah knocked again, harder this time. Still no answer. She turned, searching for his rental car, but didn't see it anywhere. A couple walked out of the office at the end of the row of cottages. She marched in that direction. Inside the small space, a fan blew warm air in an attempt to cool the room. It didn't work, but it was better than nothing. The Pensión wasn't nearly as nice as the place where Sarah was staying. It was like comparing a Hilton to a Motel 6, but worse. When she asked him the day before why he'd chosen the place, he replied, *"It gives me more of a feel for how life really is here for residents. When you stay in a hotel, you're just a tourist. You don't get the whole picture. I need the whole picture to photograph it and write about it."*

"Excuse me," she said to the elderly man at the counter. He stared at her as if he didn't understand.

She tried again. "Disculpe, Anthony de Luca, ¿por favor?"

The old man smiled. "Sí. Señor de Luca, dejó el hotel esta mañana." He saw the blank look on her face and tried again. "He leave. Comprende?" Obviously, the old man knew little English, but what he did know didn't escape Sarah's understanding.

"He left?" The look on her face must have registered even if her words didn't quite sink in.

"He leave." The old man looked at her and his eyes softened. He saw the hurt registering on her face. "Lo siento, Señorita."

"He left," Sarah said more to herself. She turned to walk out the door. The warm air in the small office was stifling. Once outside, she could breathe a little easier, but only just. He left without saying goodbye. He left without saying anything at all. He didn't even tell her he was leaving. Sarah didn't know what to think. *Was it something I said? Something I did?* The hurt was more than she had expected to feel. It wasn't as if she didn't know they would be saying goodbye and never seeing each other again, but she thought, at least, it would be when she left to go to Berlin. She thought he would at least say goodbye; kiss her goodbye. *But he did, dummy. Last night, that was his goodbye. When he kissed me and held me with such tenderness.* That last thought didn't comfort her wounded heart or her pride. She didn't know what to do with these feelings, with the unexpected pain of loss.

She walked back to the main street and looked around. Clouds gathered threatening to rain soon. It suited her mood. A row of taxis on the other side of the street beckoned. She glanced both ways, then crossed. She hopped inside the first available one and told the driver to take her to the beach. He thankfully spoke a little English and tried to inquire as to which beach.

"The closest one. One that lots of tourists go to. Preferably with a bar." She tried not to sound forlorn.

The taxi driver rolled his eyes at the American girl. He pulled out and headed toward one of the most frequented beaches in Barcelona. Sarah remained lost in thought the entire drive. She didn't bother to notice all the beautiful places they passed. She wasn't looking out but rather, reflecting within. *So, it wasn't so easy to walk away from someone with whom you've had sex, it seems.* Everything that she'd read hadn't prepared her for this feeling of abandonment when a man walks away. *You'd think I was familiar with that one when Dad left to be with his girlfriend!*

Sarah didn't know how to deal with this. Somehow, sitting at a bar at a beach seemed the best answer for the moment. *Well, I came here alone. I'm leaving alone. So, what's the difference? Just because some amazing man rocked my world doesn't mean my world ends when he's gone, does it? Hell no!* The inner pep talk wasn't working. She redoubled her effort and attempted to at least pay attention to the passing scenery.

They arrived at the beach and Sarah paid the fare. She got out, not really knowing where she was. It didn't matter. She'd just catch a cab later back to the hotel. There was a bustling bar with loud music and lots of tables out on a deck overlooking the sand. Beyond that, the ocean rolled in on frothing waves. Kids played in the sand while their parents lazed on towels, soaking up as much sun as they could. The clouds continued to gather, slowly blotting out the bright rays. Thunder boomed in the distance causing dozing adults to sit up and look around for their children. Sarah thought about how she would have loved to have shared this with Anthony. She walked to the bar and sat down at one of the tables.

A nice-looking waiter came to take her order. His name tag said he was Pablo. He had big hazel eyes and dark brown hair. He looked like he was in his mid-twenties. His physique showed him to be very active, and his tan said "surfer."

She asked for a Piña Colada. He smiled and told her in a lovely deep voice with accented English that he would have it to her, pronto.

Sure, he will. Is that how they all are in the beginning? Eager to please? Ready to do anything, say anything that you want? Then they leave without so much as a by-your-leave? Wow, this really sucks.

Sarah sat and watched the waves grow more peaked. The wind whipped up and rain began to fall. Some of the beachgoers came and sat under the roof of the bar while others made a dash for their cars and left. The beach emptied, now looking as desolate as she felt. Three drinks in, she was feeling warm and fuzzy. Four drinks later, she wasn't sure she would be able to walk steadily to the bathroom. By the fifth drink, Pablo the waiter decided she'd had enough and began bringing her water. She tried to protest, but he insisted.

"Where are you staying? I can call you a taxi." His concern grated on her nerves.

"I'm fine!" Sarah tried to order another drink, but he just wouldn't take her order.

"Señorita, you should really go back to your hotel. I don't want anything bad to happen to you." Pablo noticed how she seemed to tear up while she muttered to herself over her water. She was obviously sad about something; probably a man. She was too pretty to be so sad.

"I'm calling a taxi for you." He left to do just that. When he returned, he'd taken off his apron and name tag.

"Someone is on the way. Come, we'll wait outside now that the rain has stopped." Sarah tried to rise but toppled back into her seat. She wasn't used to alcohol at all, and five drinks had knocked her on her ass.

Pablo reached around and lifted her to her feet. "Put your arm around my waist. I'll help you."

Sarah tried again. This time she didn't feel quite as wobbly. Together, they walked out into the rain-scented air. He made her stroll up and down the sidewalk as they waited for the taxi. After a while, the steps got easier and less unsure.

"Where did you learn such good English," Sarah asked.

"I studied for a year at the University of Southern California. I was visiting with friends." Pablo went on to tell her about his plans to become a veterinarian, about going to school while working at the bar. "The pay is terrible, but the tips are great during the summer because of all the tourists."

A taxi pulled up. Pablo walked her over and helped her in. Sarah fell over slightly in the seat, laughed, then righted herself.

"Where are you staying," he asked again.

"The Hotel Claris." She hiccupped and then listed over sideways—again.

Pablo sighed. His sister's face came immediately to mind. Graciela was about the same age as this intoxicated blonde. It wasn't long ago that she'd lost a friend, one who disappeared without a trace. The two girls met at the European Interscholastic Young Adult Debate Competition six years ago in Berlin. They kept up the friendship over the next year, even planning for the girl, Marlessa, and her parents to visit Barcelona the next summer. Graciela had been excited at the prospect of seeing her friend again, but just weeks shy of the end of the school year, Marlessa went missing. Graciela might have never known about the tragedy except for the German detective who'd contacted his family attempting to find the girl. Pablo didn't remember all the details, but he remembered the detective's name. Heinz. He also remembered how devastated Graciela was over the loss of her friend and the frustration at being too far away to keep up with any news in real time. As the weeks following the girl's disappearance lapsed into months, Pablo saw a change come over his outgoing sister. She grew quieter, became more careful of who she associated with and where and with whom she went. She also became more focused on her studies, shifting her sights away from business studies to law. Years passed and Graciela's friend Marlessa had still not been found.

Inside the car, the pretty blonde hiccupped.

Knowing how quickly a situation could go south, he opened the back door to slide in next to her. He didn't trust that she'd be able to get out of the taxi successfully, much less walk up to her room. He also didn't trust the taxi driver, who looked Sarah over through the rearview mirror. He felt the need to make sure she got back safely.

"Scoot over." Sarah scooted and Pablo sat next to her.

"Hotel Claris, ¡por favor!" The taxi took off as Pablo pulled Sarah to an upright position. The ride back was a blur. She was sure he kept talking to her, but she felt groggy, and her eyes kept closing. She was aware of a hard, warm shoulder and the pleasant scent of fabric softener.

"Don't fall asleep, Señorita. Wake up. Wake up, now." He kept giving her a little shake to keep her alert.

It was like a fuzzy dream, a remnant of some faded memory. Somehow, she got back to the hotel, walked through the lobby, and rode the elevator up to her room. *Did I pay the fare? How did I get in my room?*

"Anthony....why'dyouleave?" Her speech slurred and tapered off.

The sheets felt cool on her skin. The light dimmed and the world went blank.

"Shhh. Just go to sleep," the voice spoke, but she didn't hear it. A small snore sounded. Pablo looked at the woman he'd just half-carried up to her room and tucked in. It was probably the nicest thing he'd ever done for a beautiful woman. His mother would be proud. So would Graciela. He laughed to himself, turned to toss the room key on her dresser, and then left. The door locked automatically behind him. He gave himself a mental pat on the back for remembering to put out the 'Do Not Disturb' sign. It wouldn't be nice to have housekeeping walk in the next morning and catch her unaware. She should sleep it off; both the alcohol and the heartbreak. Whoever this "Anthony" was shouldn't have left someone so naïve all alone. It was a good thing she found her way to his bar and not some other. She might not have made it home safely, or at all, he thought.

Chapter 6

The flight back to New York was fraught with turbulence and one extra whiny kid. Why the hell they let kids into business class was beyond him, but Anthony knew he was somehow being punished. It was not like he'd never just up and left a woman he'd had a fling with before, but Sarah was the first virgin—his first virgin—and he'd handled it badly. He knew it.

Traffic through town had been just as aggravating as his flight, and the high cab fare from all the various jams and delays further grated on his already raw nerves. Still, he was finally home.

Inside, his townhome felt stale and lifeless. He set about putting his bags down and opening some windows. Fresh air blew in and chased away the gloom and dust. His answering machine light blinked rapidly, showing it had more than ten messages waiting. They could wait a little longer. He just wasn't in the mood to deal with work and family right now.

Anthony finished unpacking, tossed his clothes into the washer and turned it on. Once the Downey ball was added, he walked into his galley-style kitchen and pulled down a clean high-ball glass from the dark walnut cabinet. He added a couple of ice cubes from the freezer and poured his favorite brand of whiskey over the top. He barely swirled the ice around twice before he tossed it back and poured another. He carried this one, along with the bottle, over to the couch. He finished that drink and then poured another.

She probably hates me now, he thought. *I'm such a fucking jackass. I could have at least let her know I was leaving and said goodbye...something!* "Fuck!" Anthony ran his hand over his face, feeling the day's growth of stubble. He remembered how Sarah seemed to enjoy its tickle on her skin; particularly her neck when he kissed her, and her inner thighs when he would lick and kiss his way toward her hot, wet..." Goddammit!" He couldn't get her out of his head. Memories of her so open and passionate haunted him. She'd been so uninhibited, so eager. Her natural curiosity combined with her innocence had intoxicated him more than any bottle of booze. She had no idea what she was about or how to conduct herself in an affair...and it had been refreshing. Thoughts of her with her head tossed back, lips parted, panting for him as he penetrated her deeply—a place no man had ever been before him—tumbled around his head.

She's better off without me. She'll find someone new, maybe settle down. The thought of another man touching her made him angry. He finished off the third drink and poured a fourth. *What if she does meet another guy? Will she fuck him too? She was pretty eager with me!* He fumed, and drank, and fumed some more. He thought of her in all the ways he'd had her, how she felt, sounded, tasted, and then the thought of her with another man interrupted his mental replay. "Fuck it!" Anthony threw the now empty glass of whiskey across the room where it smashed into the wall. Fragments of glass flew everywhere, and plaster chipped away at the point of impact.

His anger withered along with his spirit. He laid his head on the back of the couch and drifted. "I fucked up..." he muttered brokenly before drifting into a troubled, jet-lagged, drunken slumber.

Barcelona, Next Day

Sarah woke up feeling sick. Her head pounded and her mouth was dry as evidenced by her tongue sticking to the roof of it. She lay in bed, trying to remember exactly what happened yesterday. She remembered going to the beach and sitting at a bar. She remembered her first few drinks, and maybe a waiter in there somewhere who had brought them to her. After that, she didn't remember much. It was all fuzzy and unclear. She sat up and the room spun a little. She tried standing and immediately sat back down. She counted to ten and tried again. It was a little better this time and she slowly shuffled to the bathroom. The mirror was not kind when she beheld her reflection. Her hair was disheveled. Her face had tear tracks and smeared makeup running down her cheeks. Her lips looked chapped, and her clothing was wrinkled. At least she'd managed to take off her shoes, but she didn't remember doing that.

She pulled her jeans and underwear down and fell hard on the cold toilet seat. Every drink she'd had and a few extras poured out of her bladder. It seemed to take forever. Sarah chuckled wryly, then stopped because the action hurt her head. She stood up and removed her wrinkled clothes. A shower would help. Sarah turned on the water and tested the temperature. When it was steaming, she stepped in and let the warm liquid run over her. It felt good. She scrubbed her hair and washed her body while looking around at the tiled walls remembering the incredibly amazing moments she shared with Anthony in this same spot, under this same spray. Suddenly, she began to tremble, feeling cold. Sobs wracked her as she cried. Sinking down onto the floor of the shower, she wrapped her arms around herself and rocked back and forth. The pain of what was surely a broken heart tore her up. *He just left. He just left. He just left.* She kept repeating these words in her head. Abandoned again. First, her dad, then her mom, and now Anthony. It was too much.

She sat in the shower for nearly an hour, crying. When the tears stopped, she rose and turned off the water, then dried her body. *Never again. I'm not going to cry for a man ever again. I won't let one get close to me like that anymore.* She eyed herself in the steam-covered mirror. Anthony was her first and he'd made the experience special. She supposed some kind of attachment was natural but hadn't counted on it or the pain of loss thereafter. All she could do now was move forward.

Her stomach growled, but she was afraid to eat anything. Something told her to take it easy. She'd never had a hangover before. *Maybe just some coffee and toast.* She dressed and blow-dried her hair. She didn't even bother with any makeup, just a little lip gloss. Nothing would hide the dark circles under her eyes anyway. She put on her glasses instead of the disposable contacts. The pair from the day before had gone straight into the trash since she'd slept in them. Grabbing her purse and room key, she headed down to the café.

⊱⋅ ⋅⊰

Sarah sat in the café sipping coffee; black with one sugar. She was afraid to add cream, afraid it might not sit well on her tender stomach. The waitress came by and offered a refill. Sarah declined but asked for a glass of water. She felt dehydrated. Her eyes wandered to the people passing by. Some were old, some young, and most were paired off, holding hands and sharing knowing looks and teasing smiles. It made her heart ache.

The waitress returned with her glass of water. She picked it up and drank it down. The cold liquid felt so good in her mouth sliding down her throat that Sarah drank nearly the whole glass in one shot. She returned to sipping her coffee. The couple at the table next to her backed up their chairs and rose to leave. He was around fifty-ish with gray hair and a mustache. He was dressed in the best clothes money could buy; probably an Armani suit. The woman was younger by at least fifteen years, perhaps more. Her peach silk shirt dress barely covered her derriere. She was jacked up on six-inch Manolos which made her legs look incredibly long. The bright red belt around her middle emphasized her tiny waist. Her updo, French manicure, Chanel bag, and flawless makeup screamed "I love money!" Sarah noticed the man had a wedding ring on his left hand, but the woman with him did not. *Mistress. A pampered mistress. Enjoy it while you can, girlfriend. Eventually, you'll wake up and he'll be gone—no explanation.*

The first seeds of cynicism took root. Recognizing innocence lost, she sighed. There was no magic in Barcelona anymore. No reason to stay any longer.

Sarah went up to her room where she changed her travel plans, departing a day earlier than scheduled. She set out her travel clothes for the next day. After she finished packing last-minute things, she sat down on the side of the bed and called the front desk to order a five-a.m. wake-up call. Her plane was scheduled to leave at a quarter past eight in the morning and she would need to be at the airport at least two hours ahead of time. Finally, she lay back in the bed she'd so recently shared with Anthony—the bed where she'd lost her virginity to a man she barely knew. It was in this bed, in this room in Barcelona, where she'd fallen so briefly in love, and where she'd experienced her first major heartbreak. Sarah thought the best thing she could do would be to leave all those feelings behind, packed away inside these four walls where they would linger like a ghost of what might have been. She would never forget her time here at the Hotel Claris, but after experiencing such raw abandonment, both of her heart and body, and of being left behind, she knew that dwelling on why Anthony had chosen to walk out on her without a word would serve no purpose. She'd come to Europe for a reason; to explore her own boundaries, discover who she was in every form. This was merely one of those forms.

A tear trickled down her cheek as she closed her eyes. Sleep was hard to find, but she eventually succumbed to Morpheus' lure. Tomorrow, a new adventure awaited her. Berlin would mark a new chapter in the education of Sarah Brown.

Chapter 7

A loud pounding woke Paul from a drunken slumber. The banging was harsh and insistent. He threw off his blanket and walked to the front door, scratching his eyes and adjusting himself through his boxer briefs. He tripped over the edge of his easel, cursing roundly.

"Who the fuck is it," he grated out.

"Open up, you lazy *rekening* fool!" Paul knew that voice and he stopped dead in his tracks. Uncle Peter's voice still had the power to instill morbid dread and fear in him. It was the voice that haunted his nightmares. Since turning legal age, he'd avoided his uncle and managed quite nicely to steer clear of him for the most part. Since becoming a man in his own right—a man with more than enough strength to inflict great bodily harm on the old codger should he need to—he knew he could protect himself. But when he heard that voice, he forgot about being a grown man; forgot his own height, strength, and agility, even forgot his own rights and felt once again like that five-year-old boy lured by a friendly smile, a piece of candy or a toy, onto the lap of the seemingly giant man whose hands held him immobile while he fondled and molested that innocent child; that trusting nephew.

Paul reached into the drawer of the side table for his handgun, checked the chamber for rounds, and then cautiously proceeded to the door. He left the chain in the lock as he inched the door open. He peered through the opening at the weathered but sophisticated man on the other side. His silver hair was neatly parted to the left and his gray twill sports jacket covered a cream-colored turtleneck sweater. As usual, his uncle looked every bit the gentleman and not in the least like a child-molesting creep. To Paul, he looked like a monster.

"What the hell do you want?" Paul was in no mood for this and knew he didn't want to hear anything his uncle had to say.

"Are you going to keep me out here in the cold," he asked, smiling benevolently. It was the smile of a crocodile before it eats you.

"Yes! What is it?" Paul grew more agitated.

His uncle's smile fell, and all hints of civility faded away like flecks of ash in a stiff breeze. "I have a job for you. It's rather urgent."

Paul could smell the stale alcohol and tobacco on his breath. It threatened to revive memories best left forgotten.

"I don't work for you, Uncle." Paul started to close the door, but Peter Knudson stuck his booted foot in the jamb.

"Not so fast. I know you need the money. Your mother said you'd come 'round asking for a loan to tide you over. She also said she refused to lend it to you."

It was true that Paul was low on funds. He worked odd jobs here and there but hadn't ever settled into any particular career. His paintings never sold. He never even tried, thinking them not good enough, just the manifestations of his inner turmoil and attempts at creating art. Because of this, he'd ended up many a time on the scummy side of employment in the sex trade, turning a few tricks, and even working in a few porn films to make ends meet. He liked his playboy lifestyle, but he'd never learned to work for it. He was lucky he hadn't fallen too heavily into drugs, although he'd dabbled often enough. He liked a fast buck because it afforded him the time to play, and here was his loathsome uncle on his doorstep dangling another carrot in front of him, again. He'd learned not to reach for this particular carrot because there were always strings attached; strings that tied him up both metaphorically and physically, leaving him broken inside and hating himself.

Paul stared back at his uncle in frustration. "My finances are none of your business."

"Everything about you is my business. You're my nephew." Peter's voice softened and the benevolent smile returned; the one that always preceded that "bad" thing. Paul knew it and yet he still felt drawn in. It was like every one of his nightmares.

"I am always concerned about you, Paul. You're not settled. You drift from this to that. Don't you know that I worry about you?" The honeyed concern dripping from his voice was like acid to Paul's soul. It burned slowly, drop by drop.

"State your business so I can say no one final time and then go!" Paul had lost his patience and in doing so, brought up the gun in his right hand, aiming it straight at Peter's chest.

Peter's eyes shifted to the barrel pointed at him and his face tightened with near-imperceptible anger. "What's this?"

"Speak!" Paul didn't bother to hide his impatience.

"Well," his uncle cleared his throat, "as you are aware, I have several business interests in the Red-Light District—"

"Yes, yes." Paul waved the gun in an attempt to hurry him along.

"There's a domme in Berlin I wish to bring into my club. She's one of the best in the business, but she's reluctant to leave the club she currently works for. I want you to travel to Berlin and convince her to come work for me."

"That's it? That's your big job?" Paul was skeptical. He knew his uncle's perversions, and he wasn't personally into being dominated, so why did he want this dominatrix? He preferred being in control, and he preferred it with young men...with boys.

"This is business. I have a list of high-end customers who would pay a fortune for her. Do this. Go to Berlin and convince her. For your part, I'll pay your travel expenses, plus fifteen hundred euro."

Paul's eyes opened wide in surprise. "Fifteen hundred euro? You'll pay me that much to recruit a new dominatrix for your club? Why can't you go and do this yourself? What's the catch?"

Peter replied in a half truth. "I am blocked from entering Germany. Therefore, I need to send you as a representative for Club Tiberius since you can travel unrestricted."

"Why are you blocked from entering Germany?" In his heart, he knew why. He knew his uncle had probably gotten into trouble while visiting Berlin. His penchant for pedophilia was surely the reason.

"That's none of your business," he replied angrily. Peter's face smoothed over, and the crocodile smile slid easily back into place. "So, nephew, will you do it?"

Paul weighed all the pros and cons. He knew getting involved in anything his uncle orchestrated would somehow cause him a problem, but he couldn't quite figure out how this situation would. Plus, it paid well, and he did need the money. All he had to do was go to Berlin, all expenses paid, and charm some dominatrix into coming to work for Peter. She would not be in any danger from his uncle since Peter's tastes didn't include women. Should he grab the carrot this time?

"All expenses paid?"

"Yes."

"Payment up front?"

"Half now, and half when you succeed." Peter looked sincere, but he always looked sincere. That was how he'd managed to fool Paul's mother into thinking her son was safe in his care whenever she would ask her brother to babysit while she went to work. That was why she never believed Paul when, as a child, he'd tried to tell her what was going on with Uncle Peter.

"What am I to tell this young woman? Who is she and where will I find her?" Paul lowered the gun to his side and Peter knew then he'd won.

"I'll send you all the details of my offer to her, her information and so forth, along with your airline ticket. I'll have it delivered this afternoon. You'll leave in the morning." With that, Peter retracted his foot, which had been in the door the entire time, then turned and left.

Paul stood there with the cold blowing in through the crack in the door. It was chilling, a foreshadowing perhaps. Finally, he closed it and thought, *what the hell did I just get myself into?*

Chapter 8

Tegel International in Berlin presented as a small, but efficient airport. It was the cleanest airport Sarah traveled through so far, although so far, she'd only seen San Antonio International, a brief flight change in Atlanta, and Barcelona. Still, the cleanliness of it hadn't escaped her notice. Even the bathrooms were spotless, and she noted that they were separated into men's, women's, families, and disabled. *The Germans certainly pride themselves on spotless toilets*, she thought.

After utilizing the facilities and brushing out her hair, she picked up the handle on her suitcase and went in search of an exchange where she could acquire euros for her American dollars. She looked around for the word *wechseln*. She located the booth and stood in line. Down one corridor were rows of fancy shops where one could purchase beautiful gifts like German crystal, chocolates, clothing, leather purses and wallets, and even fun novelties duty-free. Sarah listened to the people walking by speaking in multiple languages; Chinese, French, Italian, and German. Back home in Texas, she mostly heard Tex-Mex, a localized version of the Spanish that originated from Mexico and evolved over decades north of the Río Grande. Other than that, she was used to Americanized English spoken in various dialects depending on what region of the United States people came from. Being a military city, San Antonio attracted all kinds and Helotes sat at the northwest side of Military City, USA. Spain didn't sound any different. Castilian Spanish fell upon her ear with the same rhythms as Mexican Spanish. Hearing all the different tongues speaking at once without any of the usual audial salsa, she truly felt like she was finally in Europe.

"Ich mochte Geld wechseln, bitte." (*I would like to exchange money, please.*)

"Wie viel?" The kindly woman behind the glass asked.

"Eight hundred U.S. dollars." Sarah's brief grasp of German ended with numbers.

With the exchange to euros complete, she set out to find a taxi. One happened to be in the queue out front, and she headed for it, running straight into a tall man with dark hair, causing him to drop the handle of his luggage.

"Sorry!" Sarah stopped and looked up, smiling her apology.

The man opened his mouth, prepared to curse at the clumsy person when his eyes lit upon, instead, a beautiful woman smiling up at him. His expression changed immediately. Like a chameleon, the anger left his eyes, and the tight lines around his mouth smoothed out.

"Entschuldigen Sie, Fraulein." Blue eyes locked onto the woman, taking her measure from head to toe, and then began to crinkle in the corners as a smile spread across his attractive lips.

The taxi driver looked up from his newspaper at the two and raised an eyebrow.

"I'm sorry. I have no idea what you said, but it was all me. I wasn't paying attention," Sarah babbled, reaching down for his luggage.

"I simply said '*excuse me,*'" he replied, ducking low to retrieve it from her hand. His fingers brushed hers as he gripped the handle. "You are American?" The man continued to smile down at her.

He could have been a model that just walked off a runway in Milan. *Seriously*, she thought, *are all the good-looking men in Europe because they never look this good back home? They certainly never dress this well in Texas, either*. Sarah noted the dark blue tailored suit, and the Italian leather shoes. He didn't have one hair out of place. He even smelled good.

"Yes. I guess the babbling gave me away."

He chuckled. "Not at all. It was just your charming accent."

"I don't have an..." she began to say and then realized to anyone not American, she did, indeed, have an accent.

"But you do, and it is as charming and lovely as yourself." He continued to stand and stare down at her with a smile on his face. The moment stretched out awkwardly.

"Well, thank you. It was nice to meet you." Sarah began walking again toward the taxi.

He followed. "You're just arriving? Maybe we could share the taxi? I'm on my way into the city, to my hotel." He reached past her and opened the back door. The cab driver stepped out and stood looking from one to the other to see whose luggage he would be depositing into the trunk.

She looked at the cab driver, who simply shrugged. Looking back at the tall, handsome man, she hesitated. A red flag waved somewhere in the back of her mind. *Sure, he's good looking*, but she was still a stranger in a strange land and for all she knew, he could be a serial killer.

"That's okay. I can wait until the next one. You go ahead and take this one," she said.

He smiled; one eyebrow raised in amusement. "No, no. You must take it. I can wait till the next one rolls through." He indicated with one look to the driver that he should take the woman's suitcase. The man did and loaded it into the boot.

"Well, thank you then." She slid into the seat.

The man gave her what was surely a practiced grin that made his blue eyes twinkle. "You're most welcome." With that, he closed the door and then walked around where the cab driver was locking the trunk. They spoke briefly before the tall man stood back again on the sidewalk and waited as another taxi rolled to a stop behind Sarah's.

Her driver hopped into the front seat and put on his seatbelt. He looked back at her and asked, "Where to," in half-way decent English.

"The Holiday Inn Express on Stressemannstraße, please."

The driver turned the wheel and began pulling out. Sarah twisted around and saw the handsome man give her a wave before he got into his own taxi. She faced forward and laughed to herself.

She caught the cab driver's eye in the rearview mirror. He was an old man with quite a bit of padding around the middle. His wrinkled face attested to many long years of hard work. He gave her a wink and a laugh and then wagged his finger at her like a grandpa having a little fun at a grandchild's expense.

Sarah shook her head, grinning. They drove off the airport property and merged onto the highway. Berlin loomed large before her eyes and she looked forward to exploring the city and all it had to offer, including some of the darker attractions.

The ride into Berlin took about half an hour with the traffic. The driver turned around on the street and pulled up in front of the hotel. It was a flat faced building with large windows on the first floor. Out on the sidewalk, the cab driver handed over her luggage. She paid him and offered a generous tip. The old man shook his head and laughed at the crazy American who over-tipped him.

She crossed the sidewalk, which had both a cobbled walkway and a bike path—she'd read that it was wise to stay off the latter unless one wanted to get run down by bicycle traffic—and entered into the lobby. Inside, there was a reception desk straight ahead, and off to the right was a large cafeteria-styled dining area. She approached the desk and checked in.

Passport back in hand, key in the other, she wheeled her suitcase around to the left to find the elevators. On the way up to the third floor, she read the brochure in her hand. Dining hours were outlined within. Stepping out of the lift, she turned right and searched for number 317.

Her room was contemporary in design. The bed was platform-styled, and the furniture looked like the clean lines of Ikea. Her window faced out onto the courtyard below. She unlocked it and the glass leaned in forward, tilting from the top. The fresh air wafted in, clearing out the stuffiness. It was quiet below.

She unpacked her toiletries and placed them on the sink in the sizeable bathroom. A quick shower and a change of clothes, and she was ready to head out and explore before dinner. It was three in the afternoon and overcast. The air promised to be much cooler once the sun went down, so Sarah grabbed a sweater to tie over her shoulders.

Back down in the lobby, she walked out the front door. Across the street was a German restaurant and what appeared to be a convenience store. *Good to know.* She looked left and right, trying to decide which way to go. There wouldn't be much exploring today since it was already late afternoon, and she was hungry. She came from the right, so she went left. About two blocks down on the other side of the street was an Italian restaurant. Diomira. It looked clean, and Italian food appealed to her in that moment. However, there was a cluster of police vehicles parked in the road out front.

Police surrounded an unmarked delivery truck. One uniformed officer had what she presumed to be the driver of the truck on the ground, face-down, hands cuffed behind his back. Two plain-clothes officers, an older man with streaks of gray hair at his temples and a petite woman wearing a black suit stood to the side speaking with a second uniformed officer. The older man questioned the uniform while the woman took notes. A third uniform directed traffic around the scene. As Sarah watched, the second uniform turned, approaching the cuffed driver. Words were exchanged and the first uniform pulled the driver to his feet, escorting him to the back of his police car. A tow truck arrived, maneuvering in front of the delivery truck. The plain-clothes officers returned to their vehicle and left.

Seeing no need to worry, Sarah made her way across the street safely and entered the establishment. Inside, the décor was rustic and quaint. The food smelled good. The wooden tables reminded her of western-styled country stores back home in Texas. Red checkered tablecloths covered those tables. There wasn't a lot of seating. It was quite small inside, but a waiter with long hair tied back in a ponytail greeted her.

"Just one, Signorina?"

"Yes. You're Italian?" Sarah was surprised.

"Sì," he said, smiling. "This way." He led her over to a table for two by the window.

"Thank you," she said. Sarah sat down and he handed her a menu.

"Our special today is mushroom lasagna with a salad or shrimp scampi over angel hair pasta."

"Mushroom lasagna sounds wonderful. I'll try it." She didn't bother to look at the menu. Her stomach growled.

"Very good. What kind of dressing you want on your salad?" His English was decent, but not perfect.

"Do you have Thousand Island," Sarah asked hopefully.

"Eh, no, ma'am. We have House Italiano, Red Wine Vinaigrette, Creamy Italiano, and American Ranch."

"Oh. Creamy Italian then."

"Very good. And what would you like to drink?"

"A Coke would be fine."

"Sì, sì."

He walked away with her order and returned with a small bottle of Coke and two glasses. One glass was empty for her Coke and the other was filled with cold water. The tiny Coke bottle amused her. She was used to unlimited fountain drinks. This, however, didn't scream unlimited.

He left again, returning with some breadsticks and herb dipping oil. "I'll have your order out soon." He smiled and walked away, leaving her to savor the breadsticks.

Sarah watched people walk by the window. It seemed more people were on foot or on a bike than in cars. The vehicles she saw were mostly parked, and parking was packed up and down the street. A red-haired woman walked by wearing jeans, knee-high brown leather boots, and a brown leather jacket over a green shirt. Her face was exquisite with light-colored eyes and red lips. She looked like a model. Most people walking around Germany—and even in Barcelona—looked like they consulted Vogue before leaving their homes. Not at all like the Walmart couture she was used to back home. The woman walked into Diomira and approached the saloon-style bar.

She spoke in rapid German. Sarah didn't understand what she said, but the woman behind the counter reached down to pick up a brown paper bag that contained an order. The beautiful woman paid for her meal and then turned to leave. She caught Sarah's eye and smiled, nodding. Sarah smiled back. The woman left.

Her food arrived and she dove in. The greens were crisp, but the tomatoes were a little mushy. Still, it tasted good. Soon after, the waiter brought her lasagna. It was all perfectly portioned. The cheese, noodles, and mushrooms melted on her tongue in complete harmony with each other. Delicious. The portion migh be on the small side, but it was packed with lots of calories. She could taste each one.

As she finished her meal, her thoughts strayed to Anthony de Luca. She wondered where he was now and imagined how different this meal might've been if shared with her lover rather than all alone. Shaking off her melancholy, Sarah paid the bill, intent on enjoying herself. It was time to explore; not dwell on things she couldn't change.

Chapter 9

Anthony scrolled through the thousands of pictures he'd taken on his trip through Brussels, Belgium, across Germany, and through southern Spain and Barcelona. He needed to separate them out, choose the best, and catalogue the rest for possible use in future books or articles.

Brussels was great. The food he found in that city ranged across every culture. He'd made a few side trips to other smaller cities including Bruges where he'd hired a guide to take him by boat down all the canals and waterways. He planned a special guidebook for the best places to travel near water, and nothing beat the beauty of Bruges except maybe Venice, but Venice was far more crowded, and he liked the places off the beaten path.

Germany had been traveled by both train and boat. Starting on the western side near Dusseldorf, down to Trier, and over through Frankfort, down to Munich, and up through Bavaria before hitting the Eastern Bloc in Berlin. Berlin was more modern and had a lot to offer both in and outside the metropolitan center. A traveler could find just about anything in Berlin including, as he accidentally stumbled upon, prostitution. He found those images of the man beating the young blond male and thought to himself, again, that he should've reported it. But he hadn't. Instead, he finished his own tour of the city in photos, thinking that what he'd witnessed probably happened all the time and the street walkers most likely didn't want the police involved. The pictures caught the moment of brutality in vivid color. The cane, which upon closer inspection seemed to have a metal animal head, struck the young blond hustler across his temple. Blood spatter was forever suspended midair in the images. Menace raged on the older man's face as dark brows were pulled down over fierce eyes. The goatee only added to the demonic visage. The young man's eyes screamed fear and outrage as his body language clearly indicated self-preservation. The digital display was disturbing to behold. Anthony quickly separated those out of the mix and into a folder marked "random."

Spain was productive until Barcelona. Barcelona was something different altogether. Sarah. Barcelona was all about Sarah. Her face came into focus on his nineteen-inch HD monitor. Beautiful, sexy, soft, natural, and provocative in an innocent way. Her brown eyes framed by dark lashes looked at him with promise. Her smile hinted at a secret, and her lips, as always, begged for a kiss without even asking.

He had a lot of pictures of her; walking ahead of him as they explored the shops and tourist destinations, at the beach with her toes in the sand, laughing, sampling new recipes at a food truck, and even sleeping after he'd made love to her for hours. She didn't know about those pictures. He'd taken them while she dreamed, while he thought about why he liked her so much more than other women he'd passed time with on previous trips. He thought then that it must've been because she was a virgin, and had chosen him as her first, but after a while, he couldn't justify that as his excuse. Sure, it was part of it. Every man liked knowing that he was the first; that he'd been where no other man had been before, but somehow, she wiggled her adorable ass right under his skin. He liked talking to her afterward, after the sexual adventures and great orgasms. She was smart and well-read. She was funny. She seemed genuinely interested in his work, and not in that fake way of other women who simply asked the expected questions, passing the time until they could get him up to their rooms. She cared. And he liked that she cared. And then he'd up and left her without a word.

Anthony paused, acknowledging that asshole move. He looked over at his mug of coffee sitting on the desk and picked it up, taking a sip. "Ugh!" He wrinkled his nose. "Fucking cold coffee." He put it down and reached for his backpack, digging inside for his notebook. The blue spiral contained all the information from his various shoots, including business cards, brochures, pamphlets, and personal notes. He opened the book and leafed through. Seville, Valencia, Madrid, Barcelona, and then found Sarah's information.

He looked at the address. He'd asked her for her email address after exploring the shops along the beach. He wanted to send her the pictures, he'd told her. She seemed giddy and high on all the fun from their afternoon of stolen kisses and illicit touching they'd engaged in whenever they thought no one was looking. She'd readily agreed and rattled off her information, including her cell number, "just in case."

He thought about calling her but then changed his mind. He thought about texting her, but again, *what would I say? Sorry I just up and left without saying goodbye. I'm a big dick that way. I didn't want you to get attached. I didn't want to get attached. I'm an asshole... I was scared.*

"Shit." He closed the notebook. Picking up the cold cup of coffee, he got up and went to the kitchen where he dumped it into the sink and ran the mug under the tap to rinse it out.

He looked around for something a little stronger and found nothing. He'd already killed his bottle of Wild Turkey and had yet to hit the liquor store to replace it. Making a quick decision, Anthony grabbed his jacket and picked up his wallet off the desk, slipping it into his back pocket. Keys in hand, he left, heading down to his favorite pub. He'd finish up going through the pictures later after a few drinks. He began texting Derek, his best friend.

Hey, fucknuts. O'Brien's?

His cell vibrated as he reached the stairs.

Fucknuts? Fuck You! That better be some autocorrect shit where you meant Handsome, Awesome, Best Buddy. Yeah, Twenty minutes? I'm just leaving the office.

⁕⁕⁕

Berlin, Marriot Hotel

Paul spent the afternoon catching a quick nap before his business appointment that evening. It had been difficult to arrange at first, but once he explained that he represented several clubs in Amsterdam looking for talent, the prospective employee reluctantly agreed. He was scheduled to meet her at half past ten. To seem more on the up and up, he'd asked her to include any others who might be interested in moving their business to the Netherlands where they would enjoy higher pay and better benefits. Everything was set. He lay in the queen-size bed in the Marriot silently cursing his uncle, and then himself for getting sucked into doing the prick's bidding.

He planned on running up a tab tonight. His uncle Peter said he'd pay the expenses of the trip, so Paul didn't plan on being frugal. It would be nightclubs, the appointment, a little fun after that, and a late dinner in the heart of downtown Berlin. Much like New York City, it didn't close after midnight.

He would need his rest for the night's coming attractions. He would need to be on his A-game. All he had to do was convince this woman to come work for his uncle—*the shit*—and when he got back home, he'd get the other half of his pay and be done with that evil monster.

He closed his eyes and tried not to let the usual nightmares in. They always came when he was alone. Maybe that was why he enjoyed being around women. They kept the bad memories at bay with their smiles, chatter, and sexy bodies. With a beautiful woman or two in his bed, he was distracted and drawn into the comfort of warm arms wrapping around him, and soft lips kissing him. Women loved him. And he loved women. The more the merrier.

Thinking about women he'd already had, some he still fooled around with on a more regular basis, and the possibility of meeting one or two tonight helped him fall asleep feeling happy. It wasn't long, though, before the monster intruded, pulling him in, promising candy, and ordering young Paul to pretend he was just holding a cane like the one leaning against the arm of the chair. Pretend and hold it "just like this," said a familiar voice. A voice coming from the foul mouth of the devil himself. Paul tried to scream, but no sound came out. Instead, hands covered his mouth, and he couldn't move or breathe. His suspenders were being pulled off his shoulders and down over his school uniform shirt. Hands reached, touching, grabbing. He could see his mother in the kitchen chatting away while she prepared dinner, but she never turned around, never came to his rescue. The monster had him, again, and he was abandoned, alone.

In the single occupancy hotel room, Paul tossed and turned on the bed, sweat gleamed on his forehead, and he repeatedly opened and closed his mouth, looking like a fish out of water, making small sounds that were cut off; that never quite reached a full scream. Outside, the sun began its descent toward the horizon as the day faded. His eyes opened suddenly, and he was released, finally, from the horrific grasp of the dream. He lay there in the dim light of late afternoon, tears sliding down his face. *Motherfucker! Fuck him! One day I'll kill him. One day,* he promised that little boy still trapped inside the nightmares.

❧ ❧

Sarah didn't know where to start. She walked a few blocks, enjoying the architecture in downtown Berlin. The streets were the cleanest she'd ever seen. Throughout the more urban areas, trees and small manicured patches of grass caught her eye. The high-rise residential buildings all seemed to have miniature parks within their courtyards where many locals were walking their dogs, riding their bikes, or just strolling like she happened to be doing. With each building painted a different color—yellow, green, red, and blue, it was all quite beautiful to behold. There were bakeries and small fresh produce markets on just about every corner. The pubs were quaint and looked like what she expected in a metropolitan city like Berlin, but some were more old-fashioned, and could be described better as 'taverns.' In all, the eastern bloc of Germany had a wonderful mix of old and new. Pre-World War II and post-modern architecture swirled together to make it unlike any city she'd ever seen—so far, that is.

She was near Potsdamerplatz when she realized it was getting late. The sun would soon set, and she had no plan of where to go or what to do. She stopped into a tourist shop near the Bahnhof and picked up a few trinkets for her co-workers—a cuckoo clock refrigerator magnet for Marge, a silver spoon with 'Berlin' on the handle for Terry, who collected them, and a T-shirt for Jim. Sarah paid for her items and stood, looking like the American tourist she was as she wondered why the salesclerk didn't put them in a bag for her. She stepped back and watched as two other customers paid for their items, picked them up, and then walked out with them in bags they had carried into the store. Looking around, she found a blue tote bag with a picture of the Brandenburg Gate on the front. It cost three euros. She purchased it at the last minute and then stowed her travel treasures inside.

Outside, daylight waned. She walked faster back toward the hotel. Lights began flickering on along the brick and concrete sidewalks. Storefronts closed, and restaurants and bars glowed like welcoming beacons to those seeking dinner and after-hours fun. Passing one of the many courtyards full of people coming and going only an hour earlier, Sarah found it to be empty save for a red-haired woman leaning against a tree, talking into her mobile. She looked familiar, but since she knew no one here, the thought flew out of her head. Suddenly, Sarah tripped and fell forward onto her hands and knees.

"Shit!" She sat back on her heels and inspected her right hand, which had smacked the ground hard enough to scrape her palm.

"Bist du verletz?" The red-haired woman approached and dropped down next to Sarah.

"What? I'm sorry. I don't speak German."

"Ah, American. I asked are you hurt?" The red-haired woman's green eyes were filled with concern.

Sarah held up her right hand. It was bleeding.

"Here, let me help you." The woman grabbed a scarf stuck inside the pocket of her jacket and wrapped it around Sarah's hand. "If you come with me inside, I can clean it up for you." Sarah started to rise, and the woman offered a helping hand.

Sarah reached with her left hand and stood as the woman tugged gently. "That's okay. I'm not far from my hotel. I can take care of it."

The woman looked at her with kindness. She was stunningly gorgeous in a way that Sarah knew she never would be. Flawless skin, emerald eyes, flowing red hair, and a svelte, shapely body like a runway model.

"Oh! You're the lady from the restaurant." Recognition lit Sarah's eyes.

"Excuse me?" The red-haired woman's eyes grew larger, if that was possible.

"Earlier today you picked up some food at the restaurant down the street. I saw you there."

Red laughed. "Ah, I see. Yes, yes, that was me. Now I remember you. You were eating alone."

Sarah's smile fell at the reminder of dining alone. "I'm Sarah." She started to offer her right hand, then remembered it was injured and wrapped in the woman's green scarf.

"Elsa. Please, now we are not strangers, and you must come inside and let me tend to your hand." She took Sarah's left hand and led her toward the faded yellow building.

"I don't want to intrude…"

"Who's intruding? It's just me and Anno, and we don't bite." Elsa was smiling as she opened the door and walked inside toward a small lift.

Sarah didn't like small spaces and the cramped interior had her holding her breath.

"Who's Anno? Is that your husband?"

"What? No! Anno is my little brother. No husband. Just us."

"That's an unusual name, Anno." Sarah followed as Elsa pulled the gate open and pushed the door out onto the fourth floor.

"It's short for Johann. Quite common, really."

"How old is he?" The hallway stretched straight down and then dog-legged to the left. It was around that corner where they stopped in front of a door marked '4A.' Elsa pulled out a key and unlocked the latch.

"He is fourteen, but he will tell you *almost* fifteen." She laughed. "His birthday is coming up in just one month. He is a pain in the ass, but I love him."

Sarah smiled and looked around the entry hall. The tall ceilings were topped with crown molding in their pre-WWII décor. At the end of the hall was a spacious living room with three high windows facing out onto another building and a partial courtyard.

Elsa continued to pull Sarah along by her good hand into the bathroom. The black and white tile on the floor was matched by a similar backsplash behind the pedestal sink. Elsa reached into the medicine cabinet above and pulled out hydrogen peroxide and some ointment. She unwrapped her hand and turned on the water.

"Stick your hand under there for a few minutes," she instructed. Elsa threw the scarf into the waste basket.

Feeling guilty, Sarah said, "I'm so sorry. I'll repay you for it."

"Nonsense! It was old and I want to buy a new one anyway." Elsa turned off the water and opened the peroxide bottle. "This might sting a little," she cautioned, pouring it over Sarah's hand.

Sarah sucked in a breath. It stung like hell.

"Sorry." Elsa smiled and then blew gently onto Sarah's palm. She couldn't remember the last time a woman had been so nice and motherly toward her, not even her own mother. This beautiful woman didn't appear to be much older than herself, but she had that motherly quality—maybe because she took care of her brother, but she didn't know the full story on that, so she didn't want to speculate. Still, it was nice. Sarah's eyes welled up with tears.

"Here now. It wasn't that bad, was it?" Elsa noticed the tears and instantly grew more concerned.

Still holding her hand, Sarah shook her head, feeling foolish. "No, not at all. It's just, well, a lot has happened lately, and you're being so kind."

Elsa popped the top off the antibiotic ointment and rubbed a little of the gel gently onto Sarah's scraped palm. It was soothing, just like her demeanor.

"Hold still." She grabbed a roll of gauze and wrapped up the hand.

"Now you are all good. Come. We will have a coffee and some girl talk, and you can tell me all about it."

The tears flowed faster. Elsa stopped walking toward the kitchen and turned back to envelop Sarah in her arms.

"Shhh. It's okay."

Sarah cried. All her emotions burst past the flood gates—her mother's illness and passing, her father's at-will absence, and Anthony's abandonment all tumbled out in a rush of tears and almost incomprehensible words over the next hour. Elsa listened with compassion and kept Sarah's coffee cup filled. They sat together on the couch with legs drawn up beneath them. The sun had set, and night was upon them.

A key in the lock interrupted the ebbing of grief and intermittent hiccups.

"Anno, is that you? It's about time! Where have you been?" Elsa sounded more like a mother than a sister.

"Geez, Elsa, I was only at Erik's," replied a voice down the entry hall. "Relax."

A beautiful blond teenage boy rounded the corner into the living room and stopped. He looked at Sarah.

"Sorry, I didn't know you had company." He thrust his hands into the pockets of his jeans and stood awkwardly, staring at the woman with the tear-stained face.

"This is Sarah. She's visiting from America. Sarah, Anno. Anno, Sarah."

Anno offered a small wave. "Hey."

Sarah sniffed and laughed. "Hey. Nice to meet you, Anno."

"So, what's for dinner?" He walked to the kitchen.

"I don't know. What are you cooking?" Elsa asked him and laughed at the horrified look on her brother's face.

"Me? Why me? Elsa, I'm starving!" He opened the small refrigerator and looked at it like it might suddenly spit out a full meal.

Elsa followed and reached around him, pulling out the bags of food she'd picked up earlier at the restaurant.

Sarah stood up, preparing to leave.

"Where are you going, Sarah?"

"I should get back to my hotel. You guys need to eat, and it's getting late."

"What? No, no. You're having dinner with us and then we'll get you a taxi. Sit. Eat."

Elsa wasn't taking no for an answer. She heated up the pasta with chicken and vegetables and quickly put together a salad of cucumbers, tomatoes, and onions. Anno scarfed his down as if he were truly starving and then went off to his room to play video games.

Sarah helped Elsa clean up. Afterwards, Elsa excused herself to change clothes and grab a duffel bag along with her purse.

"Anno. I'm going to take Sarah to her hotel and then I'm off to work. Stop playing those videos and do your homework. I'll see you tomorrow. Love you."

She kissed the top of his head and walked out of his room as he threw a shoe at her saying. "Stop kissing me!"

Sarah smothered a laugh. The relationship these two had was obviously a loving one. She'd never had a sibling, so she didn't know what it was like, but it looked nice.

On the way down the lift, Elsa explained. "Our parents were killed five years ago in an auto accident. I've been taking care of Anno ever since. I was only eighteen then. Anno was a surprise since he came along so late in my parents' marriage, but he's my special little man."

"God, you were so young to be taking on that kind of responsibility. How did you do it? What do you do? Where do you work?" Sarah was full of questions.

Elsa opened the door to the courtyard, and they walked out into the night air, which had grown chilly.

"Wow. It sure gets cold after dark." Sarah was unprepared, with only a thin sweater over her T-shirt. Elsa wrapped an arm around her shoulders, and together they walked to the street where she hailed a taxi.

As they slid into the backseat, she said, "I work in a sex club."

Sarah's eyes widened and her mouth dropped open.

"Where to?" Elsa asked.

"What?" Sarah couldn't believe what she heard.

"Which hotel? Where are you staying?"

"Oh. At the Holiday Inn Express, just down the street."

Elsa gave the direction to the driver. Sitting back, Sarah stared at her.

"What? You're shocked? It's honest work. I'm a dominatrix. I basically spank bad men for money. It pays well, and I can afford to keep a nice flat and take care of my brother."

"It's not that. You just caught me off guard, that's all. Really? You spank men?" Sarah's expression changed from shock to curiosity.

"Yes. I tie them up, whip them, degrade them, make them lick my boots, and spank their bottoms or whatever else they want spanked."

The cab driver coughed and looked at them in the rearview mirror before quickly looking away.

"How fascinating." Sarah was intrigued.

Elsa noted that Sarah wasn't being judgmental at all, but rather, seemed like she wanted to know more. Realizing she didn't need to defend herself, Elsa relaxed. "Would you like to come visit me at work? I could show you around later."

"Yes!" Sarah didn't hesitate. Elsa chuckled.

"I have a few appointments, and then some man from Amsterdam is coming by. He wants to recruit me for one of his uncle's clubs. I'm not interested in moving, but maybe some of the other girls might be. A few of them will be showing off for him, so you might find that interesting. But after that, say around eleven-thirty, I could show you the dungeons and maybe you can watch what we do there. What do you think?"

"I think I need to know where to go and how to get there," Sarah replied as they pulled up in front of her hotel.

"It's best if you take a taxi since you don't know your way around." Elsa leaned forward to speak to the cab driver. "Can you come back and pick up my friend at eleven and take her to this address?" She wrote it down on a piece of paper, then wrote it again on another for Sarah just in case. "I'll pay you in advance."

"Oh, I can pay for the taxi," said Sarah.

"I got it. No worries, as you say in America." The cab driver told her he'd be back at the appointed time and then wrote it in his schedule book. The look on his face was inscrutable.

"Okay, I'll see you later, Sarah." Elsa hugged her and kissed her cheek.

Sarah got out and stood on the sidewalk. She waved as the cab pulled away. Turning to go inside, she began thinking about clothing. *What does one wear to a sex club?*

She had at least three hours to spare before she would be leaving again. She decided to take a nap for the first two hours and then get changed in the last hour. She set her travel clock to wake her at ten. Sarah fell asleep faster than she thought possible considering her level of excitement, but she had traveled most of the day, walked around the city, fell, and cried her heart out. All of it took a toll on her, and exhaustion hit hard. It was the best two-hour nap she'd had in a long time.

Chapter 10

The pinging of the travel alarm woke her. Sarah lay in the dark, slowly coming to consciousness. For a moment, she forgot where she was, and then it all came flooding back. She was alone in bed in Berlin. Not next to a warm, sexy man in Barcelona. The last thought was quickly suppressed.

Sarah shook herself and then got up, picking out a lavender sweater dress with three-quarter sleeves. It was a lightweight, soft, cashmere material. The length of it ended about two inches above her knees. Beneath it, she wore a darker purple thong but decided to skip the bra. It was a risky move because the material sliding over her nipples felt like a constant caress and they remained erect. She slid into thigh-high black leather boots and cinched a wide black leather belt with a silver buckle around her waist. She left her hair down but added a few curls. Keeping her makeup simple, she added plum eye shadow and black eyeliner that made her brown eyes smoky, and a plum-colored lip gloss. Standing back, she checked herself out in the bathroom mirror. A sexy stranger stared back at her; not the mousy librarian from Texas at all anymore. This was not a girl, but a woman. Her mother would not have approved, and somehow, that thought made Sarah smile. She'd suffered too long under Mary Brown's strict rules and warped religious rantings. Had she seemed even remotely happy with her life, Sarah might have listened more to her mother, but she'd always been angry and miserable, never enjoying life. Mary Brown viewed being a woman as a horrendous burden, a trial by fire bestowed by God to test unworthy souls.

It was all bullshit.

She was free of all of that now. There was nothing holding her back. The bounce in her step as she exited her room, purse in hand, told a story of a young woman confident that she looked her best. She may not fully believe it herself, yet, but like the caterpillar in its chrysalis, she was coming into her own. Men standing around the lobby waiting to check into their rooms noticed her as their heads craned around to watch her walk out. One man received a slap on the back of his head from his annoyed wife.

Outside, the taxi waited as promised. The driver did a double take as he looked at her. Gone was the girl next door from earlier and sliding into his backseat was a supermodel! He smiled and offered a slight nod of his head. They drove off to the club on the other side of town. She was excited to see what the night would bring. She wondered if Elsa might let her wield the whip once just to see what it was like to have that kind of control, that kind of power.

Better yet, she wondered what it would be like to be the one controlled. Illicit thoughts raced through Sarah's head as the taxi passed the Galleria and sped over waterways lit up by lanterns. The night air was cool as it blew through the window, ruffling her hair. *Almost there,* she thought. Nervousness gripped her even as excitement coursed through her body, settling in her stomach like a swarm of butterflies eager to be freed.

New York City

Anthony awoke late in the afternoon to one hell of a hangover. He and Derek hit the shots a little hard the night before. He sort-of remembered spilling his guts about a certain young woman, and then he remembered Derek laughing at him and making whip cracking sounds. As he tumbled further into drunkenness and slurred speech, Derek managed to remain upright and coherent. *Fucking Irish fuck!* Derek could drink every day of the week and all day on Sunday and still pass a sobriety test. It was like he just pissed it out without it affecting him at all. *Never trust a ginger. Those bastards can outdrink anyone.*

He rubbed his face and groaned. His head was pounding like a jackhammer. He got up and walked carefully to the bathroom. Looking into the mirror on the medicine cabinet, he made a face. A shitty visage greeted him, almost snarling. He had exactly two 500mg Tylenol left. *If I'm going to be drinking with D, I'll need to buy the economy-size bottle.*

He sighed, then popped the pills onto his tongue and leaned down to cup handfuls of water into his mouth to swallow them. A quick shower helped ease some of his torment, and a cup of coffee would fix the rest. Anthony dressed in jeans, T-shirt, and hiking boots, then headed out to the kitchen. He skipped the coffee maker and opted for instant. His head wasn't up for any delays, and he needed his caffeine ASAP.

Hot, black, and in hand, he walked to his desk sipping the brew. Each swallow seemed to bring him a little more back to the land of the living.

His desk looked like a hurricane had hit it. He barely remembered going through all his pictures again when he got home in the wee hours. Several of Sarah were still up on the screen. There she was, smiling, laughing, looking gorgeous. His notebook was out next to the keyboard and glaring at him from the open page was her email address.

"What the fuck was I doing last night?" Anthony suddenly felt sick. He sat down and opened his email. Maneuvering the mouse over his 'SENT' file, he clicked. The file opened.

"Shit!" Anthony's hands reached behind his head as he leaned forward, chin to chest and eyes closed. He counted to ten.

He opened his eyes again, hoping he was just seeing things, that he was having some post-alcoholic delusion. But no. There it was. An email to Sarah with several of her photos attached. That wasn't the worst part. It was the message, a drunken slur-typing by a complete ass.

I fucking miss you.

He hadn't signed it, but with all the images attached and the email address of adelucaphotography@outlook.com, it couldn't be more obvious who it was from, who wrote those words.

"Sonofabitch!" He sat forward and read it again. He'd meant it, but to what purpose? What would he do with her besides the obvious? He wasn't the guy who had committed relationships. He just wasn't *that* guy!

There was no way he could recall the email, either. All he could do was wait, and if she answered, he'd explain that he'd been drunk, hoped she was doing well, and that she enjoyed the pictures. She was a smart woman. She'd get it. She'd understand the brush off.

Somewhere in the dark recesses of his brain, he seemed to recall Derek saying, "Just call her, man." In his mind, he could see D's face looking both concerned and annoyed at having to listen to him whine on and on about a woman. *So, it was D's fault.* He'd make sure to repay that favor later.

His email pinged and then showed a red number "1" in new mail. He cringed. *Here we go,* he thought. Anthony hesitated a moment longer, dreading having to say the necessary words to discourage any more contact even though he was the dumbass who'd initiated it, and also fighting a feeling of...joy...over hearing from her. He clicked the mouse.

It was from his agent, Joe Wyznewski. He felt simultaneously relieved and disappointed. He read the letter.

From: jwyzlitagency@JWLit.net

To: adelucaphotography@outlook.com

De Luca,

Amsterdam Canal Cruises has requested you to come take pictures of their city from the point of view of a canal cruise and do a guest write-up about their business for their website. They've offered all expenses paid, lodging, trips on all six of their fleet up and down the canals of Amsterdam, and a per diem. Additionally, they'll feature your latest book and a link to your other books online. They're offering payment of $3,000, your usual for a week. They'd like you to start right away. Interested?

Joe

"Hmm, Amsterdam." Anthony sat thinking. *It might be a good idea to stay busy. Plus, it is a great paid gig. Who would turn down three thousand dollars and an all-expenses paid trip with a per diem? Not me!*

He sat forward and began typing his reply.

To: jwyzlitagency@JWLit.net

From: adelucaphotography@outlook.com

Hey Joe,

Yes. Arrange my ticket and let me know when to leave.

Although he'd only just returned from Spain, he didn't feel bad at all about taking off again. He could work on his book anywhere and working kept him from thinking about her. And he got paid, so it was a win-win.

"Red Light District, here I come," he joked with himself as he got up and carried his coffee to the window, looking out over the street below. *See? This is why I stay single. I couldn't possibly just take off on a whim or a quick job with a girlfriend—especially a wife. Women just don't understand that sort of thing.* Anthony comforted himself that he was doing the right thing, but deep down inside, he wished he could take Sarah with him. *She would love Amsterdam.*

Chapter 11

The address where the taxi driver let Sarah out looked dark and seedy. In that moment, she felt apprehensive and began questioning both her sanity and her safety at agreeing so readily to come to the place. The cabbie pointed toward the stairs leading down to the entrance. Sarah took a deep breath and began her descent. As she stepped inside, she saw a small reception area with a door along one wall and an old-style ticket booth on the other. Behind the glass was a shirtless man wearing a studded leather collar. He was blond, muscular, and rugged. Just as she decided he looked intimidating, almost terrifying, he glanced up from his cell phone and a wide, friendly smile spread across his face. In the split second it took to change expressions, he now appeared approachable. Dimples peeked out on either side of his lips, and his blue eyes crinkled at the corners just a bit.

"And you are Sarah, Ja?" His German accent matched his looks.

Apparently, she was expected. Sarah let out the breath she didn't know she'd been holding. "Ja, I mean, yes. I'm Sarah." She walked up to the counter.

"Elsa is expecting you. She told me all about her new, lovely American friend. I'm Hans. Hold on, liebling. I'll be escorting you personally."

Hans stepped out of the booth through an unnoticed side door and came into the reception room. He reached out and took Sarah's hands in his own and leaned forward to kiss each cheek. His graceful stride indicated to Sarah that Hans preferred the company of men—just as she did.

Indeed, Hans seemed to have a better catwalk than most runway models which was out of sync with his warrior physique. And to think, for a minute, she'd thought him terrifying. He led her by the hand through a maze of hallways, past doorways from which both screams of pain and moans of pleasure could be heard. He seemed completely unaffected by it while Sarah's curiosity was at a fever pitch, wanting to see what was happening behind each door.

They came to a large double wooden doorway, the kind a person expects in an old castle. "This is Mistress Elsa's dungeon, liebling. She's just finishing up with a customer, so be very quiet. You can watch, but don't let her Sub know you're there. There's a chair in the corner," Hans said, and then they quietly crept inside.

The 'dungeon' was a large room with walls painted black and decorated with gilt mirrors and frames around what must be copies of famous works of art. Sconces lit the room in a warm, but not quite fully illuminated glow. It smelled dank and moldy with a hint of sandalwood. She noted incense burning on a shelf above a free-standing table toward the back. On the right was a large mirror in the wall. Next to it in the far corner was a plush throne-like chair. Hans indicated this as the place where she could sit and observe. He turned to leave but stopped to have a quick peek at the flesh on display. On the left-hand wall was a rack. A naked man wearing a leather hood over his face was tied by the wrists and ankles spread-eagle. There was a zippered opening over his mouth for breathing. He had gray chest hair, and his genitals were exposed for all to see. His penis stood at full attention and his legs quivered at the knees as her new friend, Mistress Elsa, attached medieval metal clamps to his nipples. Elsa wore red leather boots that rose to mid-thigh, and a black bustier and thong. The mask over the upper half of her face reminded Sarah of Mardi Gras masks. It was black, red, and gold, and made her look mysterious. It probably also helped protect her identity. She glanced back at Sarah and gave an almost imperceptible wink. Sarah smiled. She noticed Hans standing and staring and shooed him out the door. He left with a flounce and a pout, making it difficult for Sarah to not laugh at his antics.

Elsa stood back and picked up her flogger. She began speaking in a commanding voice. "Ich glaube nicht, dass du meiner Peitsche würdig bist!" (*I do not think you are worthy of my flogger!*)

She flicked and snapped the tethers against her boot. The man shook with excitement and moaned, "Bitte, Herrin, Ich bin Ihr würdigster Sklave." (*Please, Mistress. I am your most worthy slave.*)

Elsa reached out and pinched her fingers over his left nipple clamp. He screamed. Then she ran the leather tethers softly over his engorged member. He whimpered and pleaded with her, "Bitte, Herrin! Bitte."

With that, Elsa whipped the man across his belly, then his thighs, and belly again, leaving red, angry welts to rise on his skin before actually swatting his genitals with the flogger. He moaned and screamed with equal delight. Sarah was fascinated. It was intriguing to be watching this man's pleasure/pain without his knowledge. Voyeurism wasn't something she'd ever thought about before, but there was definitely something to watching another person receive pleasure. She wondered what it would be like to be watched, as well.

Elsa turned slightly and pointed her finger at Sarah, crooking it and beckoning her over. Sarah got up and walked as quietly as she could over to the rack. Elsa handed her the flogger and stood back. Sarah looked at Elsa with wide eyes. The domme tried not to laugh but pointed at the man's stiff rod and mimicked flicking the flogger. Sarah blushed but took a deep breath and swung the tethers in a snapping motion, catching the man across his testicles and thighs.

"Ja! Bitte, Herrin, wieder!" (*Yes! Please, Mistress, again!*)

Sarah flicked him again across his thighs, then focused on his small, quivering, gray-haired member. After five good swats, the man shot gooey white fluid out like a fountain.

Elsa indicated Sarah should swat him several more times. Apparently, the man enjoyed it. After leaving several red finger-like welts on his chest, abdomen, and legs, he slumped over and cried, "Nicht mehr." (*No more.*)

Elsa took the flogger back and pointed Sarah toward her corner. She walked back, feeling powerful and strangely excited. She sat down and waited.

Elsa spoke softly to the man as she untied his wrists. She lifted the hood on his head up enough to expose his mouth as she bade him to bend down and kiss her boot. He did so with reverence, or as much reverence as he could muster wearing the leather head covering. He licked the boot and lavished his mistress with praise. When she'd had enough, she kicked at him to make him stop. He rose, and she told him to go and not touch himself at all until their next appointment. He promised he would not and wandered out of the room to another where he would change out of his bondage gear and back into the three-piece business suit he arrived in.

When the door closed, Elsa laughed and slipped off her mask. Her green eyes sparkled with mirth as she sauntered like a cat over to where Sarah sat.

"Hello, my new friend!" Elsa leaned down, kissing Sarah on each cheek. "You did very well."

"I was so scared I was going to actually hurt him, but he seemed to like it." She looked surprised.

"Herr Schulz relishes pain and especially enjoys being flogged. The first time he came to me, he begged me to kick him in the balls with my boot. I refused and wouldn't do it until his third visit. Not because I was afraid, mind you, but because I wanted him to learn that his pleasure is dependent upon my discretion and not his pleas." Elsa sat down on a foot stool, legs spread wide and arms resting on her knees as she continued to chat. Sarah tried not to notice how beautifully perfect Elsa's legs were—long, shapely, with creamy skin that looked smooth as silk. She wasn't sure why she would notice such on a woman or why noticing would cause her mouth to go dry. She licked her lips. The thought occurred that perhaps it was because she just hadn't been around many people in an intimate setting growing up.

Elsa watched her, a half-smile on her red lips.

Sarah swallowed and licked her lips again before asking, "What did he do when you finally kicked him?"

Locking eyes, the redhead responded, "He squirted all over my new black leather Ellie's. I'd just bought them the day before."

Sarah laughed. "So sorry to hear that your boots were collateral damage."

"Not at all. I made old Schulz lick them clean and buy me a new pair which he delivered at his next appointment. His lack of control earned me an extra pair of boots in another color." Elsa noticed Sarah looking at her legs. She gave her friend the once-over, appreciating how she looked tonight.

A knock on the door interrupted their conversation.

"Enter!" Elsa commanded.

The door swung wide, and two women dressed similarly to Elsa walked in. One was a blonde wearing a hot pink lacy bra and panties with white stilettos, and the other had long black hair and olive-toned skin. Her dark, almond-shaped brown eyes were lined in black kohl and her lips were painted dark red. She wore a sheer black, ankle-length negligee and bright red stilettos that had laces crisscrossing up her shins and tying at the back of her knees. They approached looking Sarah over from head to toe, taking her measure.

"Sarah, these are my co-workers, Nadia and Nicolette. Girls, this is my new American friend, Sarah Brown."

Nadia was the olive-skinned woman, and she smiled like a cat at Sarah, reaching her hand out to shake. Nicolette came right up and took Sarah's face in her manicured hands and kissed her on both cheeks, and then on the lips.

"Nice to meet you, ladies." Sarah blushed, not quite knowing how to take it all in.

"Sarah is on vacation all the way from Texas. She's had a little bad luck with men, but haven't we all?" Elsa stood and stretched.

"That is why I prefer beating them," said Nadia. She reached out and ran her hand down Sarah's hair in a comforting gesture.

"Yes, men are good for their wallets, and not much else. Women are much nicer." Nicolette cocked her head to the side checking Sarah out. She smiled with approval.

Sarah felt flushed, confused.

"Where is the Dutchman? Did he leave?" Elsa asked.

"No. We left him in the observatory." Nadia glanced at the large window on the wall to her left. "He said he wanted to watch us all work, but you're already finished with Herr Schulz, Elsa."

"I let Sarah have at him and he popped his pecker quickly. She's a natural, girls." Elsa placed an arm around Sarah's shoulders and gave her a squeeze.

"But we need to show him something or else his trip is wasted," said Nicolette, looking at Sarah.

"Who is this man again, and why does he need to see you work?" Sarah asked the million-dollar question of Elsa.

"He's a representative of a club owner from Amsterdam, the one I mentioned in the taxi, out here scouting for new talent for his dungeon. I'm not really interested, what with Anno still in school, but Nadia and Nicolette don't have any ties and could work anywhere if the pay is good, so I introduced him to them." Elsa offered the explanation.

"He's quite handsome...for a man," said Nicolette. She reached out and touched the belt around Sarah's waist. "We could work on you, Sarah," she purred.

"Me? But I don't like pain." She laughed nervously as the blonde German woman invaded her personal space.

"You never know what you will like until you try it once," said Nadia. "And we could go easy on you. Simple things like a good spanking, nipple clamps, a little roping..." She seemed to be warming up to the idea while Sarah felt nothing but fear and apprehension at being placed in bonds.

"Please, Sarah?" Nicolette stepped closer and wrapped her arms around Sarah's waist while Elsa stood back watching the American closely.

"I won't let them hurt you, Sarah. If you say yes, you'll be helping them out, and I can promise you will truly enjoy the experience." Elsa's tone was sincere, much like their conversation earlier that evening.

"But this Dutchman will be watching the entire time?" Sarah's voice trembled, both with fear and excitement.

"Yes. He will be watching. We will be watching you too." Nadia smiled knowingly. Somehow, she sensed that Sarah secretly found the whole idea quite erotic.

She looked at all three women one at a time, hesitating still, then answered, "Okay." Nicolette hugged her tight, and Nadia clapped her hands together, proclaiming, "Sehr gut!"

Elsa took Sarah's hand and disentangled her from Nicolette's arms. She led her to the center of the room where silken cords hung from the ceiling. She looked toward the large double window wall mirror and nodded, indicating that they would begin.

Elsa picked up a black scarf from a side table and proceeded to wrap it around Sarah's head, covering her eyes. She tied it tight. The blindfold would help her new friend feel less self-conscious. If she couldn't see the expressions on everyone's faces, their reactions, then hers would be more natural, uninhibited. "Now strip." The order to take off her clothes made Sarah rethink going through with this whole thing, but before she could chicken out, hands began to unclasp her belt and slid down her waist to her thighs where they reached under the hem of her sweater dress and lifted upward beyond her stomach, tickling her breasts as the material was pulled over her head carefully so as not to remove the blindfold. Another pair of hands came from behind and hooked into the sides of her thong, sliding the panties down. The boots were left on and Sarah stood naked and blindfolded while hands tied silk cords around her wrists, raising them up and outward over her head just enough to immobilize her, but not uncomfortably. She could hear them breathing, feel them moving around her, but could do nothing as she was stretched, forcing her to stand on her toes.

She noticed the air cooling her skin, could smell Nicolette's perfume on her left, and she even felt body heat at her back, but she didn't know if it was from Elsa or Nadia. A foot kicked her feet apart exposing her to the air and all who cared to look. Nicolette whispered in her ear, "Du bist ser Schön, Sarah." Manicured nails skimmed over her left thigh, leaving a trail of tingles.

"I don't understand, Nicolette," she replied, not comprehending the compliment.

Smack! A hand spanked her buttocks hard. "Ouch!"

"That is Mistress Nicolette to you, and you will speak only when ordered."

Sarah realized they were quite serious now. *What did I get myself into?* The hand that spanked her began rubbing that spot in soft, circular motions. Then it smacked her again three times more before returning to the caressing movements. Sarah tried not to be vocal, but she sucked in her breath with a hiss.

"Do you like that, slave?" Nadia's voice asked the question.

"No, Mistress Nadia. I don't." Smack, smack, smack! Three more spanks landed on her backside, followed by more rubbing. The heat that began to build up on her bottom spread and Sarah realized she was getting wet.

"I did not say you could speak, slave. Perhaps you need more punishment?"

Sarah wanted to scream "*no*" but feared she would get spanked hard again. The caressing motion was beginning to feel good, and then she felt something pinch her nipples simultaneously. Nipple clamps!

The pain was tolerable, so she said nothing. As Sarah hung suspended by silken ties, Nadia picked up a fine suede riding crop. She smacked it against the table and watched as Sarah's head turned in her direction, trying to figure out what would happen next. She didn't have to wait long as she felt something soft slide up the inside of her thigh, moving ever so slowly toward her slit. There, it rubbed gently. Sarah sucked in her breath, feeling her nipples harden, which increased the pressure from the clamps. Smack! Another hand spanked her naked bottom while the soft thing tickled between her legs. Sarah moaned.

"I see you are warming up to us, slave. You like this, don't you?" Nadia asked and Sarah knew not to respond this time. She hadn't been ordered to speak.

Fingernails that once lightly skimmed over her legs now raked down her back just enough to be this side of painful. Sarah arched her back. One of the mistresses repeated the act, and the soft piece of leather that had been rubbing her gently began, instead, to tap at her flesh, each time a little bit harder. She pushed her hips forward ever so slightly, seeking the pleasure/pain. Smack! Her bottom was spanked and then rubbed again. It felt hot. So did her entire body. She felt swollen and completely engorged. She remembered that behind the mirror, a supposedly handsome man was watching as she was stretched, spanked, and tortured. Her nipples were painfully hard now. Five hard taps against her swollen folds were followed by momentary rubbing motions from the riding crop. Three more taps were accompanied by two hard spanks on her bottom. Receiving the hits on both ends at the same time nearly put her over the edge. Sarah was panting now as a fine bead of sweat broke out over her entire body.

"Tell me what you want, slave. Speak your desire."

Nicolette finally gave her permission to speak, and all Sarah could think to say was, "More, please."

They stopped. Her body screamed at her to be released from all the pent-up desire. She wanted to cry. She arched and wiggled, trying desperately to reconnect to the crop or a hand, anything that would help end this sexual frustration. Nothing. Then she remembered what Elsa had told her about Herr Schulze, about how he begged her to give him what he desired so she withheld that very thing to keep him on the edge, to keep him coming back. But she wasn't a regular customer. She was on vacation and wouldn't be here long. Sarah didn't know what to do. She was tied up and at their mercy.

The nipple clamps were taken off. Blood rushed back into the sensitive peaks, and they begged for attention. Soft hands began to massage her breasts and then, miraculously, she felt a warm, wet mouth wrap around one while a hand continued to rub, massage, and tweak the other one. From behind, she felt someone kneel at her feet, and fingertips ran up and down her legs from the outside to the inner thighs. Lips kissed her heated buttocks, and a tongue licked a slick line from that tormented area downward to the part of her that begged to be touched. The first flick of a tongue on her anus shocked her, and then it traveled forward circling like a hungry predator, finally delving deep which made Sarah's knees go weak. She slumped, held up only by her wrists. She grabbed at the ties with her hands, holding on. The two women worked her over while Elsa watched from the corner chair previously occupied by the lovely American who was now displayed so provocatively in the center of the room. It was incredibly erotic, so much so that Elsa couldn't watch without reaching down to stroke herself with her leather-clad hand. No one paid her any attention as she pleasured herself. The perks of the job, some might say.

Nadia worked Sarah's nipples hard, biting just a little while Nicolette lapped at the moaning girl. As Elsa watched, Nicolette reached around and used her fingers to take over the rubbing motions and slipped her tongue deep inside Sarah. With her other hand, she inserted one finger into the innocent woman's anus and with all areas covered, the two professionals brought Sarah to a magnificent shuddering climax.

Nadia and Nicolette left Sarah hanging as they wrapped around each other, kissing, licking, and touching while they sank to the floor and maneuvered into 69, pleasuring one another.

Elsa stood and walked to Sarah where she began untying her wrist restraints. Sarah could barely stand. She reached for her blindfold, then felt Elsa's hands stop her. "Not yet," she said.

"What? More? There can't be more! I don't know if I can take it." The small smile on Sarah's face showed she was not displeased at all, but instead, incredulous.

"Just lean on me. Now sit here." Elsa led her to a table up against the back wall. It was, like everything else, covered in leather. She could feel it against her skin. She sat. Elsa indicated she should lie back. She did. Then she felt the beautiful German woman climb on top of her and straddle her hips. Sarah could hear the wet kissing and moaning coming from Nadia and Nicolette. She tried to imagine how they looked entwined together. She also wondered how she looked with a beautiful redheaded woman sitting on her hips, and how it all must look to the Dutchman watching from behind the two-way mirror.

Lips touched hers in a light kiss. The kisses were soft and sweet but then deepened as she felt Elsa's tongue slip inside and explore. Her hands moved down her arms and skimmed back up. She tasted good, and Sarah couldn't believe how urgent her body began to feel again. Those lips trailed down over her cheek and to her neck where they licked and gently bit.

Elsa sat back and reached up on the wall for a two-way strap-on. She pulled aside her thong as she inserted the phallic shaped vibrating portion into herself and hooked the belt. Then she lifted Sarah's legs, pushing her knees wide apart and placed the tip of the soft silicone dildo at her opening. She inched her hips forward and felt it sink into the wet, pink flesh. Elsa rode Sarah with the skill only a woman would have or even know about when it came to pleasuring another woman. To Sarah's surprise, her body welcomed Elsa's ministrations. Hands squeezed her breasts and Sarah reached up to reciprocate. The two women explored each other's bodies and found a rhythm that tightened their insides with every stroke. The dungeon had turned from its usual non-penetrating sadism into a girl-on-girl orgy.

Chapter 12

Paul couldn't believe his eyes. The woman on the other side of the glass being pleasured by three women was none other than the pretty American he'd run into at the airport. *What luck!* The sexy sight of these beautiful ladies performing cunnilingus on the tied-up woman was almost too much. He was hard to the point of pain, stroking himself and wishing he was the one fucking the blonde American. He completely forgot why he was there in the first place; forgot about evaluating the dommes, forgot about his uncle, and forgot his senses as he simply enjoyed the amazing visual of these women pleasuring each other. He was enraptured. He would never in his life forget witnessing this. He almost wanted to send his damned uncle a thank you card. Almost.

The American wrapped her legs around Elsa's waist as the domme put her back into it, shoving the dildo deep and receiving her own pleasure from the vibrator moving inside herself. This, he thought, was art. *Vermeer should've painted such beauty!* As the ladies all reached their climaxes one after the other, Paul shot his load into a tissue conveniently available for those who probably sat in this room often, indulging their fetish for voyeurism. This had to be one of the best jobs he'd ever taken on.

One thing he knew for sure. He needed to meet this woman again before he left Berlin. Such a sensual and sexual creature should not go unnoticed or unappreciated by himself. He smiled. Looking down at the center of the dungeon floor, he watched as Nadia and Nicolette pulled apart and got up. They stood and both looked at Elsa doing the American. They began clapping their hands at the marvelous performance and then walked over to the table where they each, in turn, leaned down to give her a kiss on the cheek. Elsa sat back and withdrew the dildo. She grinned like a cat as she slipped the blindfold off of the blonde American's head. The show was over.

Nadia and Nicolette walked out, waving their goodbyes, and a moment later, entered the observatory where Paul sat, now tucked away and straightened out.

"Ladies, what a perfectly charming performance." His devastating dimples peeked out around the edges of his full lips.

"You liked, Paul?" asked Nicolette.

"Oh, yes. Not exactly the S & M you usually do, I'm sure, but I quite enjoyed it. You both would be wonderful additions to my uncle's dungeon. Shall we talk about it back at my hotel room?" Paul, always thinking ahead, worked to get both women to join him for a little more of what he'd just watched, but he planned to participate this time.

Nicolette was quick to decline. "Ah, no thank you, liebling. Not my cup of tea." She wagged her finger at him.

"What about you, Nadia?" Nadia liked both men and women, and the handsome Dutchman was appealing. "Only if you buy me a drink first. I'm parched," she replied.

"Of course," he laughed. Slipping his arm around her shoulders, he steered her toward the door, intending to leave straightaway. Down the hall, Nicolette could hear him asking, "And who was the lovely guest of honor in there? How did you find her?"

Nicolette looked through the glass at Sarah and Elsa, watching as they put their clothes back on. She had enjoyed the pretty American. It wasn't every day that she got a little break from spanking old, wrinkly men and instead, got to enjoy herself with a hot woman. Sometimes, she, Elsa, and Nadia had fun with the Subs, but this was the first time they all had really let loose, the first time she'd seen Elsa enjoy a woman. She'd wondered whether or not Elsa swung both ways. Now she knew, and she'd be sure to capitalize on that next time. Nicolette desired Elsa. Now, she knew there was a chance.

✥✥✥✥✥ ✥✥✥✥✥

Driving back to his hotel, Paul's thoughts ran wild. He intended to enjoy himself with Nadia and would try to convince her to come to Amsterdam for his uncle, as well. Sure, she wasn't Peter Knudson's first choice, but what difference did it make as long as the dominatrix was good at her job? He planned to pump Nadia for information about the American who he now remembered was named Sarah. His plans didn't end there. The images of women touching, spanking, sexually torturing, and pleasuring each other were fresh in his mind and unbelievably, he had another erection.

A hedonist through and through, Paul did not feel bad for one moment about mixing business with pleasure or even having multiple women back-to-back while on vacation or at home. Life was pleasure and so he lived to please himself.

Chapter 13

Sarah arrived back at her hotel around four in the morning, completely exhausted. She kicked off her boots, whipped off her belt and lay there with an incredulous smile on her face. She recalled the extraordinary anxiety, fear, and excitement. Having so many hands on her at once was overwhelming. Mouths sucking and lips kissing while fingers stroked, and naked flesh pressed against her own was something she knew she would never forget. Standing on weakened legs, Sarah pulled her dress over her head and tossed it on the chair in the corner. She made her way to the bathroom where she relieved herself. It was then she looked down and realized she wasn't wearing her thong. A laugh bubbled up and escaped, echoing off the tiled walls.

Her body throbbed with the beginnings of the aches and pains it would feel full-on the next day, so tired or not, Sarah forced herself into the shower to bathe off quickly under a hot spray. As she ran the soap over her breasts, she cringed just a little. They were sensitive to the point of pain. *Nipple clamps,* she thought. *Never again with those, but that leather crop, now that was something else...*

She finished her shower, dried off, and threw on a T-shirt. Crawling into bed, she considered what she would do tomorrow. Her eyelids felt heavy, and as they closed for the final time that night, her last thought was, *I wish Anthony was here.*

In the Berlin Marriott, Paul strained against the backside of the woman face-down, on all fours. Nadia pushed her bottom up against the handsome Dutchman, enjoying the last waves of her orgasm. He pulled out and stepped off the bed, yanking the condom off as he walked to the toilet. She rolled over and looked up at the ceiling, listening to the loud stream of piss coming from the other room.

"Why are you so fascinated with the American?" Nadia endured many questions about Sarah when she and Paul had left the club. Even as she asked questions about her new job in Amsterdam, he had peppered their conversation with queries like "How do you know her?" and "Where is she staying?"

She could only answer that Sarah was a new friend of Elsa's and she had no idea how they knew each other or where the woman was staying. It had become annoying, so Nadia had shut him up with a kiss that ended, well, it ended just moments ago. If he was still interested in the American after all that, then she didn't know her stuff!

Paul stepped out of the bathroom, naked and God-like, and Nadia was once again struck by his male beauty.

"It's nothing. I simply found her performance entrancing." Nadia pouted and Paul saw that he needed to apply a Band-Aid to wounded female pride. "Of course, it's completely obvious now that she was only so eye-catching because of the dark-haired beauty wielding the crop." Nadia smiled like a contented cat.

Paul leaned down and placed his hands on either side of her head as he lowered his body on top of hers, wrapping his arms around her torso and rolling her over on top of him. Nadia squealed delightedly as he slid his hands down to palm each cheek of her lush buttocks. He squeezed and wiggled her hips over his own. "The way you whipped her wet little cat had me so fucking hard that I could have broken down that mirrored wall with my mighty hammer." He kissed her deeply and then trailed his tongue down her neck to her shoulder.

"You're insatiable, Paul, Liebling...or should I call you Thor?" She felt him harden once again. She hadn't been with such a man before, one who could keep loving a woman's body until she begged him to stop. Maybe he was the god of legend after all. She spread her thighs to straddle his hips and slid back and forth over the length of him. Paul let her do what she liked as he enjoyed watching her ecstatic facial expressions. He found himself wondering what Sarah would look like riding him. The memory of her face as the two dommes worked her over filled his mind. Golden-haired and radiant, she looked like a sacrificial virgin as the leather crop smacked her most sensitive part repeatedly. He imagined she would taste of sex and honey. He closed his eyes and let Nadia find her pleasure while he relaxed, absorbing the slick sensations stimulating him once again.

He knew later he would contact Elsa and work his charm toward finding Sarah. Nadia need not know. She was an incredible woman, and he appreciated her. His uncle would appreciate her work in his club, he was sure. The loss of Elsa was the gain of Nadia in his mind. *What difference does it make?*

"Ah..ah...ah..." Nadia reached her climax. Paul still had not found his. She looked down at him. "Not yet, eh?" She slithered down and wrapped her lips around him. Paul smiled. Women always came easy to him. He barely ever had to ask.

As his breath hitched and his pleasure peaked, he envisioned a blonde head in place of the brunette. Nadia swallowed, another point in her favor.

As she settled next to him, falling asleep, he reached over and picked up his mobile and texted his loathsome uncle.

Mistress Elsa is not interested, but I secured another worthy domme, Mistress Nadia. She's fantastic and is willing to start in two weeks.

❧ ❦

In a damp office in Amsterdam, in the early morning, Peter stared at the message on his phone. His brow furrowed and his face turned an angry shade of red. *He failed! The worthless shit failed. I send him to do one simple task, and he fucks it up.* He thought about the sublime blond boy. *Oh, my angel...*

Peter flung his phone across the room where it smashed into the opposite wall. Surprisingly, it was still in one piece, which should have pleased him, but instead, it made him angrier. The thought of the beautiful boy being out of his reach stirred an inner rage. He'd lost Paul when Paul grew up. Therefore, it should be Paul's responsibility to find a replacement and Peter knew who he wanted. The Berlin angel. Failing to secure the sister meant losing the boy, and if he had to lose something, then is stood to Peter's reasoning that Paul should lose something of equal value. But what? Or more to the painful point, who?

He pressed his hands together in front of his brooding visage and pondered a fitting punishment for Paul. Peter's reputation for viciousness was no joke as all his staff knew not to cross their boss. Paul Christiansen was about to be reminded why he feared his uncle so much for so long. *He will pay for this.*

Chapter 14

Anthony stepped off his flight into the hustle and bustle that was Schiphol airport in Amsterdam. He walked through the cavernous space, dodging people coming and going. He was lucky that he had only his carry-on which contained his clothing for a week, his camera, and iPad. He passed all the shops on his way out of the secure area and into the general section of the airport leading out to the street. Outside, tulips of all colors filled planting beds. Taxis lined up along one lane of traffic while shuttle buses occupied the lane closest to the sidewalk. Eager cab drivers wearing black suits stood by their dark Sedans waiting for customers. *Not your typical New York City cabbies at all,* he thought. These drivers were far more professional in appearance, more like personal drivers for the rich and famous. Despite the summer month, the air felt more like spring with a crisp breeze. Gray clouds thick with the promise of rain hung low in the sky. Not the brightest welcome one could hope for. Anthony flagged one of the many secret-service-looking cab drivers and gave him the name of his hotel located in the heart of the city. It was a bed and breakfast, which he preferred. As they drove off the airport property, he found himself looking forward to the day cruises. His driver, who introduced himself as Carl, kept up an amiable chat asking Anthony about his trip to the Netherlands and recommending various spots he might visit.

He even hinted at a "great place to relax and meet a nice woman" in the Red-Light District.

Anthony chuckled. He never paid for sex. Never needed to, but he smiled and thanked the man kindly without indicating whether he would take him up on the offer.

The words "a nice woman" caused flashes of seductive brown eyes framed by mussed blonde hair—hair he'd mussed with his own hands as he'd cradled that face and kissed her ripe lips senseless—to fill his mind. Sarah. He still couldn't shake thoughts of her. Maybe he just craved one more tumble in the sack. *That's probably it,* he thought. *Sometimes it takes a little longer for sex to grow stale when it comes from someone as fresh and sweet as Sarah.* He'd only had a few days with her; not nearly enough time to wear out the welcome mat at the altar of her incredible womanhood. Hers was an altar he could stand to worship at a few more times. Not many women managed to hold Anthony's attention for more than a few weeks. Most only managed a few days, but most weren't Sarah. Most were jaded and knew the score. Craving more of this particular woman must simply have to do with him being her first. It was a kind of heady feeling knowing that no other man had touched her, caressed her, tasted her as he had.

She was like a new toy, wrapped in packaging that no one had ripped through already. Pristine. He was the one to tug at her ribbons and watch as the shiny paper fell away, and the delicate tissue parted revealing the treasure inside. He was the one to lay hands upon that treasure and claim it for his own. It was his. She was his. Or she had been, until he tossed her aside and walked away. *Dumbass!* He wondered, as the car passed rows of Dutch homes along the canals, what she was doing now—who she was doing now. The thought of another man touching her made his skin hot and his fists clench in his lap. Would she respond to another man the same way she did with him? Would she so easily invite someone else back to her hotel? No.

No, not his Sarah. She wasn't that type. Had she received his drunken email yet? Anthony looked down at his mobile. No messages.

As the cab pulled up to the B&B, he gave himself a mental shake and a quick reprimand to stop thinking about her. Amsterdam and its canal cruises awaited him, and he was eager to see the sights. Carl waited patiently as Anthony paid the fare and added a generous tip. With a tip of his hat, the driver was off once again, and Anthony headed inside just as the wind picked up and the rain began to fall.

Chapter 15

The sun shined brightly through the crack in the curtains hanging over Sarah's hotel room window. It found its way to her eyes and pried them open. They felt gritty, as if sand had been sprinkled into them. She reached up and rubbed them with the back of her hand. A nagging beeping sound came from the bedside table. It was her cell phone. Still half asleep, she picked it up and peered at the screen through one eye. YOU HAVE MAIL.

Sarah pressed the email icon and waited for it to open. Images, one after the other, began to flash across the screen of herself smiling, shopping, and standing in front of tourist spots in Barcelona. Then a picture of herself sleeping with a sheet barely covering her modesty. In that one, Anthony's face looked out at her from his spot next to her slumbering, completely unaware form. He was smiling that smile that made her heart flip-flop. Dimples on either side of his full lips taunted and teased from amidst five o' clock shadow as his eyes looked...satisfied?

Anthony had sent her these pictures. And there was a message. *I fucking miss you.*

Sarah sat up and stared at the phone. Tears stung her eyes, and hope filled her wounded heart. It was quickly replaced by anger. "You miss me?" she said out loud to an empty room. "But you're the one who left! No goodbye or a note or anything!"

She slammed the phone down onto the other side of the bed. Covering her eyes, she struggled not to give in to the emotions that threatened to overwhelm her. Tears fell and because they did so, she became angrier. She didn't want to cry for a man who would just walk out on her like Anthony had done. She forced herself to breathe in and out slowly. It took five minutes to calm down. She laid back down and looked over at the phone. Picking it up, she began viewing all the pictures again. There were a few selfies they'd taken together. *I fucking miss you.* The words echoed in her thoughts. *He misses me,* she thought again. She smiled, a watery, wobbly smile that was a fusion somewhere between joy and pain.

She wondered if she should reply, and if so, what should she say? She couldn't think of anything that wouldn't sound naive or desperate, so she decided to wait. Maybe Elsa could help her figure out the best way to deal with this new development. And with that, Sarah recalled the night before. Her cheeks pinkened at the memory of Elsa wearing a realistic strap-on, deep inside of her and kissing her—everywhere. The memory was damned hot and exciting, even in instant replay. Almost as good as the real thing had been with Anthony. She wondered what Anthony would think if he knew she'd had sex with another woman—three other women. *Maybe it's time to find another man and see if there is a difference?*

"But he *fucking* misses me," she said. With that, Sarah wondered if she could be with another man and not think of Anthony, not feel like she betrayed him somehow. Being with another woman didn't feel quite like cheating. *Wait! Cheating? But we're not a couple. You can't cheat if you're not part of a couple and emailing how much you miss me doesn't make me yours, De Luca! You don't get to walk out without a word and then come back with a few sweet words and make me feel guilty."*

Sarah was back to indignant and self-righteous anger. She got up, heading to the bathroom to shower and get ready for another adventurous day. She texted Elsa.

Lunch?

Ping. Sarah saw a quick reply from her new friend.

I'm starving! I'll pick you up in thirty minutes so be ready. Bringing Anno. He says he's starving too.

And with that, any feelings of awkwardness over the previous night's activities disappeared. It was easier with women. They understood each other's needs. It took Sarah all of twenty-five minutes to quickly shower, dress, and brush out her hair. A little mascara and lip gloss were her only makeup, and jeans, boots, and a T-shirt seemed perfect for a casual lunch outing. She grabbed her purse and room key and headed down to the lobby to meet her friend and her friend's little brother.

Although wearing her glasses instead of contacts today, Sarah glowed. With her hair down, new wardrobe, and emerging sexual confidence, men noticed the once nearly invisible young woman. Gone were the calf-length pencil skirts in dull, drab colors. Gone was the schoolmarm bun she used to twist her hair into. Gone were the neck-high button-down shirts and Catholic novice white underwear her mother used to buy for her. Now, figure hugging tops, bottom-hugging jeans, sassy lingerie, and free-flowing hair transformed her into a strikingly lovely woman. There were hints of secrets in her eyes, and a playful upturn to her lips. The butterfly emerging from its chrysalis.

Out on the curb, a beat-up red Peugeot waited. Inside, Elsa seemed to be dancing in her seat while her brother, Anno, leaned over the passenger seat trying to change the radio station. As she approached the car, Elsa noticed and reached over her brother to pop open the door.

Anno came up complaining and Elsa swatted him good-naturedly on the back of his head.

"Hallo, my friend! Sexy specs."

"Hello, Elsa. Hi, Anno. Nice to see you again." Sarah climbed into the seat and was quickly engulfed in a hug from Elsa accompanied by the standard kiss on each cheek Europeans are famous for. She pushed her glasses back up on her nose.

"Hey," Anno replied as he sat back, giving Sarah room.

"So, how are you feeling?" Elsa gave her a knowing look with laughter on her lips.

"Hungry! I could eat a horse." Sarah tried not to blush, and then she laughed out loud.

"A horse? Americans eat horse?" Anno looked disgusted.

"It's only an expression," said Sarah. "We don't actually eat horse. It just means I'm so hungry, I could consume a lot of food right now."

"Oh. You don't look like you eat a lot. You're so tiny, well, in all the right places." Anno said this with the candor of a soon-to-be fifteen-year-old boy, one just now caught eyeing her boobs.

She laughed and turned to Elsa. "A real smooth talker he is."

"Ja, a real horny boy is more like it." Elsa looked at her brother in the rearview mirror as they drove away from the hotel. She chuckled as she saw the embarrassment creep into her little brother's face.

Sarah turned and looked at Anno, noting his discomfort. "Thanks for the compliment, Anno." He half-smiled, mollified.

"So, what kind of horse are you in the mood for?" Elsa asked.

"Hmm, I don't know. What do you recommend?"

"Oh, let's go to Oma's." Anno sat forward with his arms resting on each of their seat backs.

"You always want to go to Oma's. I swear, you could live there." Elsa turned to Sarah. "It's a very good German restaurant, though. The food is homestyle, and they have very good house beer."

"Sounds good. I'm up for anything."

"I know this!" Elsa winked at her friend, and they headed off to Oma's as Anno filled Sarah in on the dishes they offered, listing Rouladen, Bratkartoffeln, and Sauerbraten as his favorites.

By the time they reached the restaurant, Sarah's stomach was growling like a bear. As Elsa parked in between two other vehicles on the street, her mobile rang.

She looked at the screen not recognizing the number but answered anyway. "Hallo?" Sarah and Anno climbed out of the car as Elsa continued talking on the phone.

"Ja. No, I'm just getting ready to have lunch with a friend. Sure, sure. Well, if you're close by, you can join us. I think that would be okay..." Elsa eyed Sarah and her brother, who was shuffling back and forth on his feet with his hands in his pockets irritated at the delay.

Sarah had no idea who she was talking to, but if she wanted to invite a friend to join them, it was okay with her, so she gave Elsa the thumbs-up.

"Okay, sure. We're at Oma's on..." Elsa proceeded to give the address and directions. "See you soon." She hung up and closed and locked the car door.

"Who was that?" Anno asked as he led the way inside. "Do we have to wait until someone else arrives before we can eat? I'm starving, Elsa!" Sounding every bit like the ever-hungry teen, Anno waited for her answer.

"He won't take long, so I think it's safe for you to order before you wither away and die." She made a serious face as if that might be a real possibility.

Sarah laughed and patted Anno on the shoulder. He sidled up closer to her, laying his head on her shoulder as he wrapped one arm around her waist. "See? Sarah understands. She loves me more than you do." Both women laughed at his antics.

"That was Paul Christiansen, the scout from last night. Can't take no for an answer, I guess. Still, he seems nice, so if he wants to try and pitch me again, I'll let him. Especially since he offered to buy us all lunch!" They followed the hostess to their table and let her know one more would be joining them.

"You mean the man who was on the other side of the...?" Sarah stopped short of finishing her sentence, remembering that Elsa's brother was right there.

"Yes. No worries, though. He's quite charming, and very handsome." Elsa checked out the drinks menu and decided on a cherry beer, then asked Sarah what she would like.

"I'll take one," Anno said, expectant.

"You're not old enough yet, young man. Not until you're eighteen."

"I'm not versed in beer, so I'll try whatever you're having." Sarah looked at the menu, which was written in German.

"What does this man want, sis?" Anno asked as he reached for the rolls the waitress brought to their table.

"He's trying to convince me to come work for his uncle in Amsterdam." Elsa leaned over to help Sarah decipher the dishes on the menu.

"What? We can't move to Amsterdam. All my friends are here," Anno said, alarmed.

"I know this, little brother, and that is why I already turned him down. Nadia will be going, though," she said to Sarah.

"Oh, really? She decided to take him up on the offer?" Sarah asked.

"Ja, she doesn't have anything tying her down here." Elsa reached for a roll and slathered butter on it before taking a bite.

"So, I'm just tying you down, huh?" Anno said this over a mouthful of bread.

Elsa laughed. "Brother, you are my anchor, not my tether. I don't have any desire to move, and although I wouldn't want to uproot you, it has more to do with me."

"So why did you invite him to lunch?"

"Because, darling, free food!" Elsa laughed. "And he's easy on the eyes. Sarah might enjoy meeting him."

Anno looked put out, not caring for any competition for Sarah's attention. "He's probably bald and fat."

The waitress came back and took their order for drinks. "Two cherry beers and one Coke."

The ambience of Oma's was quintessential old Bavaria with gabled ceilings, wood beams, and quaint curtains on the windows which all had flower boxes filled with blooms on the outside. A jukebox played a polka and everyone seemed to be having a good time. The waitresses all wore peasant blouses and kirtles. It was the Germany tourists expected when visiting. Their waitress, a blonde woman with an overflowing bosom spilling out of her top, brought their beer. Anno blushed when she leaned over to hand him his Coke. She smiled, knowing the effect she had on the boy. Elsa laughed.

"That's why Anno loves coming here. He's a breast man."

"Shut it, Elsa," he said, glancing at Sarah.

"It's okay, Anno. I get it. You know, girls go through the same thing at your age. I remember noticing the boys for the first time, and how embarrassed I used to get when one noticed me back." She reached over and placed her hand on his, causing twin red spots to blossom on his fair cheeks. "You are a handsome young man, and the girls will be flocking to you, I promise. Just remember to be kind and treat them with respect."

Feeling brave, he turned his hand over and clasped Sarah's fingers. "You think so?"

"I know so." She spoke sincerely. Anno, seizing the moment, lifted Sarah's hand and kissed her fingers.

"Anno!" Elsa said as she burst out laughing. "Stop trying to seduce my friend."

"What? I was being chivalrous." He gave his sister a look that said, *'Don't ruin this moment.'*

"I think you're very charming, Anno. No worries." Sarah winked at him and then let go of his hand.

He looked at her with puppy-dog eyes.

They were interrupted.

"Hallo, Elsa." Sarah looked up and into the face of a male model. He was gorgeous. Jet black hair and crystal blue eyes in a face chiseled by an artist of the Renaissance stared back at her. Full lips smiled and dimples enticed as he stood casually wearing a dark gray suit and white T-shirt.

"Who are your charming guests?" he asked, feeling like lady luck was on his side when he noticed that Elsa's friend just happened to be the very American woman he hoped to find with her help.

"Oh, Paul, you made it. This is my little brother, Anno, and my friend, Sarah. Guys, this is Paul Christiansen." Elsa stood and shook Paul's hand. Sarah offered her hand when he reached out. He leaned over and kissed her fingers, whisper-soft, while maintaining eye contact. She blushed and Anno interjected, shoving his hand between them to shake.

"Anno." Paul gave the boy a hearty handshake. He noticed the warning look the boy gave him and glanced over at Sarah knowingly.

"Paul," said Anno, effecting a much deeper voice than his normal speaking range. Elsa smothered a giggle.

"Have a seat, Paul. We've only just ordered drinks." Everyone sat back down as Paul waited for the ladies to seat themselves first. Anno sat, then stood up again following Paul's lead.

"I believe we've met already," Paul said as he looked at Sarah. She blushed, knowing he was the man from the night before behind the two-way mirror.

"You have? When was this?" Elsa asked as she sipped her beer.

"At the airport. You are the charming American, Sarah Brown."

Sarah laughed as the memory emerged. "That's right! We were both trying to get into the same cab."

"Exactly. I would have preferred sharing it, but alas, she thought I might be some kind of pervert." Paul laughed.

"Well, aren't you?" asked Elsa, grinning.

"As often as I can get away with it, my dear." He perused the menu and when the buxom waitress came over to take his order, asked for a Jopenkerk. The blonde made a point of flirting with Paul, leaning over and offering him a full-frontal view of her breasts as she wrote down his order—something she didn't do when taking the orders from the table earlier.

"Poor Anno may never forgive you for coming to lunch, Paul. You've captured the attention of both his women!" Elsa joked, not caring about embarrassing her little brother as she deemed it her right as big sister.

"What's this? Oh, Anno, I apologize. Which one is yours?" Paul's eyes twinkled. "Is it the luscious waitress or our lovely Sarah?" Sarah blushed and felt Anno's discomfort.

"Neither, of course," he mumbled. Paul looked at the boy, knowing exactly how he must feel having been there a time or two as a young man. He was a good-looking kid on the very edge of manhood, but not quite yet. Then something clicked. Something sinister. Anno was exactly the type of young man his uncle went for. Perfect male beauty, as yet, pre-pubescent. His smile faltered a little. *So that's why he wanted Elsa. Shit.* The specifics of his uncle's demand, the slip about being banned from flying into Germany could not be a coincidence. He knew now that by failing to employ her, he had denied his uncle of what he was truly after. The boy. *That sick fuck! Good.* Paul was suddenly angry, and yet he felt joy at depriving Peter of the child, and joy at inadvertently saving the boy by fucking up. He knew there would be hell to pay for this. He only hoped Nadia would not be the one to pay that price, or himself, but he knew that this last hope would be asking too much.

He pasted a smile on his face and continued. "Take heart, young man. Soon I will be old, ugly, and wrinkled eating Muesli with a straw while you'll be strong and handsome and having your way with the ladies."

Sarah snorted. "Ha! As if you'll ever be ugly."

Anno huffed. Paul beamed his most devastating smile at her causing a red flush to run up her neck into her cheeks.

"So, Elsa, let's just get the business portion out of the way so this luncheon can be written off for taxes, and then we can all simply enjoy. We would like to offer you a job in Amsterdam." He left out what type of job, considering that her younger brother was sitting there.

"Thank you, Paul, but as I've said before, I'm not interested in moving. I have my life here, and my little brother to care for." They shook hands, and Paul felt relieved that she hadn't changed her mind. He'd hate to be the reason her brother was put in harm's way. He wouldn't wish that on any child, not ever.

"Very good. Now, let's order some food, more drinks, and Sarah can tell me all about her visit here in Deutschland."

Lunch was ordered, and the afternoon proceeded with good conversation. Sarah listened to Paul tell tales of his travels, and she occasionally gently kicked Anno under the table when she noted the boy feeling left out. It made him smile.

Paul watched Sarah closely when she spoke of life in Texas. Despite all of his charming tactics, she seemed unfazed. It wasn't that she didn't have the look of a woman noticing a handsome man. She did. But she wasn't gushing and falling all over herself vying for his attention, like their waitress who kept returning and asking if he needed anything else. He was intrigued. This, combined with memories of her submissive performance last night, had him aching to blow past her barriers. He would have to work for this one, something he was not used to doing. But he enjoyed a challenge. In his head he decided, *challenge accepted!*

Chapter 16

Anthony completed the first of five canal cruises. He'd taken about eighty pictures of the scenery from the boat, passengers enjoying themselves, the crew at work, and more. It was a good start. As he stepped off the ramp onto the dock, he saw a man walking by carrying a cane. He stepped out of his way quickly to avoid forcing him to stop and walk around him. The gentleman was older, wearing a tweed jacket and hat. His white goatee stood out on a rugged face topped by thick, dark eyebrows. He had powerful-looking shoulders for a man his age. As Anthony side-stepped, his eyes were drawn to the wooden cane with the metal handle. It was a lion's head. Something about it seemed familiar. The man gave a perfunctory nod of acknowledgement in his direction without looking his way.

He passed and headed toward a bench near a stand of trees planted alongside the canal. As Anthony looked on, the gentleman pulled his mobile out of his pocket and looked at the screen. His face was pinched in anger. He appeared to be muttering to himself. Two boys on bicycles rode past the older man toward the food kiosk on the far side of the dock. The man looked up at the boys and the lines of anger in his aged face smoothed out. A smile replaced the frown. He put his phone back in his jacket pocket leaving his hand there and continued to watch the two boys jump off their bikes and eagerly purchase snacks.

Something about the way the man watched the boys struck Anthony wrong. His eyes never left them. The boys picked up their bikes again and headed off with their purchases in hand. Still, the man watched them.

Cursing silently, Anthony knew. He knew in that moment that this man was a pedophile. He stayed put, keeping an eye on the boys until they were out of sight. The man also watched until he could no longer see them. He was smiling a small half smile when he turned his head and caught Anthony's eye. The old man knew that he'd been caught ogling the boys. His happy expression morphed to a fierce scowl, but Anthony didn't blink. His own eyes narrowed, the message reflected in them, *'I know what you are, asshole! And I'm watching you!'*

The man stood, and grabbing his cane, walked quickly away. He glanced back at Anthony once and then turned a corner. Right then, Anthony knew why the cane seemed familiar, why the man caught his eye. It was him, the old man from Berlin that he'd photographed beating a male hustler. *But what is he doing here?*

He knew the man wouldn't recognize him since the incident in Germany took place at night and he was a fair distance away from the scene of the crime. He'd run off anyway. Anthony had the advantage in that his camera provided clarity through the telescopic lens. The pictures seemed up close and personal but had really been shot from a goodly distance. As far as the old man was concerned, Anthony was just someone who happened to catch him in the act of fantasizing about the two boys. But for Anthony, it felt far more personal since he had the images of the Berlin incident in a file on his laptop.

If he'd still been in Germany, Anthony knew he would've gone ahead and notified the police about the old man. Anything to protect kids from people like that. Violence rose up inside him and all he could think about was beating the man within an inch of his miserable life. As a child, Anthony had spent time as an altar boy and he clearly remembered one Sunday after mass when Father Flaherty had invited him and Nick, his neighbor and friend, to his office. There, Flaherty had offered both boys some of the sacramental wine to try. "But don't tell your mothers," he'd said. The priest stood between them and kept his hands on their backs, rubbing up and down in a soothing manner while they drank. When he and Nick finished the small amount, Father Flaherty offered more. Anthony remembered thinking this odd, and thinking if his mother found out, if she smelled it on him like she did his dad on Friday nights, she'd be as pissed at him as she often was with his Pops. He declined, but Nick held out his cup. That was when Flaherty told Anthony that he should go join his parents who "were surely looking for him by now." Nick stayed behind thinking only about having more wine. He was like that, often getting into trouble doing stuff that his parents wouldn't approve of. As Anthony walked out the door, the last thing he saw was Flaherty sitting down in his desk chair and pulling Nick onto his lap. After that day, Nick wasn't the same. He became withdrawn and did everything he could to avoid going to church. His grandmother said he was just a 'bad seed,' but Anthony now knew the truth. Nick had fallen prey to someone exactly like the old man. He was a kid then and could do nothing, but he was a man now and wouldn't let that bastard near those boys. The problem was, what could he do now that the old guy had left? He had no idea where to find him, and he couldn't report a crime more than half a year old perpetrated in Berlin to authorities in Amsterdam, especially without a name or a complainant. He felt the familiar frustration of being powerless all over again.

He counted to ten and then headed off to explore the city. Anthony had to console himself that at least he managed to keep the pervert away from those two boys and also put him on notice that people are watching. It would have to be enough for now. But if luck would favor him with another meeting in the future, he wouldn't be so nice.

Six blocks over, Peter Knudson entered his office and sat down at his desk. *Do-gooders. They are always so self-righteous and interfering,* he thought. *Who is that man to judge me? Every man has his dark side,* his inner diatribe continued. *The difference, however, is that I embrace mine while men like the one standing on the dock deny theirs. So be it. Deny yourself while I indulge and squeeze every ounce of enjoyment from my predilections. Let those do-gooders sit in self-righteous judgment while living miserable lives of self-denial while evil old fucks like me smile, licking our fingers of each and every drop of sweetness taken from innocence.*

Grinning to himself, Peter pulled out his cellular and fired off a message to Paul.

She is not the one I asked you to secure. Since you've already offered her employment, I'll give her a probationary period. But as you've failed in the initial task, you've forfeited full payment for the job. Return home.

He then reached over, picked up his desk phone and hit the intercom button. "Daniel, call Aleks Gruber and tell him I require him at my office in one hour. I have a job for him."

"Yes, sir." Daniel hung up, wondering what in the world his boss was up to now. Aleks Gruber was not someone anyone would want to be associated with unless involved in criminal activity. The man was the type any sane person avoided on the street by walking in a wide circle around him and praying not to meet up with him in a dark alley. Daniel knew he had spent some time in prison. Gruber was covered in prison tats and sported a Mohawk. Visible on the shaved sides of his head were swastikas and other neo-Nazi insignia. Daniel knew, also, that Gruber was the man Peter Knudson sent to lure and secure many of his working girls. His face showing distaste at the task, he pulled out the number on file for the thug and dialed. He answered on the second ring. Daniel relayed the message.

Looking up, he caught Greta's eye. Greta handled all the bureaucratic paperwork on the working girls. She had a tougher shell than Daniel, but she wasn't without compassion or sense. She knew that Knudson skirted the law, and she also knew how he treated the women in his employ, herself included, but not to the same degree since Peter needed her expertise to handle all the legalities for his business. She shook her head in the negative, acknowledging Daniel's wordless message warning that the thug was coming in soon.

Greta had been in Knudson's employ almost from the beginning. She knew more about their boss than anyone and once intimated that his sexual preferences ran to the sickest side of human behavior—young boys. She even hinted that he'd victimized his own nephew, Paul. No one ever filed charges against him, however, so there was no proof that this was true, but Daniel somehow didn't doubt it. His boss gave him the creeps. Sometimes, Knudson invaded his personal space in a manner that made him very uncomfortable and having him that close set off every alarm bell inside of him. Instinct. He was a firm believer in trusting it.

He also noted on each occasion when Paul had come to the office, which amounted to only four times in the three years Daniel had worked here, that the good-looking man seemed reticent, as if entering the building was completely distasteful to him. But it was the hint of fear in his eyes that struck Daniel and tore at his heart. He thought Paul was the most beautiful man he'd ever seen, and although he knew Paul was not gay, he still longed to hold him, shower him with love. Greta spoiled him, and she seemed the only one Paul was ever happy to see on those few occasions he'd come in. He was polite to Daniel, but Daniel didn't get the big hugs Greta received from the gorgeous nephew. He treated her flirtatiously, and yet also with the same kind of affection a son would show to his mother.

Greta said she'd known Paul since he was twelve. By then, the damage to the boy had been done. It stunned Daniel that the woman could continue to work for Knudson if she knew this was the kind of man he really was. He'd asked her once why she hadn't quit and found employment elsewhere. She responded that she'd put in too much time, invested too much into the business to give it up because of that monster. She said she was the only real buffer the girls had against Knudson. This was true as Daniel knew Greta had helped more than one working girl get her passport back and escape their boss's clutches when things got really bad. On those occasions, Knudson railed at Greta, threatening violence for which she would calmly respond with a practiced line. "I know everything about you, Peter. I have documentation of all your nefarious dealings filed away, and if you make a single move to harm me, or send anyone to harm me, those documents will be released to authorities. You'll spend your life in a jail cell."

The mere threat of prison, of being locked away always forced the monster back inside his cage. As he noted earlier, Greta possessed a tough shell. He could take a page from her book and add it to his own by working on growing a thicker skin, but Daniel just wasn't the type. He felt everyone's pain. Too much heart. It made him a very loyal friend, even a loyal employee despite the fact he didn't like his employer. In this business, there had to be some good guys to help counter the bad ones like Knudson. When Yeline found herself on the receiving end of their boss's wrath, Daniel and Greta stepped in to help. He understood why Greta stayed, even if he still thought they both would be better off elsewhere.

So, they continued with work, waiting for Gruber to arrive. Whatever Peter Knudson wanted with the man, it would not be good. Daniel worried about Yeline, who continued to refuse unsavory clients, albeit less often now. He and Greta did all they could to conceal this from Knudson, hoping to get the girl out of the country soon and working in a new career field, one that didn't involve prostitution. But having Gruber called in could mean bad things for the Ukrainian woman. The clock on the wall ticked by at an excruciatingly slow pace as both Daniel and Greta contemplated what was going on and whether they would need to act quickly to save one more Red-Light District casualty.

Chapter 17

Paul's mobile vibrated in his pocket as he sat enjoying lunch with Elsa, Sarah, and young Anno. He was laughing at a terribly bad joke told by Anno as he pulled it out.

"A Roman walks into a bar and holds up two fingers. How many beers did he order?" He looked from his sister to Sarah, and then at Paul.

"It's a trick question. Two, of course!" His sister said this as she waited, knowing it was probably the wrong answer.

"Wait, is he in Germany or Rome?" asked Paul, laughing.

"What difference does that make?" asked Anno, irritated that they weren't taking him seriously and answering the question.

"Well, if he's in Germany, it would depend on which two fingers he was holding up. Are any of them the thumb, or no?" Paul struggled not to laugh.

"Oh, that's right," said Sarah. "I remember someone told me that the thumb counts as number one, and then the rest of the fingers are two, three, four, and five, but if a person holds up the second and third finger, it would be three, not two. That's how native Germans peg American tourists at bars!" She clapped her hands together looking at Anno. "So, which two fingers is the Roman holding up?"

Anno rolled his eyes and put his hands over his face. "Not you, too, Sarah. You guys really know how to spoil a joke." He sighed.

"Aw, come on. What's the answer already!" His sister kicked him under the table.

"Five. Five beers. You know, you hold up two fingers in the shape of a V and it makes a Roman numeral five." Anno held up his fingers to demonstrate.

Sarah and Paul started laughing. Elsa shook her head while wagging her fingers at her little brother. "You're a real comedian, Johann."

"You suck, Elsa." Anno tried to stay mad, but seeing everyone laughing around him made that impossible, and a smile broke out across his face as he succumbed to the moment.

Paul finally looked down at his phone and saw he had a message from his uncle. He opened it.

She is not the one I asked you to secure. Since you've already offered her employment, I'll give her a probationary period. But as you've failed in the initial task, you've forfeited full payment for the job. Return home.

Paul saw red. *Rotten bastard! Damned if I'll let him have Nadia now.* He decided he would call Nadia after lunch and explain that the offer had been rescinded. It was a lie of sorts, but it would protect her from Uncle Peter, and what would surely be his wrath if she went to Holland. *Return home, indeed.* He would not be ordered around like a child. Peter did not have that kind of hold over him anymore, and he knew it. He would stay and continue to enjoy himself on his uncle's dime another day or two. After all, he still planned to pursue Sarah. He did have the first half of the money, so he wasn't worried about funds. The hotel was on his uncle's credit card, *so the bastard was stuck with that bill.* He also had his airline ticket and could simply change the return date by calling Lufthansa. *Fuck you, old man. No new dominatrix for you, and you will absolutely* not *get your hands on this boy.*

"Is something wrong, Paul," Sarah asked, concern in her voice. Elsa also appeared worried by the expression on his face. Paul quickly replaced his frown with a smile. He began to lay the groundwork for his lie.

"No, no. Well, it's just that my uncle has texted me that he no longer needs to fill that position in his business, and I'm left with the unpleasant task of breaking it to Nadia." He looked both upset and worried.

Elsa reached out and put her hand on his arm. "No worries, Paul. Nadia is fine right here where she is. I'll help you tell her if you like." And with that, Paul knew that this, at least, would be all right. Nadia hadn't yet quit her job or made any irreversible changes or decisions. However, there would certainly be hell to pay when he arrived back home. He knew it just as surely as he knew the sun would rise. It might get ugly—very, very ugly. Still, Paul had no clue how bad the situation had become, and as he sat in Oma's enjoying the company around him, his uncle was busy making plans of his own.

Paul regretfully excused himself after their lunch was over. Paying the tab as promised, he set out to see Nadia and deliver the news in person. "It's the least I can do after having lifted her hopes about the job," he told Elsa. "I appreciate you offering to come with me, but you should stay with Sarah and Anno. Have fun. Show Sarah some sights." He turned and shook Anno's hand.

"Very nice to meet you, young Anno. I leave the women in your capable hands. Look out for them."

Anno's chest puffed out a bit at this. He decided Paul wasn't so bad after all.

Paul turned focusing on Sarah, taking her hands in his, and kissing her on both cheeks, lingering just a little longer than necessary. "Sarah, it has been such a pleasure meeting you again. Perhaps I can entice you to share dinner with me before I leave? Tomorrow?"

Sarah blushed. After spending a few hours in his company, she concluded he was a nice man, and not some crazy, stalker pervert. "That would be nice."

"Where are you staying? I can pick you up at six."

"The Holiday Inn Express, the one on Stressemannstraße." He continued to hold her hands while she answered him. His gaze said he was checking her out. Sarah considered the possibility of Paul sexually, but she had some doubts, a nagging hesitation. *Damn it. A perfectly gorgeous man is asking me on a date, and I'm thinking about someone else.* She wanted to kick herself.

"Very good. I'll pick you up there." He lifted her hands, kissing her fingers before releasing them and stepping back. He waved at everyone as he headed off to hail a taxi.

"Well, well, Sarah. Conquering hearts, are you?" Elsa dug her elbow into Sarah's side in a teasing manner.

"What? It's just dinner," she answered.

"Are you really going out with him? He's just trying to get you into bed, Sarah." Anno looked so forlorn, and so serious that Sarah smothered the laugh that threatened to bubble up.

She reached out and hugged him. "You're so sweet to worry about me. Don't, though. I won't let him have his way with me, I promise." And she meant it. In that moment, she knew she wouldn't do anything with Paul other than eat dinner tomorrow night.

"Seriously, Sarah. You're too good for him." He changed his mind about Paul again as he hugged her back. Elsa put her arm around both. Sarah smiled, feeling a sense of family for the first time in a long time. She was falling in love on her crazy jaunt around Europe, it just wasn't the kind of love she expected. Turns out, it was better. It was the kind of love for friends who were beginning to mean the world to her. *Okay, maybe you don't have girl-on-girl sex with your friend, usually, but hey, what are friends for, right?*

She turned to look at Elsa. "I got a text from him this morning."

"Who? No! Him? Barcelona? Why didn't you tell me sooner? What did he say?" Anno stepped around to Sarah's right side while Elsa linked arms with her on the left. Together, they walked to Elsa's car, chatting away about Anthony's surprise message.

"You have to help me figure out what to do. Should I ignore it or write him back? If I write him back, what do I say?" They climbed into the car.

"Hmm. Well, first of all, he has some explaining to do." Elsa started the car and pulled out into traffic.

"And who is this guy?" Anno sat forward in the back seat and gave Sarah the eye.

"Sarah loves him." Elsa supplied the information.

Sarah's eyes popped. "I do not love him, Elsa! I just like him a lot." Elsa smirked, and Anno blew out a frustrated breath.

"How many *guys* do you have? Honestly, how are we going to work out as a couple if you have *guys* all over the place?" Anno's eyes were serious, but there was a tell-tale tug at the corner of his lips.

"I'm so sorry, Anno. I promise, no more *guys*. Just this one, and he left me, so I suspect you have absolutely no competition, and I'll patiently wait for you to grow up and take me on a real date." Her speech was solemn, but her eyes danced with mirth.

"That's better. And you won't have to wait long. My birthday is coming up next month."

"But you'll only be fifteen, little brother! I'd say waiting another three years is quite a stretch." Elsa pointed out the obvious.

"Don't ruin this for me, El. If she says she'll wait, then I'm holding her to it." Anno put his hand on her shoulder and gave it a squeeze. Sarah burst out laughing.

"So, he wrote you after leaving you? What did he say?" Anno grew serious with this question.

"He said he misses her. Can you believe it? After he just up and left without a goodbye," Elsa explained.

"Well, we men are kind of stupid sometimes, Sarah. We do dumb shit, especially around beautiful girls." His expression was pure honesty.

"Oh, sweetie. Thank you. You know, I don't really have any experience in this department. It's kind of all new to me, so I'm not really sure what I should do. I do like him, but I wasn't looking for a relationship, of any kind, when I set out on this adventure. Yet here I am faced with one and finding and making great friends with you and Elsa." Sarah turned in her seat so she could more easily address them both.

Elsa reached over and covered Sarah's hand with her own. "And we are friends, Sarah. You feel like family already."

"So, what should I do?" Sarah looked at her.

"We'll put our heads together and figure it out. No worries. You know, it will all really depend on what you want to happen. So, take a little time to decide whether you want to see Herr Barcelona again. If so, it shouldn't be too hard since it seems he wants to see you too. If not, then simply don't answer him back. He'll get the hint." Elsa pulled off the main road onto the side street near her building and began looking for a parking place.

"In the meantime," she said, "we'll park the car, and take the tube downtown for a little sight-seeing, okay?"

"Okay!" It was a good plan, and Sarah was in good company with her new friends. As they parked and exited the Peugeot, she asked herself, *"Do I really want to see Anthony again? Will he just leave again, or will it maybe pan out to something more, something stronger?"* And then she thought, *"Of course I want to see him. I miss him too."*

Chapter 18

Paul broke the news to Nadia...eventually. Thinking he had come back for more, and happy about that fact, Nadia had welcomed him with open arms. It mattered not that they'd just parted in the early morning hours. As soon as she received his call asking if he could come by, she was ready for the next round. It was unexpected since he'd told her he had some business to deal with that day. Still, it was gratifying that he would come back again, so soon, to her bed. The news he delivered afterward, however, was not.

"I don't understand." She sat up in bed, pulling the sheet up over her breasts.

"The business I had to attend to today, that is when I was told the offer of employment no longer stands. I wasn't informed as to why, only that I should tell you straight away that my uncle must rescind the offer. I'm so sorry, Nadia. Please know that the decision had nothing at all to do with you, and everything to do with business."

She looked at him for a long time, gauging his words. Something felt off. "Was there ever really a job? Are you really who you say you are or was this some scam to get me into bed? Or Elsa? That's who you really wanted all along. You came to offer her the job originally, didn't you?" Her dark eyes turned stormy as she worked herself into a rage.

"It's true. My uncle sent me here to recruit her, but she wasn't interested, and I made an executive decision to offer it to you instead.

You're a real talent, a wonderful asset to any club." He tried to smooth things over with compliments.

"But your uncle didn't want me. He wanted her, and you failed to secure her. You didn't really have the authority to hire me, did you?" She got up off the bed, and stood clutching the sheet around her, denying him the sight of her nakedness.

Paul sighed. He wasn't going to get out of this one unscathed. Nadia was no fool. There really was nothing he could say that would make this any better, so he rose, grabbing his clothing, and began putting on his pants. When he finished dressing, he turned to her, looking her straight in the eye, and simply said, "I'm sorry, Nadia."

He walked out of her bedroom to the front door. She followed, and the storm he knew was coming began.

"That's it? That's all you have to say? You promise me a job and use my body, and then yank it away and all you can say is 'I'm sorry, Nadia?' Just who the hell do you think you are?" The sheet slipped as she punctuated each word with hand gestures. Her Italian temper erupted like Mount Vesuvius. If he didn't run, he was going to be burned alive.

Paul opened the front door, but turned back to see her standing there, furious and glorious at all the time. Despite feeling terrible about treating her this way, he knew he'd done the right thing. She would never know that he had saved her from a very bad situation. So be it. He looked her up and down one last time and grinned.

"You're truly magnificent. Good luck." With that, he blew her a kiss and left. A loud bang resounded against the door after he shut it, and he knew she'd given in to her fury by throwing something solid and quite heavy at his retreating back. Good thing he'd walked out quickly, and that the door had caught hell instead of the back of his head.

It was late in the evening by the time Paul arrived back at his hotel. The hours he'd spent with Nadia had flown by pleasantly until the end. He showered and then ordered room service. He was intent on racking up the bill, so he ordered porn, although he was too lost in thought to pay any attention to it. It didn't matter. As long as the charges drove the bill up, and his uncle was left with no choice but to pay it, he was happy. Tomorrow night, he would pick Sarah up for their dinner date. He couldn't wait to see what it would take to pick the lock that led to her treasure. It had been a very long time since he'd felt challenged by a woman. She was different. Not raised with European values, but rather, American inhibitions.

After hearing about her life growing up in Texas, he was genuinely surprised by her uninhibited escapade the night before with the three women. The Sarah he witnessed last night from behind a two-way mirror was not the same woman he had lunch with today.

He wondered which of the two was the real Sarah Brown. He sincerely hoped for the sexual creature from the dungeon but also found that he wouldn't mind the young lady with whom he'd shared a meal. *Of course, a combination of both might steal my jaded heart,* he thought. Paul laughed out loud, knowing full well that wouldn't happen any time soon. At least, he didn't think so.

He thought about Uncle Peter. He knew once he got home, the shit was going to literally hit the fan. Standing up to him was never easy for Paul, who always forgot his own maturity, strength, and size in the presence of the monster of his childhood. It was time he remembered, and past time he dealt with Peter once and for all. Paul was not a religious man by any stretch, but he prayed for guidance; not for the degenerate man he was today, but for the innocent child he'd once been. Had it not been for Peter Knudson, Paul thought he might've stood a chance in this life to be successful. But he remained haunted by the past and incapacitated by fear and insecurity that kept him from realizing his full potential. Surely, God, if he exists, could understand and lend a helping hand. *But if God exists, where the hell was he when*

I needed him all those years ago? I was just a child. A child, for Christ sakes!

He would not, however, wait for God to protect Anno. He'd done that himself, even if by accident. *Peter will never get his lecherous, perverted hands on that wonderful boy.* Knowing he'd at least thwarted that crime he felt a tad better. A knock on the door alerted him to the arrival of his dinner. He signed the room service ticket and added a generous tip, all to be added to the bill, of course. As Paul sat down to his Filet Mignon and a 2005 Cabernet Sauvignon, he considered how best to approach Sarah the following evening.

She did seem adventurous, but it appeared she needed to feel a certain amount of comfort before taking the leap toward pleasure. She trusted Elsa, therefore she allowed the experience to happen. He would have to gain enough of her trust or else she might shut down on him completely. The only way he could think of accomplishing this would be to rein in his desire, and seek no more than a goodnight kiss, an innocent one at that. If he could show her patience, she would open up on her own, become the aggressor. He made his plans whilst savoring the texture of a good steak and sipping a fine wine. *Delicious. But then, free food always tastes better.* His plan would take at least two dates, possibly a third, but that would be stretching it. He could pull this off.

He turned his attention to the triple X-rated movie currently playing. A red-headed Irishman dressed as a leprechaun was vigorously plowing a blonde woman's 'pot o' gold' and asking, "Whose gold is it?" The woman was screaming her pleasure. "Yours!" It was silly, but he didn't mind. Paul cleaned his plate and worked on polishing off the Cabernet. By the end of the bottle, his eyes drifted shut. He managed to shove his tray outside the door and hang the 'Do Not Disturb' sign. He hated being awakened by housekeeping too early. He fell asleep thinking about Sarah, but she kept asking him where he hid his gold. He couldn't find it no matter where he searched, and she could only point at his heart unable to speak. He didn't understand, so he looked under his tiny leprechaun bed, and a monster jumped out, landing atop him. He screamed silently in terror, paralyzed inside the nightmare. No one came to help.

Chapter 19

When Paul didn't arrive back in Amsterdam by that evening, Peter Knudson put his plan into action. He knew his defiant nephew would react to the message by simply ignoring it, staying in Berlin on his dime. He called the Marriott and confirmed Paul was still registered and hadn't checked out. In fact, he'd ordered a very expensive dinner on the room tab.

The little bastard! He tried canceling the reservation so they'd throw Paul out, but the desk clerk informed him that such short notice would result in a rather large fee.

Knudson handed an envelope of money and an airline ticket to the tattooed man with the Mohawk. Gruber opened it and counted the cash, then folded it and placed it in the pocket of his leather jacket. He nodded once and then left the office. It was late. Knudson stood looking out his window onto the street below. Men walked in and out of the doors next to the display windows glowing bright red neon. Inside each, women in various degrees of undress beckoned passers-by to come in and sample their wares. Peter could only think of his blond angel, and how he was snatched away by his ungrateful nephew. The inaccuracy of his viewpoint didn't translate for him, the knowledge that he'd never actually had the boy, but neither did he acknowledge the immorality and criminality of his selfish pleasure-seeking predilections. He didn't care who he hurt, as long as he got what he wanted.

Since that didn't seem possible at this time, he was now making sure to discover what Paul cared about. Once he knew, he planned to viciously yank it away from him forever.

The idea of exacting revenge felt good, and Peter smiled. His vision blurred, and a sharp pain ricocheted across his chest and down his left arm. He shook himself, rubbing the arm. *Not yet. Not yet, you damned devil. I'm not ready.* He slowly ambled over to his chair where he sat down and rummaged inside his desk drawer, seeking a small bottle of pills. He quickly extracted one and placed it under his tongue. He closed his eyes and counted to ten. The dizziness abated, and the pain subsided. He still felt weak, but at least the tightness in his chest eased.

My angel. Peter drifted off into memories of the blond boy tossing a baseball in a park on a lovely spring day. He imagined again, the smile that caught his attention, and convinced himself that smile was for him alone. While prostitutes plied their trade outside, inside, a monster fantasized a child's worst nightmare. He fell asleep sprawled over his desk chair.

⚜ ⚜

Across town at Schiphol, Gruber boarded a KLM redeye to Berlin, Tegal. He carried only a small army-green duffel bag filled with necessities. In his hand was a business card for a gentleman known for making his money gun running on the black market. He slid the card in his wallet and shoved it into the back pocket of his jeans. After buckling himself in, he pulled out his iPod and pushed the earbuds in his ears, loudly playing the Sex Pistols' *Anarchy*. Next to him, an older woman glanced nervously in his direction. He noticed and grinned at her, displaying the holes in his gumline. Chuckling evilly, he winked. She looked quickly away.

The plane took off, expected to land on time at four-thirty in the morning. Throughout history, mothers of the world have iterated over and over to their children that there is nothing good out in the world after midnight. In this particular case, arriving in Berlin in the wee hours, every mother was dead to right.

Chapter 20

"What should I wear, Elsa?" Sarah spoke into her iPhone as she rummaged through the clothing hanging in her hotel closet. "I don't even know where he's planning on taking me." She picked up a navy-blue sleeveless sheath, and held it up to her body, glancing down to see how it looked. Her phone began to slip, so she quickly cocked her head back over to the side.

"Go for simple and classy. I think he likes that about you or else he'd be taking Nadia out instead." Elsa knew Paul and Nadia had spent the night before together but didn't feel it was necessary to say anything. Both Sarah and Paul were only visiting Berlin so a single date was no big deal, and her new friend might enjoy herself. Paul was very handsome and polished. Seeing no harm in withholding the information, Elsa figured Sarah might have some juicy stories to share afterward.

"Nadia? You think?" Sarah asked as she moved two more outfits out of the way and eyed a white skirt with red flowers that fell to just above her knees. The skirt had a red halter-style top that went with it, and she'd purchased strappy red heels to match. In all, it was fun, flirty, and sexy, yet still classy.

"No, not really," she prevaricated. "I was just throwing it out there." Elsa, who was at work on her day off cleaning her instruments and sterilizing leather bed cushions, nipple clamps, and penis pumps before putting them into the on-site autoclave, laughed.

"Will you be having some fun with our Dutchman, Sarah?"

"What? No! Remember, I promised your brother I'd behave myself, and I would hate to break my word to the man I love." The cheeky grin on Sarah's face translated through the phone.

"I'll be sure to let him know you said that since he's been depressed all day and keeps asking me if you're interested in Paul. I've never seen him so put out, poor pup. Seriously, though. If the mood strikes, remember you're an adult and can do whatever it is you please."

"I know. But I'm still not sure it's what I want. I can't get Anthony out of my head. Speaking of, I haven't decided what to do about his email yet, either."

Elsa sighed. "You'll know when you know. In the meantime, it's good that he's realizing he messed up."

"What makes you think he thinks he messed up?" Sarah sat down on the edge of her bed and began removing her clothes to shower.

"Because, darling. He emailed you. A man who doesn't want any more contact with a woman doesn't do that. He's been thinking about you, bet on it. So, letting him wonder a day or two more is okay. He left you wondering. You leave him wondering. Then, if you decide to answer his message, you have the upper hand. You set the pace and the rules."

"Hmm." Sarah chewed her lower lip, thinking. "Well, you know more than I do on that score, so I'll take your words into consideration. Okay, I have to jump into the shower. I'll call you later if you're up and let you know how it all went."

"Yes! Call me. I want all the juicy details," Elsa said, laughing.

"No juicy details. Stop that, Elsa! And tell Anno I said hello." Sarah's mood lifted. It was nice having a girlfriend to share with, to talk things over.

"Okay, okay. I'll tell him. You go have fun. Tusch!"

Sarah walked naked into the bathroom and turned on the shower. She stood, looking at her body in the mirror while the water heated up. An expression of consideration settled in her eyes. She stood there, quietly, as steam filled the room. Blinking, she turned and stepped under the hot spray and washed away the day.

❧❧❧ ❧❧❧

A knock on the dungeon door made Elsa jump. She wasn't expecting anyone. No one besides Hans was around. It was early yet. Club hours didn't begin until later that day. "Enter," she said.

Nicolette peeked around the corner and then sauntered in. She looked at Elsa, who was polishing medieval ankle chains with a soft cloth.

"Oh, hey. What are you doing in today?" Elsa, noting it was just Nicolette, went back to putting a shine on her equipment.

"Same as you, only I'm finished. Need some help?" Nicolette stopped in front of Elsa, who was sitting on one of her rolling stools, and casually shoved her hands into the back pockets of her jeans. The action pushed her unbound breasts forward, displaying their shape under her white T-shirt.

Elsa looked up and came face to face with Nic's nipples, which poked through their cotton covering. She licked her lips quickly and looked down, polishing the second ankle clamp.

"I've got it, thanks." Nicolette rarely came into her dungeon except on very few occasions, and only with Nadia or Hans in tow usually. It was no secret to Elsa that she only had relationships with other women, and it did not go unnoticed that Nic had, sometimes, shown a marked interest in her. Elsa didn't mind a dalliance now and again with another woman, but her primary sexuality was heterosexual. Still, she admitted to herself that she'd wondered about Nicolette from time to time. She was quite a beautiful woman, after all.

"Are you sure?" Nicolette's hand covered her own as she sank down to her knees before Elsa. Her fingers caressed the soft hand working diligently to shine up the metal. Heat crept up Elsa's neck at the contact.

Nicolette watched Elsa's face for a reaction, reassurance. She had taken a great risk in attempting to seduce her colleague, her work-place friend. But the opportunity presented itself with both of them here alone. If things went wrong, it could backfire in a most unpleasant way, creating a tense working environment. But if it worked out...she dared hope it would. Slowly, Nic took the cloth and ankle clamp out of Elsa's hands and set them down to the side. She inched forward on her knees, slowly spreading Elsa's apart to fit in between them. When their faces were inches apart, she ran her hands up Elsa's arms all the way to either side of her face where she gently sank her fingers into the thick, red hair. Naked desire shined in Nicolette's eyes.

Elsa sat, frozen, holding her breath and waiting to see what Nic would do next. Her heart raced and her body caught fire. The blonde woman held her gaze, seeking reassurance, and whispered, "So schön." It was spoken with reverence. Then, Nicolette leaned all the way in and kissed Elsa full on the lips. It was a soft, tentative kiss at first, but then it exploded into a passionate tangle of tongues. Nicolette tasted the inside of Elsa's mouth, nipped her lower lip with her teeth, and deepened the kiss even more as she slid her hands down from her face, and around her back where they roamed freely up and down, cupping her hips and pulling her closer.

Elsa's hands caressed Nic's sides and found their way to her back where they, too, slid down over her derriere, squeezing as their hips ground into each other. Breasts rubbed through cotton, further arousing them both. Nicolette brought a hand around to cup Elsa's breast. She slid her palm over the hard nipple, then circled her fingers around it before pinching it just enough to elicit an exquisite pain.

"Oh!" Elsa moaned into Nic's mouth. Encouraged, she pulled Elsa's shirt up over her head and quickly unhooked her black cotton bra. Pulling back, she stared at the small, pert breasts and rose-colored nipples. There was a charming sprinkling of freckles across her chest, a natural phenomenon for most redheads. The contrast against her white skin was breathtaking. Fearful it would end before it began, Nicolette leaned down and took one of the rosy peaks into her mouth and rolled her tongue over the tip, sucking lightly.

Elsa held her head close, and arched her neck, sighing. Nic moved to the other nipple and began unbuttoning Elsa's jeans. She pushed her back while using one arm to help lift her off the stool and guide her onto the floor. On her knees between Elsa's legs, she shimmied the jeans down and pulled them off, tossing them to the side. Her panties followed. Taking on the role of Top, Nic pulled her own T-shirt off, exposing her full breasts. Elsa's eyes zeroed in on the firm globes as she reached up to run her fingers over the dusky, beige nipples. She sat up and began licking them, reveling in the feel of tight, velvety peaks on her tongue. Nic pushed her pants down, and somewhat awkwardly released them one knee at a time. Kicking them off from her ankles, she leaned over Elsa, forcing her onto her back and began a slow, wet assault with her tongue over her breasts and abdomen. Her hand caressed downward to her athletic, creamy thighs, and then tickled softly over red pubic hair. She repeated the action without delving deeper, and Elsa's eyes pleaded with her.

"Nicolette, please." Her body was aching to be touched. Elsa's hands wanted to roam over the tanned body. They itched to feel her skin. Eyes met, and needs communicated. Nicolette turned and straddled Elsa's shoulders, offering a spectacular intimate view. She was pierced, something Elsa never knew. As she marveled at the sight before her eyes, her hands caressed up and down Nic's thighs. Below, Nicolette dove deep. Elsa nearly exploded. Pulling Nic's bottom down, she returned the pleasure lick for lick. Together, they found a rhythm, riding it out until they crashed together in a spectacular climax.

Through the two-way mirror, a man witnessed the scene going on between the women. He waited until they were finished, uncomfortably adjusting himself a time or two along the way. The blonde woman lingered, kissing the redhead often. She asked the redhead to join her for dinner that evening, but red declined saying she had to get home to her little brother. She was kind in her rejection, but the disappointment was clear on the blonde's face. Red tried to reassure her with promises of "another time."

Mollified, the blonde finally got dressed and left, but not before blowing red a kiss. Red sat on the floor for a while. After what seemed like an eternity, she pulled on her clothes and put her cleaning items away. She walked out of the double doors into the long, dark hallway and headed toward a back exit. He followed quietly as she went out into the twilight and headed toward the UBahn station. There, she descended the stairs and waited on the platform for her train. He stood back, waiting. When the tube arrived, she hopped on. He entered one door down and sat where he could watch her. She was engrossed in texting on her cell phone.

A ten-minute ride brought her to her destination where she got off and walked up the stairs to the street. He stayed back, but watched where she went, then trailed. As she walked a few blocks, crossed to the other side, and entered a building, he ran the short distance from the pathway and stuck his foot in the door before it could close and lock. Inside, he found the lifts and looked at the floor numbers as the elevator climbed. It stopped on the fourth floor. When it began its descent once again, he knew that it was her floor. He opened the door to the stairs adjacent and ran up four flights. Roaming the hallway, he stopped and waited. *Click.* The sound of a door closing on the far end of the hall alerted him to her whereabouts. He walked down and around the corner. Only one flat was on this side. The man made a mental note, then went back to the lifts, caught a car down, and went out to the street where he hailed a taxi.

"Where to?" The cab driver noted the man's appearance and reached a hand under his seat slowly, finding his handgun. Assured it was still there, he waited for a reply.

"Das Marriott, bitte." The Mohawk and swastikas tattooed on the man, and the menacing look in his eyes put the driver on edge. All he could think to do was get him where he wanted to go quickly. He took off and treated the city streets like the Autobahn.

Chapter 21

S arah checked herself in the mirror one last time. With her hair up in loose curls, and the red halter top and floral skirt adorning her body, she looked 'Tre Chic,' in her opinion. She was going on a date in Berlin with a handsome Dutchman. *When did my boring life get so exciting?*

Paul sent her a dozen red roses that arrived at the door as she was getting out of the shower. The woman from the front desk smiled hugely at her as she presented the bouquet.

"Nice boyfriend, eh?"

Sarah was amused and pleased. No one had ever sent her flowers before. *Well, that's brownie points for you, Paul Christiansen.*

"Not my boyfriend. Just a date," she told her.

"Well, that's a good start then." She wished Sarah a good night and left. Setting the flowers down on the table in the corner, she looked for the card. It was handwritten.

Hope we are still on for six. My number in case you need it is below. Can't wait to see you again...~ Paul.

She'd laid the card down and completed getting ready for her date with the scent of roses filling the room.

Standing before them once again and remembering the moment they arrived just a short while ago, a smile spread across her face. Sarah picked up the card and put it in her wallet. Then she took a picture of the roses with her cell phone. It was a moment she would always remember. Considering this, she plucked out one of the blooms and laid it on the table. She would need to purchase a hardback book so she could press the flower between the pages. The book would matter, too, so she promised herself that she would go shopping the next day and find something befitting this moment.

Sarah picked up her purse and room key and headed down to the lobby. International date night was about to begin.

Paul's taxi pulled up to the hotel at exactly six. Sarah walked out the front doors and crossed over the walkway and bike path to the curb where Paul, dressed up and looking even more like a cosmopolitan male model fresh off the front page of GQ, waited beside the open car door. He handed her a single red rose.

"More flowers?" She laughed and brought the bloom up to her nose, inhaling its sweet scent.

With his hands on her bare upper arms, he leaned down and kissed each cheek in greeting. "You look stunning. The lady in red." He took her free hand and spun her around like a dancer, admiring her grace and the length of her smooth legs beneath the flair of her skirt.

"Shall we?" He helped her into the back seat of the taxi. Sarah scooted in and Paul climbed in beside her. As the car pulled into traffic, she noticed the subtle scent of his aftershave. Sandalwood with a hint of lavender and moss. His hair was combed back, but the wave persisted and ended with a slight curl on the nape of his neck. His dark blue suit and white T-shirt made his already bright blue eyes brighter. He looked very handsome and smelled even better. Keeping her promise to Anno, and herself, would not be easy while on a date with such an appealing man. His thigh brushed hers as the vehicle weaved in and out of traffic. Warm, but no sudden spark like she experienced with Anthony. He glanced her way, a glint in his eye, and a small smile on his lips.

"So where are we going," Sarah asked.

Paul enjoyed her excitement and curiosity. "You'll see." He reached over and covered her hand with his own, caressing the back of it with his thumb.

"You're a tease, Paul Christiansen." She gave him a mock serious look.

"You've no idea, Sarah," he laughed. "But I promise you'll love it."

As they maneuvered down Wilhelmstraße, the beautiful architecture of Berlin revealed itself to Sarah's interested eyes. They came to a large, dome-topped building jutting out into, and surrounded on nearly all sides, by water.

"Where are we?" Sarah stared, taking in the majesty of the building.

Paul stepped out and offered his hand to Sarah. He leaned into the cab and paid the driver, asking him to come back in one hour.

"This is the Bode Museum. It was established back in the late 1800s by Wilhelm von Bode, but the idea came from the Crown Princess Victoria of Prussia, wife of Emperor Frederick III. Inside is one of the largest collections of sculptures and Byzantium art in the world. We have one hour until closing." Paul offered his arm. "Will you join me, Miss Brown, on a walk through history?"

Sarah placed her hand on Paul's arm and grinned up at him. *Damn. He's earning more brownie points!* "Yes, Mr. Christiansen, I'd love to."

She looked out over the waterway on either side as they passed over a bridge to the entrance. Twilight cast a surreal glow over the water as streetlights came on like someone flipped a master switch. The sound of waves lapping the shoreline and a bell from a buoy further out mingled together creating nature's orchestral music for Sarah's ears. It struck her that she was on a romantic date in Europe with a gorgeous man, and only a little over a week ago, she was just a library aid from a small town in Texas. Her conscience interfered, allowing one thought to sneak in. *What would this date be like if I were on Anthony's arm instead of Paul's?* She knew that was unfair to the man at her side, so she shook her head, clearing the thought away. They passed under the dome inside which led to the main hall. The height and sculptural details amazed Sarah, who nearly tripped as she attempted walking while looking straight up overhead at the grand staircase. Statues lined the circular walls and spires near the ceiling. Together, they strolled through the exhibits and displays of fine art. Paul was a wonderful tour guide; informed, but not a show-off.

"There are fifteen centuries of culture in this museum, Sarah. Imagine that. We come from such a rich history of immensely talented people touched by some kind of divinity that they have, thankfully, shared with us in their artistic creations." Paul, despite his base nature, loved art, and being able to share it with someone seeing it through innocent eyes was beyond enjoyable. He watched her face noting the joy lifting her lovely lips into a permanent smile as they came upon each new sculpture, each new mosaic or painting. She even showed interest in the ancient coins on display.

Paul extended his arm, reaching down to hold her hand. It was such a subtle shift, she didn't even notice until it dawned on her that his large, warm hand engulfed her own. It was nice, so she allowed it to continue throughout the tour.

Their time passed by pleasantly, and an announcement was made that the museum would be closing in fifteen minutes. They hadn't even seen half of it!

"Thank you, Paul. That was beautiful. I just wish we had more time to get through the rest of it." They crossed the bridge back to the street and waited for their taxi. Night had fallen, and lights twinkled along the road, casting a muted glow that tapered off into the darkness.

Paul reached up and tucked a strand of Sarah's blonde hair behind her ear. "You're welcome. I'm just glad you had fun. Art is something

I love. I paint in my spare time, but I'm nowhere near the level of what we just saw."

"I'd love to see your work. I can barely draw a stick figure." Learning that he had the soul of an artist made her think of him in a different light. He was very kind. At least, he had been to her. That, and his model good looks, was making it much harder to ignore his charms, yet he wasn't making any advances. Instead, he was a perfect gentleman.

"I'd love to show you. But you'd have to come to Amsterdam." He smiled and stared down into her brown eyes.

"So you can lure me to your home to show me your etchings, sir?" A laugh teased at the edges of her red lips as she uttered a cliched line from one of the many books she'd read.

"So I can paint you," he whispered, his voice low and oddly sexy. Caught off guard, her breath caught in her throat, and heat bloomed on her cheeks.

Paint her? The idea of posing for him was tempting, and incredibly erotic. Would she be clothed or nude? Thinking of him watching her intently while she stood naked, unmoving, made the blush on her cheeks travel all over her body. *Wow! Would I? Could I?* Then...*he's already seen me naked!* Remembering that he was the man on the other side of the mirror made her blush a deeper crimson.

He seemed to read her thoughts as a slow smile spread across his lush lips, causing his dimples to deepen on either side. They reminded her of Anthony. *But he's not here, and Paul is,* she admonished herself.

I fucking miss you. Anthony's message flashed through her mind.

A car horn interrupted them as the taxi pulled up to the curb. "Ready for dinner, Miss Brown?" Paul knew he was making progress, but he also noticed that he suddenly wasn't in such a hurry. He was thoroughly enjoying his time with Sarah. It had been a long time since he last went on a proper date—a very long time. She was sweet, fun, intelligent, flirty, and sexy. Just the kind of woman a man looks for when he's ready to settle down. He wasn't ready to settle down, but he might be ready to try a more equal kind of relationship with a woman—with this woman—rather than the usual type with which he dallied.

They slid into the back seat and headed off for a late supper. Another car followed. As they drove onto Tiergartenstraße toward the Hotel Brandenburger Hof, the vehicle behind them kept pace at a discreet distance. Inside the taxi, Paul continued to hold Sarah's hand, softly caressing her palm with his finger. Sarah tried to ignore the warm spirals running up her arm from the seemingly innocent caresses, but it was not easy. Being with Paul was a far cry from being with Anthony. They shared an animal attraction that was raw in its need to be expressed. Anthony was a little cruder in his speech, although that never bothered her. Paul, on the other hand, was cultured, quiet and kind, and his charm was subtle, yet it seemed to build upon itself in warm layers that gently peeled away her inhibitions. She was afraid it might also conquer her conviction to remain platonic. *Stay strong!* Sarah reminded herself she would take things slow and just enjoy being on a date.

The ride to their dinner destination took less than fifteen minutes. Paul informed her they would be dining at Die Quadriga, a popular restaurant inside the quaint five-star hotel. Outside, striped awnings adorned windows on either side of, and over, the entryway. Sconce lighting lit up the door, and inside the restaurant, the hostess greeted Paul like an old friend and led them to a table in the corner near the floor-to-ceiling glass doors that led out to patio dining. The wall behind their table was covered in dark wood wainscoting, polished to a shine. The white crown-molding outlining the recessed ceilings added old-world charm, and the crystal goblets sitting just so next to the white porcelain place settings and silverware, reflected the muted overhead lighting and candlelight softly shining from a hurricane lamp in the center of the table. With the doors open to the patio beyond, a warm breeze blew in, carrying with it the scent of Jasmine and climbing roses. It was almost perfect.

"Paul, this place is too much." Sarah couldn't stop looking around at everything, absorbing the ambiance, memorizing every detail.

"It couldn't possibly be too much. Not for you." Paul held the back of her chair and helped adjust it after she sat. He pulled up the chair next to her rather than across from where she was seated.

"How do you know about this place? The hostess seemed friendly with you." The observation was innocent, lacking accusation, but he played with her anyway.

"Jealous?" The waiter arrived with the wine menu.

She smiled and gave him a saucy look.

"We'll start with a Chenin Blanc," he looked over at Sarah, "and a water with lemon on the side as well."

"I'll leave the wine selection to you. I'd be no help at all." Sarah leaned her chin on her clasped hands and watched as Paul chose no less than three wines to accompany their dinner. The Chenin Blanc would pair with their appetizer—a Flavored Smoke with Kobe, pistachio, and tuna. That was followed by an asparagus soup flavored with chervil, vanilla, and rabbit. The entrée was a delicate Poussin with Rhubarb, celery, and shallots paired with a Sauvignon Blanc, and the main course of Belly of Pork served with water chestnuts, Romanesco, and summer truffles threatened to have the staff roll her out of there later in a wheelbarrow. The final wine was a dessert wine, slightly sweet, a Gewürztraminer that went well with their chocolate-hazelnut Nougat. It was the biggest meal Sarah had ever eaten, and probably the most expensive if her lack of knowledge of what half of it happened to be was anything to go by. Paul seemed comfortable with the selections and ordered it all as if he ate this way every day.

For Sarah, it was too much. Thankfully, European portions were small, but even so, with five courses, she felt she might have to skip the taxi and run back to the hotel.

"Paul, you're going to make me fat feeding me like that." She sat back and took a deep breath, her head light from the combination of good food and wine.

"Then we'll have to come up with a way to burn all these calories." The devilish glint in his eyes suggested he had a few ways in mind. He stood up and offered his hand. "Come."

Sarah raised an eyebrow and stood, slipping her fingers into his waiting palm. He led the way out onto the patio, beyond the tables, to an open area of cobblestones surrounded by topiaries in sculpted urns. The soft strains of classical music filtered through the doors and drifted past their ears, enchanting the night.

"Dance with me." Paul took her into his arms and began slowly initiating her into the steps of the waltz.

"I've never danced to classical music in my life."

His smile was infectious. "Then it's past time, don't you think? Just follow me. One, two, three, one, two, three. See? Easy as breathing." They twirled together around the patio as Sarah found her footing. It was more than any young woman could ask for—the perfect date. Almost.

No longer needing to watch her feet, Sarah looked up at Paul, who towered over her. The look in his eyes said *I want you*, but his actions said *I can wait*. In that moment, Sarah didn't want to wait. It was a vacation. After tonight or tomorrow, she'd never see this man again, and she wanted to satisfy at least one small curiosity, one that wouldn't violate her promise to either Anno or herself—not much, anyway.

"Paul?"

"Hmm?" He maintained eye contact without missing a step. His hand on her waist shifted, lightly caressing her lower back.

"Kiss me." She whispered the command with as much confidence as she could muster.

Paul stopped mid-step, the casual expression on his face turning serious. He searched her eyes, seemed to find the answer he was looking for, then pulled Sarah in for a long, soft kiss. It was lovely, but not the deep kiss she was looking for, now longing for. She reached her arms higher, wrapping them around his neck and deepened the kiss. She took the initiative, tasting his lips, sucking his tongue, and drawing him in as close as she dared.

Paul let her do with him as she wished. It was incredibly sweet and tempting. He could feel her body pressed against his, urgent and seeking. His own body responded, growing hard as his hands pulled her hips closer still, but he held back, eventually breaking the kiss. Looking down into her passion-glazed eyes, he knew he could have her but suddenly realized that was not all he wanted. He dropped soft kisses onto her cheek, and pulling her back to him, began to dance again.

Sarah was disappointed, but also thankful. The kiss was great, hot and sexy. The fact that he pulled back made her want more. Still, it was her own volition that deemed she wouldn't let things get out of control with him tonight. But it rattled a little. *Doesn't he want me?* A frown creased her brow; one he couldn't see.

But he felt it. "I do want you, Sarah. Believe me..." he said as he ground her hips against his hardness. Her body responded, heating up. "But let's take it slow. Let's savor this time and each other for a little while longer, yes?" He leaned back a bit and looked into her eyes.

After the no-holds-bar passionate affair with Anthony, Sarah didn't know what to make of this. However, she took him at his word and nodded. "Okay."

Paul kissed her lips softly. He found himself surprised that he would put off what he knew he wanted when it was falling into his lap.

She really wasn't like the type of women he usually slept with at all. Sarah was the type you treat with the utmost respect. Women like her didn't usually fall for men like him. They knew better, but she was too naïve to know this. She only saw the better side of him that he'd shown her since their first meeting. The way she reacted to that side of himself, his love of art, his gentlemanly manners, made him want to be a better man. And a better man wouldn't take advantage of an innocent woman high on romance, good food, and even better wine. He remembered her being tied up and worked over by Nadia and Nicolette, and yet he knew that deep down, she was remarkably innocent of the ways of the world.

The music ended, and he pulled back, his body controlled once again. "Let me take care of dinner and we'll walk back to your hotel. It's not far, and the stroll will be nice. Plus, it gives me a little more time with you before I must say goodnight." Paul kissed her fingers and went inside to pay the check. Sarah stood in the moonlight, in the middle of a lovely five-star restaurant garden, smiling.

Inside, Paul retrieved his uncle's company travel credit card from his wallet and handed it with the check to the waiter. When he came back, he added a thirty percent tip and signed the receipt. Noting the amount of the tab, he grinned. *Take that, you monstrous fuck.*

Sarah came up behind him, reaching around to pick up her purse. He offered his arm, and they left, exiting the hotel and heading back toward the Holiday Inn Express. They strolled arm in arm talking about art, movies, their friends and family. The journey passed by in less than an hour but didn't seem quite long enough. Paul walked Sarah up to her room, patiently waiting while she dug out her room key.

She turned and looked at him. "I had a great time, Paul."

"So did I, Sarah." He lifted his hand to caress her cheek. Leaning down, he claimed her lips in a thorough kiss, leaving her in no doubt of his desire for her. She pressed her body against the length of his, indulging in the feel of muscle beneath his suit. Again, he ended the kiss before she was ready.

"You don't have to go." Her breathy voice whispered the words, forgetting, in the heat of the moment, her promise to herself and to Anno.

Paul smiled. "Yes, I do, or I'll never leave."

She looked so disappointed that he chuckled. "But I'd like to see you again tomorrow."

Her face lit up. *So, this isn't the very last time I'll see you.* "I'd intended to go shopping for a book tomorrow."

"A book?" Surprise registered on his face. He wound a strand of her hair around his finger while tracing the tip around her ear.

"Yes, a book. I want to press one of your beautiful roses inside the pages as a keepsake." His subtle ministrations made her long for bolder caresses.

"Oh, I see. Well then. Perhaps I can help you pick out just the right book to remember me by." He liked knowing she wanted to commemorate their date. It made him feel special for a change. It was nice that a woman, this woman, thought enough of him to keep him as a treasured memory. However, he wasn't a memory yet, and maybe, just maybe he could offer her more to add to that mental treasure chest of hers. A thought was growing from a seed of an idea.

"How about I pick you up here and we go have lunch, do your shopping, and see what else we can get up to?" He leaned closer and waited for her reply.

Sarah felt heat rush up her neck to her ears, and then back down where it settled low, throbbing in need. The more reserved he was, the more her body wanted him. The whole gentleman thing was working for her like magic.

"That sounds like a good plan…" She licked her lips, feeling anticipation and some nervous anxiety.

His eyes focused intently on her movements. "Let me do that," Paul growled as he kissed her senseless, licking and sucking her lower lip. With his desire rising, and his body painfully erect, he pulled back and tried counting to ten as he held her close, breathing in the scent from her neck and hair.

"Tomorrow, Miss Brown." Once again in control, he stepped back, turning to walk away.

"Tomorrow, Paul." Sarah went inside her room and locked her door. As she leaned against the wall, she acknowledged the unfortunate, unsatisfied state of her body. Tears stung her eyes, and emotions erupted as Sarah realized she truly missed Anthony. Knowing this, she felt guilty about Paul, which made her more miserable. She lay back on the crumpled duvet and cried.

Finally, she stumbled to the bathroom where she shed her clothes and washed her face. As she came back to bed, she looked at her phone. Picking it up without another thought, she found his email and hit 'REPLY.'

Love the pictures. Thank u…I miss you too. S.

Then she hit 'SEND.'

The food, the wine, the romance, the feeling of being desired, and the sting of unrequited love for another, all took their toll, and Sarah curled up, falling into a restless slumber.

Gruber watched as Paul left the Holiday Inn Express a mere ten minutes after entering. He'd walked the woman in but didn't stay.

His observation of the way Christiansen treated the female all evening was one that showed he cared about her. He pulled out his mobile and fired off a text. This information would be of great interest to Mr. Knudson. He included a picture of the two he snapped back at the bridge by the museum. Two cozy lovebirds. Gruber smirked. He waited until he got a reply, then headed out. He had plans to make.

Chapter 22

Anthony cracked one eye open. It was dark. He'd been asleep for about an hour after spending the evening talking about cameras, lenses, and lighting with a group of student filmmakers staying at the Bed and Breakfast. Dinner was served in the main dining room promptly at six; a somewhat dry pork roast with potatoes and green beans, but the wine was good, and the company made it all palatable.

The three students, Jack, Eddie, and Elysa were all from Columbia University School of the Arts in New York City, so they immediately gravitated to Anthony, and the four of them ended up dominating the conversation at the table that included the B&B owner, Nanette, who cooked their dinner, Hugh Langley III, a mortgage banker from Lloyds of London, and Edgar and Francesca Fouquet from northern France. Everyone was interested in the college students' film project; a deeply intellectual documentary about a conspiracy theory that Ann Frank didn't die at Bergen-Belson but survived and was among the few remaining Jews liberated by the British army. Their focus was to be on the famous diary, evidence of editing after her proposed death from Typhus, and interviewing some people who claimed to have seen her in Amsterdam and even Belgium years after the war ended. The subject caused quite a debate amongst the guests before it turned to the technical side of the project, camera angles, lighting, lenses, and more. Bored with all that, Nanette, Hugh, and the Fouquets retired for the night, leaving Anthony and Jack debating Canon over Nikon for still shots, and Eddie and Elysa arguing over sequence of events in their upcoming interviews.

After polishing off four bottles of wine among themselves, everyone sauntered off to bed. Anthony was sleeping deeply when a nagging sound pulled him from his muddled dreams. PING.

He blinked. Clearing the fog from his head, he realized it was his cell phone. Someone had sent him a message via his email. *Derek, you fuck! It's the middle of the night, you drunken Irishman!* Anthony mentally cursed his best friend as he reached for his phone. Ready to send a blistering text back to Derek suggesting he both go to AA and purchase a clock, he was surprised to see that it was not from him. Not recognizing the address, he clicked on the message.

It was from Sarah. *I miss you too.*

He lay there in the dark, staring at the screen and reading her short message again. He heard a loud thudding sound and realized it was his heart beating. Her smile, and the image of her face came to the forefront of his mind with ease. He felt warm and happy. *Must be all that wine.* Rubbing sleep from his eyes, he remembered holding her, kissing her, and just talking to her. He smiled into the darkness. Sitting up on the edge of the bed, he contemplated answering. *Should I? She said she was going to Berlin. Is she still there? I could see her again, maybe get her out of my system.*

All these thoughts flooded his sleep and fermented grape-addled brain. His fingers ran ahead of his senses.

Where are you now?

SEND.

Sarah was finally asleep when her phone vibrated on the nightstand. Waking suddenly, she reached for it. She opened her inbox. It was from Anthony. He wanted to know where she was. Her fingers danced across the mini keyboard.

I am in Berlin. Where are u?

SEND.

Her phone vibrated in her hand as the message arrived.

In Amsterdam working. A.

Sarah didn't know what to make of that. Had she interrupted him? Was he saying he was working to offer some kind of excuse, so she'd leave him alone? She wasn't sure what to say, so she lay there biting her lip, thinking.

BUZZ. Her phone vibrated again.

What R U wearing?

She laughed. He included the smiley face emoticon. So, he wasn't trying to blow her off. Sarah wrote back.

If you were here, you'd know the answer to that.

Back in his room, Anthony received her cheeky reply and laughed out loud.

Send me a picture, princess.

SEND. He waited.

In her hotel room, Sarah melted. She was still his princess.

PING. An image icon flashed in his email. He clicked to open it. Bam! There she lay, naked and inviting in a tangle of sheets, just like he'd left her, but in a different country this time. "Damn!" Anthony smiled as his heart pounded, and his groin became tight, growing hard. The idea occurred to him that it would be nice to have her with him, have her by his side on the remaining canal cruises. Have her in his bed again.

Come join me in Amsterdam.

SEND.

Sarah got his message while she was putting her nightshirt back on. The happy smile on her lips spread wider as she repeated the word "princess" in her mind. It was his term of endearment for her. Not just 'baby' like he most likely called all other women, what he'd called her in the beginning before he switched over to the other. For that, she gave him an eyeful of her body, reaching for him all the way from her bed in Berlin. *Come join me in Amsterdam,* he said.

She thought about it. If she did, she knew she would not only enjoy it, but might fall harder for him, and then what? Would he just leave again when he was finished with his job, with her? Elsa said she would have the upper hand, be able to set the rules, but could she? Would he respect her demands? *You never know until you try,* she thought.

I have a few conditions, Anthony.

SEND.

She waited, holding her breath.

And what would those be? A.

Anthony knew he'd been a first-class shit, so wasn't surprised she would have reservations, but conditions?

Sarah thought.

First, absolutely NO leaving without a proper goodbye. That means I need to know when you plan to leave. That was just rude. S.

Anthony's mobile burned in his hand from her blistering words. He deserved it, he knew. He was also kind of proud of her standing up for herself like that. She was a feisty one and wasn't about to take any shit from him. Instead of making him angry, that thought caused a huge grin to spread across his face.

Okay. What else?

SEND.

Sarah lost all the wind in her angry sails when she read his response. No argument from him, just surrender.

I don't have anything else, but if I think of something, you have to do it!

She added the blushing emoticon to indicate that some of the things she might have him do would be naughty.

Anthony read more into that blushing smiley face than he should have because he was harder than Thor's hammer and she was too far away for him to nail her.

I'll do anything you want me to do...and more. And I'm sorry...

This last email made Sarah's heart flip-flop in her chest. He apologized. She hadn't expected that.

Okay. Then I'll come.

She waited, feeling warm in her heart, and all over her body at the thought of being with him again.

Yes, you will!

Anthony tossed out the line, then got serious and told her where he was staying. He asked her to text him with her flight information as soon as she was confirmed.

Sarah was so excited that she went ahead and called Lufthansa to make her reservation. She was to fly out the following afternoon. After she wrote down her information and messaged Anthony, she remembered she had a date with Paul the next day. *Crap! I'll have to call him in the morning and cancel.* She felt bad but figured that he would be okay since they'd only just met. *No big deal, right?*

She fired off a text to Elsa to let her know of her change of plans. Elsa was still up and responded immediately. Somehow, she wasn't surprised.

I knew it! You love him. Anno will be devastated.

Elsa typed her message as she walked out of her dungeon into the dark hallway, finished with her appointments for the night. Leaving out the back door, she walked quickly across the street and down toward the tube station. She nearly ran into a large man sporting a dark goatee and wearing a Trench coat despite the warm weather.

"Sorry," she said, and then moved a little faster to get down the stairs and onto the well-lit platform. The man had that dangerous look about him. Several other people waited for the next train, making her feel a little safer.

Her phone pinged.

I don't love him, Elsa. I just...like him a lot. And he apologized.

Elsa smiled a knowing smile.

You doth protest too much. But glad he said sorry. Maybe you'll come back to Berlin after you two get married.

Elsa pushed the send button and waited for her phone to blow up as she knew that would set her friend off. She tried not to laugh out loud in public.

ELSA! You're too much. I would come back no matter what. You and Anno are my friends now. Stop pushing me to marry!

This time she did laugh out loud, and a few people around her looked at her sideways.

The train pulled up, coming to a stop. She jumped on when the doors opened and found a seat. At this time of night, seating was plentiful. The ride home was uneventful. She scrolled through her playlist as she exited and picked a song. Sticking her earphone into one ear, she climbed the stairs to the street level. The sounds of a few cars passing and the wind in the courtyard trees greeted her unplugged ear. It was late and people were home tucked away in their beds.

The light over the door to her building flickered, as if it was about to go out. It gave her the creeps walking under it, and she quickly punched in her code for entry. Once inside, the silence was over-whelming. She rode up the lift to the fourth floor and made her way down to her flat. Inside, all was dark. Anno had not left on the hall light for her like usual nor was the front door locked. *What is wrong with that boy!* She set her backpack and keys down on one of the livingroom end tables after stumbling in. The only light provided came from the moon outside filtering in through the sheer curtains covering the floor-to-ceiling windows. Although it was nearly two-thirty in the morning, she was mad enough to poke her head into her little brother's room to chide him for not leaving the light on or locking the door.

"You forgot something, little brother! Thanks a lot!" Elsa's voice carried, but no reply was forthcoming. No sounds of snoring or stirring. She tried again. "Hey! You're not getting off that easy, Anno." She flipped his light switch on and off several times, then stopped. She flipped it back on again to confirm what her eyes relayed to her brain. He wasn't in his bed.

"Anno!" Elsa shouted and turned to look around the apartment. "Anno, answer me!" She looked in her room to see if he had fallen asleep there watching her television. Her room was empty, and exactly as she left it earlier.

She grabbed her phone and called his cell number. An answering ring came from inside his room. She walked back in and saw it sitting on the nightstand. Picking it up, she checked his messages. There were a few to his best friend, Erik, which ended two hours ago. She texted Erik.

This is Elsa. Is Anno with you?

She waited.

The longest minute of her life later, he answered.

No. Is this a joke, Anno? What R U up to?

No, Erik. This really is Elsa. Anno isn't home. Did he say he was going somewhere with anyone?

Elsa reached for straws. Anno was either always with Erik at his house or here at home. He didn't hang out with anyone else.

No. Sorry, Elsa. He said he was going to bed. Are you sure? Can I help?

She could tell his friend was worried.

No. I'll handle it. Go back to bed. When I find him, I'll let you know...after I kick his ass.

Her optimism didn't go beyond that text. She really was worried. She grabbed her keys and went back downstairs to look around outside. The light over the entryway door flickered, offering very little illumination by which to see. She called out to him, trying to keep her voice low so as not to disturb the other residents.

"Anno!" She walked around the courtyard. "Johann Martin Kreiss! You better answer me. So help me, when I find you, you're in so much trouble!" Her voice cracked as emotions threatened to overtake her. Silence greeted her pleas. Fearful, she dialed the police.

Within the half hour, an unmarked Volkswagon Jetta driven by two Kriminalpolizei had arrived and began taking her information. Kriminalkommissar Joseph Heinz, a seasoned veteran detective with graying hair at his temples, tried assuring her that teenagers often go off without permission to do things their parents or guardians would otherwise disapprove of. Elsa knew better. She knew Anno would not do this to her. He would not leave the door unlocked or go anywhere without her knowing where he was. She told the Kripos such.

His partner, a rather quiet, observant woman who introduced herself as Birgitta Mahler, patted her on the back and asked, "Is there anyone you can call? You shouldn't be alone. It would help to have someone to wait with you while we search for your brother."

Elsa thought of Sarah. "Yes. My friend. I'll call her now."

"Good," she said. "And try not to worry. We have his photo and have put out word. Someone will notice him somewhere or else he'll just come home on his own." She rejoined her partner, and they left with the assurance they would check back in with her in one hour.

Elsa dialed Sarah's number.

"Elsa, are you still up?" Sarah's sleepy voice answered on the second ring.

"So sorry to call you this late, but Sarah, Anno is missing!" Elsa's voice broke as the tears began to fall.

"What? What do you mean missing?" Sarah, now fully awake, sat up in bed immediately.

"I came home, and he wasn't here. I checked with his friend, Erik, and he wasn't there, either. I looked everywhere, Sarah. I called the police, and they came, but now I have to wait, and I'm so worried. Where could he be?" Elsa became almost incoherent as she sobbed.

"I'm coming over right now. Just hold on, okay?" Sarah was already jumping out of bed and pulling on a pair of jeans.

"You don't have to..." Elsa hiccupped.

"Of course I do. You're my friends and I love you guys. I'll be right there. Just wait inside." Sarah hung up and ran to the bathroom to throw on a bra and T-shirt. Slipping her feet into running shoes, she grabbed her purse, a jacket, and her room key. As she rode down the elevator, she pinned up her hair. The night clerk at the desk looked up from reading his book and watched as the blonde American jogged out of the hotel and turned left.

Sarah sprinted like a marathon runner the few blocks up to Elsa's apartment building without even thinking how crazy it was she was running down a street in Berlin in the middle of the night—alone. When she got to the entryway, she stopped. She didn't know the code to get in. She looked at the list of last names of the residents on the panel but didn't know Elsa's last name. She texted her instead.

I'm here. Buzz me in!

The buzzer sounded and Sarah opened the door, running inside to the lifts. On the fourth floor, she jogged down to the end and hooked left, stopping to knock on Elsa's door. It opened before she could finish raising her hand. Elsa, with a tear-stained face, rushed at her, engulfing Sarah in a hug. She cried.

"Where could he be, Sarah? Where?" Elsa was falling apart. Her brother was everything to her; all she had left since the death of their parents.

"Sssh. I don't know, but we'll figure it out. Let's go sit down and then you can tell me what the police said." Sarah kept her arm around her friend as they made their way to the couch.

"They didn't say much, just that he would probably come home by himself. But Anno doesn't go off like this without telling me. Especially in the middle of the night. He knows better. And he didn't take his phone with him. He never goes anywhere without it." Elsa's anxiety was affecting Sarah, who teared up while listening.

"Did you tell the police he left his phone?" Sarah's face was incredulous. How could the police think nothing was wrong when a teenage boy was missing without his phone?

"I, I...don't know! Oh, Sarah, I can't think straight." She blew her nose.

"It's okay. We just need to think." Sarah stood up and walked to Anno's room. She went inside and looked around. Elsa followed her, observing her friend searching the room.

"What are you looking for?" Sarah was on her hands and knees, looking under the bed.

She sat up and looked around. "What's that smell? It's like a hospital in here." Sarah sniffed, then sniffed again while looking in corners and all around.

Elsa inhaled, but her nose was plugged from crying. "I can't smell anything. What does it smell like?" She walked up behind her friend, looking over her shoulder.

"Kind of chemical-like." Sarah lifted the covers on the bed and leaned down to sniff. She reached for the pillow and lifted it up, finding a white cloth lying folded over. She picked it up. It was a washcloth. She sniffed it.

"This is it. Is it one of yours?" Sarah held it up to Elsa's nose. She sniffed, managing to get some air through her nasal cavity and detected the chemical scent which Sarah had referenced.

"Ugh! No. What's that smell?" Elsa's nose wrinkled.

Sarah thought she recognized the odor as one of many she smelled while her mother was in the hospital. "I'm not sure, but we should call the police and show them this, and make sure they know Anno left his phone here."

"You think someone took him, don't you?" Understanding dawned on Elsa, and then she realized that her brother may have been abducted. Tears flooded her green eyes again, smearing mascara down her cheeks. "Sarah. Oh, mein Got! What am I going to do?"

"You're going to hold it together because Anno needs you. And until we know there's something to worry about, we should keep cool heads, okay? Keep it together, Elsa." Sarah took her by the hand and led her back to the living room where she calmly talked Elsa through calling the police again. It took about thirty minutes for the detectives to come back. KriminalKommissar Heinz did not seem pleased. *But that might just be his normal countenance.* Sarah gave them the information on what they found and pointed out that Anno's phone was still in the apartment. They both looked at the washcloth, sniffed it, and immediately pulled out gloves and a plastic bag to put the cloth into.

"You should've shown us this before, Fraulein Kreiss." Heinz gave Elsa a stern look. Elsa's face registered the slight in his address, but before she could reply, her friend spoke up.

"She didn't know this when you first came. I'm the one who found it." Sarah stood and faced the detective.

"And who are you? How did you know where to find this?" He started treating Sarah like a suspect and she was not the least bit pleased with his attitude.

"I'm Sarah Brown, friend of Elsa and Anno. I didn't know where to find it. I simply did what most rational people would do and looked around his room. Elsa was with me and we found it together. You should have done this the first time you were here!" Sarah's temper blazed to the surface.

"Calm down, Miss Brown," said Mahler. She had a look of understanding on her face as if she endured her partner's prickly personality often and knew how it grated on others. "Did you say earlier the front door was also unlocked?" She made notes in a small notebook.

"Yes." Elsa found her voice. "Yes, it was not locked, and the hall light was off. Anno always leaves the hall light on for me."

The female officer walked to the entry hall and found the small credenza with the lamp sitting upon it. She reached with her gloved hand to turn the switch. Nothing happened. She found the light bulb, an old Tungsten, and gave it a twist, tightening it. It lit up.

"Does anyone else have a key to the flat," she asked.

"Just me and Anno. And the landlady, Mrs. Schmidt," Elsa offered.

"Do you have any dispute with your landlady?" She continued to make notes. Then the detective paused to check out the front door. She leaned down, noticing tiny scratches around the lock.

"No. None. I've never had any problem with her." Elsa watched the detective as she looked up at her partner and gave the slightest nod of her head. Kriminalkommissar Heinz pulled out his phone and hit the speed dial button for dispatch.

"This is Heinz, badge number five, six, two, seven. Send a crime scene unit over to the address of my last call." He hung up.

"Crime scene unit?" Elsa's voice rose and tears began to fall in earnest.

The rest of the night crept by in agonizing confusion for Elsa and Sarah as they sat on the couch being questioned again by Heinz. He also woke Elsa's landlady and questioned her. Two CSU officers dusted the front door, hall lamp, and Anno's bedroom for fingerprints. His partner made the rounds with her neighbors, asking if anyone had seen or heard anything between the hours of midnight when Anno sent out his last text to Erik and around two-thirty in the morning when Elsa came home. No one had heard anything. But Mrs. Schmidt offered that perhaps her surveillance camera picked something up.

"I have only the one camera in the main entrance. You can check it." She looked worried. She'd known Elsa and Anno for many years and had watched the boy grow up.

"Secure the tape and review it. Report anything you find back to me immediately." Heinz gave the order to his partner, who left with Frau Schmidt in tow.

He turned back to Elsa and Sarah. "You should try and get some rest. We'll keep an officer outside your door for the rest of the night, and if we find anything of interest on the surveillance, we'll let you know." He got up to leave, then turned to Sarah. "You should not leave Berlin until this is resolved, Miss Brown."

Sarah nodded her head, giving the detective a look. "I wouldn't dream of leaving my friend at a time like this." She thought about Anthony. He would have to understand. Elsa was more important right now.

"Sehr gut." He nodded at Elsa. "Frau Kreiss." The abrasive man now showed compassion and respect considering the evidence found, evidence that added up to a crime that too often ended badly in his experience. Either the boy was already dead, or he'd wish he was because he would be sold into black market child sex trafficking. Those children were never found again. And this woman, a protective sister, albeit one with a less than appropriate career in his opinion—*a dom-inatrix*—was obviously distraught and worried as any mother would be for a son. It would take a miracle to find the boy, and the world seemed pathetically low on that commodity. He went downstairs to check on the progress with the tape and then headed out the door calling his contact at the Bundeskriminalamt.

"Bjorn. Heinz here. I need you to check flight manifests coming into and going out of Berlin in the last twenty-four hours, and also for the next twenty-four. Check the rails too."

"What am I looking for, Heinz?" Bjorn's voice crackled over the mobile speaker.

"Known sex traffickers. And the sooner, the better. You know the drill." The raspiness in his voice tipped Bjorn off as to where Heinz's mindset was at, and the level of his emotions.

"Don't let yourself go there, Joseph." Bjorn's tone softened.

"Dammit, just get on it, already. Schnell!" Heinz ended the call and then pulled a cigarette out of his pocket. Lighting it up, he inhaled, taking the soothing smoke into his lungs. He exhaled as he leaned up against his car. Heinz knew he couldn't lose another child. It would be too much. It would kill the last remaining part of himself that was human. Before he knew it, his cigarette had burned down almost to the filter. He refused to light up another one. He was trying to quit. Without anything else to do while he waited, he paced around the building looking for clues—anything. Forty minutes dragged by as he poked around shrubbery and looked up at windows.

"Sir, we found something." It was his partner. She'd walked up behind him, nearly giving him a heart attack. He spun with his firearm almost clear of the holster.

"Announce yourself next time. I could have shot you!" His irritation was evident, but his need to know what she found was stronger. "What is it? What did you find?"

"A man entered the building at eleven forty-seven p.m. Frau Schmidt says she's never seen him before. There's no footage of him leaving. He must've either exited out the back or he's still in the building." She said this in a matter-of-fact manner.

"If she's never seen him before, how did he get in? Residents have a code for the door." Heinz asked the pertinent question.

"He came in after another resident left." She looked down at her note pad. "An *Herr Schumaker* from the second floor. I questioned him just now and he doesn't remember the man passing him."

"What the hell was this Schumaker doing out at that hour? Where was he going?"

"He said he was walking his dog." She looked up, waiting.

"And he didn't notice a stranger? The dog didn't bark or anything?" Heinz was getting irritated again and his thoughts turned foul. *"People are so wrapped up in their own little worlds that they fail to notice important things around them, like strangers entering secure buildings. It makes me angry thinking how easily criminals get away with the crimes they commit. Most often it's because people ignore them, and don't want to get involved. Then a child goes missing and everyone wants to know what the police are doing about it. Well, what the hell are they doing about it? If they'd just pull their heads out of their arses—"*

"No report of the dog barking. There were enough seconds that passed after Herr Schumaker exited the door before the man entered to indicate that he was probably hiding off to the side and just waiting for someone to come out. He slid his foot in right before the door closed."

"What did he look like? What's the description?" Heinz walked quickly back toward the front of the building while his partner followed.

"Tall, around one hundred eighty-two centimeters. He was wearing a dark, possibly denim jacket. Long hair pulled back, shaved at the sides. There appeared to be a tattoo on the side of his head. Looked like a crude swastika. Probably a prison tat. The integrity of the video is not the best. It's dark and grainy. Just a cheap camera to provide the most basic security surveillance." She closed the notepad.

Just then his phone buzzed. "Ja. What do you have?" Heinz waited as Bjorn read what he discovered. He looked at his partner as he listened. "How do you know it was Aleksander Gruber?"

"The passport photo matched Gruber's criminal file photo. He's traveling under the name Marcus Janssen, but the face recognition doesn't lie." Bjorn had more.

"Give it to me. What's the description of this asshole, and his priors?" Heinz waited, knowing it wouldn't be good.

"Height, one hundred eighty-one centimeters. Weight, eighty-three kilos. Wears a Mohawk. White Supremacist type. Several tattoos including swastikas on the sides of his head. Multiple piercings. His priors include breaking and entering, robbery, assault with a deadly weapon, possession and distribution of narcotics, and sex trafficking. He just finished ten months for minor possession of cocaine in Amsterdam three months ago, which is where Marcus Janssen flew in from. He plea-bargained a shorter sentence by turning state's evidence and testifying against his dealer. No record of a flight out yet. Still checking all the rail stations' surveillance."

Heinz nodded to his partner. "Bjorn, we need an all-points on this character. We have surveillance of a man matching that description entering the residence of the victim. I'll have Mahler send over footage of what we have. Get that out with a mugshot to all agencies. I want this bastard caught."

Heinz handed the phone over to his partner. "Get that video over to him ASAP and have him fax over the mugshot of Aleksander Gruber."

"Ja vol." She took the mobile and walked back toward the building, coordinating with Bjorn as she went.

Heinz waited at the car. He was seeing red, and ready to pound the suspect with his bare hands. It felt like the Schubert case all over again, chasing leads with very little time. He knew he would need to calm down enough to speak with Frau Kreiss. She wasn't going to take any of this well. And he had no assurances to give her.

Chapter 23

Dawn lit the sky in contrasting shades of purple, orange, and blue, which streaked through the sheer window covers and splashed on the opposite wall. Sarah rose after a mere hour and a half of sleep on Elsa's couch. After Detective Heinz gave Elsa the news that Anno was abducted by a known sex trafficker, she lost it, wailing uncontrollably until her body couldn't take the stress anymore. Around five in the morning, she'd finally fallen asleep. Sarah held her until her breathing was deep and steady, and then she pulled the covers over her friend, and headed out to lie on the couch. She wanted to be able to hear either the phone or the door should anyone come by or call with news. No one called. No one came by. Each hour that they didn't hear anything meant another hour Anno spent in extreme danger.

Sarah washed her face in the bathroom sink and walked quietly to the kitchen where she put on a pot of coffee. She sat at the table where only two days ago she'd shared dinner with her new friends. It didn't seem possible that it was such a short span of time. It didn't seem real that something so horrible could have happened to that sweet, innocent boy. The dam finally broke and Sarah cried. She'd come to Europe for an education, but the one she was getting was more about pain than pleasure. People she cared for either left or got hurt. It just wasn't right. She felt exposed, to both the best side of people, and the absolute worst side of human nature.

Wiping away the tears, she tried to pull herself together. She needed to call Paul and let him know what happened. At least she didn't have to tell him, '*Sorry, I'm canceling our date so I can run off to Amsterdam to be with another man.*' She would also have to message Anthony. *Would he understand?*

Glancing at her watch, she noted that it was nearly eight. It was early yet, but she had no idea what the day would bring, so Sarah pulled out her mobile and dialed Paul. On the fourth ring, he answered.

"Yes? Who is it?" Sounding gruff and grumpy, he waited for a reply.

"Paul, it's Sarah." Sarah's voice was raw after so little sleep and her tearful breakdown at the table over coffee.

"Sarah? What's wrong?" His tone shifted from irritated to concerned.

"I have terrible news. Last night, someone took Anno." She had to stop. Just saying it out loud brought a huge lump to her throat that threatened to choke her.

"Took him? What do you mean?" Paul sat up in bed. An alarm bell started ringing somewhere in the back of his mind.

"Someone broke into Elsa's flat while she was at work and took him. The police found a rag soaked in ether, and the landlady's surveillance camera identified the guy. Some sex trafficker from Amsterdam. Something Gruber."

Paul stopped breathing. Gruber. He knew the man. Knew he sometimes worked for his uncle. Knew that Gruber was paid now and again to retrieve certain types of women from small towns in Ukraine, Czechoslovakia, and Croatia, according to Greta. He was a dangerous man. Paul sat, stunned. Thoughts ran rampant through his head. He knew his uncle was behind this, but somehow, he couldn't quite believe he'd go so far as to kidnap a child and have him secreted out of the country, have the boy brought to him. Yet he was more than aware of the kind of monster Peter was—always would be. If he said nothing, the boy would be abused in ways he'd never be able to forget, to heal from. Anno would be scarred for life…just like Paul. He'd feared his uncle for so long, but then he only had himself to worry about. Now, an innocent and wonderful boy was in great danger. He couldn't just slink away and hide—not anymore.

"Sarah, listen to me. I can't explain over the phone, but I know who this man is. I know who he works for. I'm coming over. Call your policeman and have him meet me there." Paul stood, looking around for his clothes. "Wait, text me Elsa's address."

"Paul, how do you know this man? He's a criminal! Why can't you explain now?" Sarah's voice rose, and she had to force herself to take a few breaths.

"Sarah, do as I say. Time isn't on our side. Call your detective. I'll be there within the hour." Paul hung up and began throwing his clothes into his bag. He would need to be ready to get on the soonest flight back home. This time Uncle Peter would not get away with his crimes. It was time for him to meet Paul Christiansen, the man. He couldn't save himself all those years ago. He was too small, too young, and not even his own mother had believed him. No one helped him, but he'd be damned if he'd stand by and let this happen to Anno. No one was there to help him then, but he was here now to help this young man. A quick shower found Paul dressed, but unshaved. He didn't want to spare the time. Every moment would count from here on out.

He grabbed his bag and room key and went down to the lobby where he tossed the key on the desk and left. He didn't give a damn about a proper checkout. It was all on Peter Knudson's tab anyway. *Fuck him!*

He hailed a taxi and gave the driver the address glowing on his mobile screen. As they pulled into traffic, Paul called to reserve a flight back to Amsterdam. There was one leaving that afternoon. It would have to be soon enough because there were no others. *If anything has happened to that boy, I'll kill you. I'll kill you, Peter.* Paul made the silent promise, his fists clenching as he stared out at the passing buildings.

The cab finally pulled up in front of the faded yellow apartment building. Sarah stood outside, pacing back and forth. She waited for Paul to pay the driver, then could wait no longer.

"Tell me how you know this man who took Anno? Did you have something to do with this?" The anger and outrage in her voice took Paul by surprise. Never did it occur to him that she might blame him when he divulged his knowledge of Gruber.

He grabbed both of her arms, holding them at her sides and looked her in the eyes. "Sarah, I swear to you that I had nothing to do with this." The fire in her expression said she didn't believe him, but her silence told him she was waiting for his explanation.

He sighed. "But I know who did." The tension around his mouth showed in small lines at the corners. She hadn't noticed them before. He was usually smiling and behaving in a devil-may-care manner. Not today. Not now.

"I'm waiting, Paul." She crossed her arms over her chest, effectively putting a barrier between them.

"My uncle, the one who sent me here to try and hire Elsa...it was him. I didn't know what he was up to, I swear, but now I do. He only wanted her to get to Anno."

"That doesn't make any sense at all, Paul. Why would he want to hire Elsa to get to Anno? He's just a kid. He wouldn't even have met or known him!" She was getting worked up again and completely missing what he was trying to say.

"Sarah, my uncle is a very sick individual." A haunted look came into Paul's blue eyes that changed his handsome face from gorgeous to tortured; as if he'd survived the worst possible circumstances that a person could endure. "He's seen him before. I'm sure of it. He was in Berlin last fall, and then something happened. I don't know what, but he said he couldn't come into the country anymore. That's why he sent me. At first, I took him at his word that all he wanted was to hire this dominatrix for his club, but deep down, I knew better. I knew it couldn't be that simple. He was up to something. I just didn't know what it was, until you called me this morning."

Sarah blew out a frustrated breath. Then understanding dawned and her expression became horrified. "He likes boys, doesn't he? I mean, sexually?"

"Yes." Paul stood with his hands on his hips, looking down at her.

"How could you know this about him and do nothing?" She threw out the accusation before realizing that Paul couldn't have possibly known this would happen, just as he said.

The dark look clouding his light blue eyes made them appear as black and deep as the ocean in a storm. "I'm not 'not doing nothing!' Why do you think I'm here right now? And where is that detective? Where's Elsa? I need to tell her...to tell her I'm sorry. Tell her I'm going to get her brother back." Paul paced, nearly tripping over his suitcase where he'd set it down and forgotten all about it.

Sarah instantly felt bad. "I'm sorry, Paul. I believe you. I believe you didn't know, but you can't blame me for the misunderstanding. The detective is on his way, and Elsa is still sleeping. She had a bad night, so I didn't want to wake her until you got here." Sarah waited, but he didn't say anything else. He seemed lost in thought.

"Just how do you know your uncle likes boys in that way, anyhow?"

Paul came back to himself upon hearing her question. He licked his lips, looked down at the grass, and then slowly lifted his shame-filled eyes to hers.

She was horrified. "No!" She didn't want to believe it.

"Yes, Sarah. From the time I was just a little boy, he..." Paul couldn't get the words out, so he skipped over them. He couldn't look at her.

"No one believed me then. Not my mother, no one. Eventually, it stopped because I grew up. Peter doesn't like men, or women for that matter, in that way. Just...boys."

Sarah threw her arms around Paul and hugged him tight. The idea that a little boy could be so abused, and no one protected him was unimaginable. What kind of mother doesn't believe her child when he says he's being molested? Her heart broke for that little boy, and it wept for the man who, at this moment, seemed completely broken. He stood with his arms down at his sides while Sarah held him, unable to accept her compassion, her desire to comfort. He felt nothing but shame and anger. Felt completely unworthy of this woman whose heart automatically opened to him in a way his mother's never had.

"What are you going to do?" She looked up and saw the moisture in his eyes.

"I've booked a flight back to Amsterdam this afternoon. Lufthansa. I know where Gruber might take Anno. He won't be traveling by plane, but probably by train and private driver, too."

"I don't understand. How would he know how to evade police?" Sarah's naivete showed.

"Gruber sometimes...procures women from the Czech regions to come work in the brothels my uncle runs." Saying it out loud made it sound as terrible as it actually was, even though prostitution was a legal business in the Netherlands.

"He takes them? Are you serious? I thought it was legal in Amsterdam to prostitute yourself out?" She stood back, feeling outraged again.

"It is. But not every woman wants to be a prostitute, and there are illegal sides to the legal business of being a paid whore. I know. It sounds bad. It's just life, Sarah. It happens all the time." He tried to sound blasé about it, but he knew that wouldn't set well with this woman even as the words left his mouth.

"That doesn't make it right, Paul. I can't believe that after what you've just told me you went through that you'd think it was okay, that it's 'just life' for someone else to be taken and sexually abused. And you were going to take Nadia to him? What were you thinking?" She poked a finger into his chest to punctuate her last words. He felt like an ass.

She was right, of course. But until this moment, he'd not thought beyond himself. He had the good grace to feel remorseful. "I'm sorry. You're right, Sarah. But Nadia wouldn't have been in any danger. She would've worked in one of the legitimate clubs. Still, I did think about that, and that's why I made sure he didn't hire her. Uncle Peter never rescinded that offer. I just didn't want to embroil her in his sick world, so I made that up. I lied to you. For that, I'm deeply sorry. But we need to focus on Anno right now."

"So now what? How will you get him back? Your uncle sounds dangerous." She asked the obvious question, one that didn't have an obvious answer.

"That's why I need to talk to your detective. We'll need help from Interpol. But we have to act quickly. Uncle Peter must have felt desperate to go to these lengths. I don't think he'll wait long once he has Anno in his grasp."

"Oh, my God, Paul." Reality hit Sarah all over again, and she choked up, tears welling in her eyes.

Paul wrapped his arms around her and kissed the top of her head. "We'll get him back, Sarah. I've spent my life trying to avoid this man, but I'll be damned if I let him hurt Anno. I won't let it happen. I promise you."

She sobbed quietly, then wiped her eyes. Paul waited a few minutes for her to get herself together. He admired her strength, her values. He wanted nothing more than to live up to the high expectations this woman would have for the people in her life, for the man she might love. "Come on. Let's go wake Elsa."

As they turned to walk into the building, the police Volkswagen pulled up and detectives Heinz and Mahler stepped out. While they entered the building together, Paul told his story for the second time that morning. By the time they reached Elsa's door, Heinz was on his phone with a contact at Interpol, and Paul waited for Sarah to wake Elsa so he could launch into a third telling, and a most sincere apology, although he wasn't sure why he should be apologizing for Peter Knudson. He just knew that he needed to do everything he could to make things right.

Sarah sat next to him on the couch afterward. "I'm going with you. I already have the flight booked. You're not doing this alone." She put her hand over his.

"It's too dangerous, Sarah. I can't let you do that."

"It's done. Elsa must remain here in the unlikely event we're all wrong and Anno shows up. I also have a friend in Amsterdam who can help. He'll look out for me. Don't worry. But we'll both help you, so just stop arguing and say, "Thank you, Sarah.""

He shook his head and smiled. "Thank you, Sarah." It was the first time in his life that someone said they would be there for him. It was an overwhelming feeling. "Wait, you said you have a friend there? A *man* friend?"

"Yes. His name is Anthony de Luca." The look in her eyes when she said his name hit Paul with the force of a fist in the gut. He realized she had feelings for this man. *Competition. Great.* He shook himself. There would be time to worry over that later. Right now, Anno was the priority.

Heinz interrupted. "Christiansen, we need to talk." He indicated Paul should follow him. He rose and they exited the room heading out into the hallway. Elsa looked up from her conversation with Mahler. Dark circles stood out under her green eyes.

Sarah looked at her friend. "Don't worry, Elsa. We're going to get Anno back." She said it with such conviction that Elsa simply nodded in the affirmative. Her shy American friend was exhibiting a spine of steel. She might be naïve in the ways of sex, but when it came to being strong for people, she was a superhero.

Mahler, too, was impressed. A case like this had never come across her purview before. A home invasion resulting in a kidnapping was rare. More so was having anyone know who did it and for what reason. The kicker was having the intel on where to find the victim. She felt optimistic for once, and she was glad. Knowing her partner's background and what he'd seen in his twenty years in the police department, ten as a detective, she knew he needed for all to turn out well here. A case from two years back had left Heinz a cynical and emotionally distant man. That case scarred Joseph Heinz so badly that he turned to drinking, which led to divorce and the loss of his own family. He just couldn't get over it, and the perpetrator had never been caught. It was now a cold case file that sat on Heinz's desk as a constant reminder to him of what he considered his greatest failure. Sitting next to it was a picture of his family on vacation in France several years before. In it, smiling and happy, was his ex-wife and his daughter, who was twelve at the time. Both represented all that he'd lost, the time when his entire life fell apart. All he had now was his job, and even that hung by a thread for a time until he joined a counseling group for alcoholics at the request of his department head, a request in the form of a demand, one in which he could not refuse unless he wanted to hand in his badge and firearm for good.

Now, Heinz was like a man possessed with the Kreiss case. Mahler recognized the determination in his eyes. He wouldn't rest until young Anno was home safe in the protective and loving arms of his sister.

In the hallway, Heinz outlined the plan with Paul. "We'll be met on the ground by Interpol. From there, you'll head home as usual, and we'll follow from a discreet distance."

Paul stared. "We? You're coming too?" He was surprised by this, but secretly glad. He truly wouldn't be alone. Still, he had a sick feeling in his gut that despite all the help and tactical support, things were going to get ugly fast.

"You didn't think I'd let you go on your own, did you?" Heinz asked. He'd felt more than sorry after hearing Paul's personal story. No child should go through what Christiansen had endured. But now was his chance to help save another, so he would do all he could to put an end to the monster that had plagued this man, the monster who now had Anno, and he would do it gladly. In the end, he hoped all their demons would be purged. "Don't worry, Paul. You'll be tracked by GPS, and we're outfitting you with a wire. We'll get the bastard, once and for all." Heinz placed a fatherly hand upon Paul's shoulder and gave him a reassuring pat. "Now, are you ready?"

The time had come to act. It was put up or shut up, and Paul steeled himself for what would surely be the hardest thing he would ever have to do. It was "Go" time.

"I'm ready." Paul forced confidence into his voice, but fear still gripped his soul.

Chapter 24

The flight to Amsterdam was tense for all. Paul knew he was about to face his life-long worst nightmare. His gut was in knots. Beads of sweat dotted his otherwise perfect forehead. Kriminalkommissar Heinz felt the thrill of the hunt for the first time since the cold case that haunted him for the past two years. He was re-energized and ready to take down Peter Knudson and Aleks Gruber. He was even more thankful that his contact at Interpol had granted him the authority to cross international lines and participate directly in the operation rather than sit back in Berlin on the sidelines. Thanks to Bjorn explaining to the director how deeply personal this case had become to Heinz in a short period, he would experience the satisfaction of seeing Knudson arrested, and he would also be the one to bring Anno back home to his sister. His heart came back to life, beating with purpose. Hope and the advent of justice had brought him back from the dead.

Sarah was both worried for Anno, praying they would get to him in time, and excited to be seeing Anthony again. She'd messaged him to explain the change in plans. She told him what had happened to her friend's brother, and that the man who took him was right there in Amsterdam. Anthony was fully supportive and ready to offer whatever help they needed. His thoughts strayed to the older man he'd witnessed on his second day in the city, and the coincidence didn't escape his notice. As he waited at the airport for Sarah, he pulled up the images on his laptop and looked them over again. Maybe he would get that chance to turn the man in after all. The thought brought a satisfied smile to his lips.

Upon landing, the three of them were escorted off first by airport security police and taken to their headquarters where Agent Maurice Touchard, liaison to Interpol headquarters in Lyon, and Chief Niels Limmer and Officer Timon Oleson of the *Koninklijke Marechaussee, or KMar* greeted them. Touchard took the lead.

"KriminalKommissar Heinz, pleasure to meet you." He reached out to shake hands with the detective. "And you must be Mr. Christiansen?" Touchard addressed Paul, shaking his hand as well. He then turned to Sarah, offering a smile. "And you are the American, Sarah Brown. Charmed, I'm sure." His French accent sounded musical to her ears, but he had a hard look around his eyes, something all the officers in the room seemed to share. Touchard was fine-boned, almost delicate, and refined in his dove-gray suit and striped tie. Limmer had a receding hairline with white, wispy tendrils curling near his ears. He had a bit of padding around the middle that seemed to confirm he spent more time at a desk than on the move. Oleson was tall, blond, and muscular with a ruddy complexion. He had a kind smile.

"Gentlemen and lady, I'm Agent Maurice Touchard from Interpol. This is KMar Chief Niels Limmer, and his deputy, Timon Oleson. We have much to go over and very little time to prepare." To Paul and Heinz, he said, "We already have an undercover unit in place at the address you provided. They are keeping watch, and our task force stands ready two blocks away out of sight. You, Christiansen, will go directly to Knudson. You will act naturally, and when you can confirm he is present, you will give us a signal, a code word which we will monitor from the unmarked unit. We're going to wire you here, so kindly remove your jacket and shirt. Oleson will do the honors."

"What's the code word?" Paul began undressing, hanging his jacket on the back of one of the chairs pushed under the table. He unbuttoned his shirt and shrugged out of it, revealing lean muscles and a tanned chest. He caught Sarah watching him, and a smile tugged the corner of his lips.

"It's a phrase, actually. You will simply say, *I need some water.*" Touchard looked at Limmer, nodding that he should pick up the conversation.

Limmer stepped forward and paced around Paul as Oleson placed a very small wire in the center of his chest, taped it down, then wound the thin cord around his side to the back where the small powerpack clipped onto the waistband of his jeans. "You'll have to leave your shirt untucked. It will help hide the bulge, small though it is. Better safe than sorry, eh?"

Oleson stepped back and turned on the receiver sitting on the table. "Give us a sound check," he told Paul.

"What should I say?" His voice echoed from the receiver.

"Again," said Oleson. "Say your code words."

"I need some water." Paul's eyes rolled as his face showed he felt a little foolish saying it. It seemed too simple. "What happens after I say it and confirm Uncle Peter is there?"

"You leave that to us. Just go about your usual business, leave and go home." Limmer explained it as if it were elementary.

"But aren't you going to arrest him?" Paul was becoming alarmed.

"Calm down, Christiansen." Touchard placed a hand on his arm. "We have a plan to place a tracer on your uncle. We'll follow him from the office to where he's holding the boy. We can't arrest him before we know the victim's location. Even you told us you weren't sure where he might keep him."

"It's going to be all right, Paul," said Heinz. "We'll get him. Count on it." The determination in his brown eyes reassured Paul, who looked over at Sarah standing out of the way.

"And what about Sarah? What is she supposed to do while all this goes down?"

Sarah looked at her watch, wondering if Anthony had left the airport since she hadn't disembarked along with the other passengers. Her phone pinged. She looked down, noticing it was from Anthony.

Where are you?

She looked at Touchard. "It's my friend, Anthony. He's wondering where I am."

"Well, tell him you'll be escorted to arrivals shortly." Touchard alerted one of the security officers that had brought them to the office.

Sarah sent off the short text and waited. Limmer turned to her. "Be sure we have the address where you'll be staying."

"I don't get to come with you? But I should be there for Anno." She was not happy with being sidelined. She turned to Paul. "You can't go in there by yourself. It's too dangerous. You need someone with you." Paul smiled at her concern. "Wait, what about Nadia?" Excitement rang in her voice.

Paul blinked. "Nadia? What about her?" He put his shirt on over the wire and buttoned it up.

"I could be Nadia!" She nearly jumped up and down as a plan began to formulate. "Your uncle doesn't know what she looks like, does he? You never told him, did you?"

Paul began to see where she was going with this. His hands came up, gesturing she should stop. "No, Sarah. It's far too dangerous for you. And you hardly fit the description of an Italian dominatrix."

Touchard and Limmer exchanged glances. Limmer spoke up. "It might be an easier way to place the trace on your uncle. Our own plan involved the subterfuge of sending in an undercover female officer into his office seeking employment, but Miss Brown would have the advantage. She'd be in a prime position to get close enough to slip the tracer onto his person." Limmer turned to look at her. Touchard spoke. "Could you do it, Miss Brown? Could you act well enough to fool an old whore-mongering pedo?"

"I could do it for Anno. That's all that matters. I'm sure Paul will help me." She looked at him beseechingly.

"I don't like this, Sarah." He closed the distance between them and stood looking down at her determined face. "Peter is a wily old bastard, and you are completely innocent. He would sense this, believe me." Paul ran a hand through his hair, working through all the possible scenarios in which Sarah was found out, and they were exposed. He also couldn't see any other viable option because a stranger wandering in looking for work was weak at best. Peter wouldn't even see that person. Greta would handle it. She took care of all applicants or anyone who came into the office. He reluctantly gave in. "All right. If it will help Anno, then we have to try. I'll keep you safe. I swear it."

"What should I do, then?" she asked.

"Be Nadia. You've met her. You know how she is, very sexual, very straightforward." He looked her up and down. "And we'll have to do something about what you're wearing. What did you bring? Any high heels?" He looked down at her Skechers. "Something sexier? Not that you're not sexy, but to be Nadia, you really must put it out there." He indicated she should open her suitcase. She did, and Paul began helping her pick out something appropriate for an Italian dominatrix. In the end, he went with black heels, the jeans she was already wearing, and a black button-down shirt that he tied above her waist rather than buttoning it. Her cleavage was now displayed, deep and perky, in her purple bra. At his suggestion, she darkened her makeup with black eyeliner and a smoky gray shadow. Then, she applied a red lipstick generally reserved for evening.

"Let your hair down," he told her. Sarah unclamped the butterfly clip and let her hair fall. Paul stepped closer and sank his hands in, mussing it a bit and bringing it forward. He smiled, enjoying the tactile experience of her silken tresses slipping through his fingers.

Touchard, Limmer, and Oleson stood back watching the transformation of the young woman from girl next door to whip-wielding vixen. The entire process was rather intimate and made them feel as if they shouldn't be in the room.

Heinz stood with his arms crossed over his chest. He raised a hand to rub his jaw, considering Sarah's new look. "It could work. I almost don't recognize you, Miss Brown." Heinz smiled. It was the first time they'd seen this facial contortion on the detective and both Sarah and Paul were shocked. They looked at each other, sharing a moment where they struggled not to laugh.

"Someone should bring my friend in here. He'll be wondering where I am."

Touchard nodded to one of the two security officers standing on the far side of the room. "Bring him here." He looked at Sarah. "Send him a text to report to the nearest security station. They'll pick him up and bring him in."

Sarah did, then she sat and waited. Paul was suddenly aware he was about to meet this man that Sarah obviously had feelings for. He didn't like it. He paced a few steps away, wiping his hand over his face. The scent of her shampoo wafted off his fingers that had only moments ago been sifting through her hair. He didn't want it to be the last time.

Five minutes passed before the door opened, and in walked Anthony. He immediately located Sarah in the room, and then the huge smile on his face fell. Sarah, however, was so excited to see him that she ran straight into his arms and held him tight.

"Hi!" She leaned back and stared into his handsome face. Anthony's eyes were wide, taking in her attire.

"Hi." He was afraid to ask what the hell she was wearing, but he wondered just what the hell she was wearing in this room full of men. His arms went protectively and possessively around her as he looked at them one by one, dismissing them all until he got to Paul.

Sarah noted the expression on his face and tried hard not to laugh. She placed her hands on his cheeks and directed his eyes back to her. "I'm going undercover." She said it like it was something she did every day.

Anthony was confused. "As what? A streetwalker?" Sarah did laugh this time.

"Close. As a dominatrix. An Italian dominatrix at that." She seemed rather pleased with herself to see him so speechless. "Ciao!" She grinned up at him, happier than she cared to admit at being in his arms again.

Heinz stepped forward and introduced himself. "Sarah has volunteered to accompany Mr. Christiansen to his uncle's place of business. It seems Knudson is expecting a new hire for one of his clubs, but she's not coming. However, since the bastard doesn't know that, Sarah has offered to step in. In fact, it was her idea."

"Offered to do what, exactly? I'll be damned if I let yous all put her in danger!" Anthony's temper began to rise, and his New York dialect grew stronger.

"She will simply slip a trace, a very small GPS tracker, into Knudson's pocket or attach it to his collar. Depends on how close she can get and be able to deliver the device without his notice." Touchard filled him in. "I'm Agent Maurice Touchard, by the by. Interpol liaison." He extended his hand to Anthony.

Things just got crazier as far as Anthony was concerned. "Interpol? Are you fucking serious? Look, Sarah explained what happened, and this guy sounds damn dangerous. There's no fucking way I'm letting her go in there on her own."

"She won't be alone. She'll be with me." Paul stepped forward, asserting himself. The two men took each other's measure.

"This sick fuck is your uncle! How does that relation make you safe for her to be with?" Anthony stared Paul down.

Paul refused to break eye contact. The other men watched these two square off, sending sideways glances at one another. Limmer and Oleson prepared to pull them apart in the event one went for the jugular since they were obviously having one hell of a pissing contest over the woman.

Sarah was no longer amused. For this to work, everyone had to get along. "That's enough, guys. We're here to save Anno, a boy taken by a sick-minded pedophile. Remember?"

She continued, looking at Anthony and speaking softly. "Paul isn't like his uncle, sweetie. In fact, he's one of his victims, when he was just a child himself."

Upon hearing this, Anthony instantly felt like a dick. All he could think about after hearing that was his friend Nick.

Paul, on the other hand, did not want this man's sympathy and would've preferred Sarah not reveal so much. It was still painfully shameful to admit out loud, and he didn't like the stigma making him appear weak, as less than a man in his own right.

"I'm sorry, man. I didn't know." Anthony offered an apology. Paul acknowledged Anthony with a tight nod.

"Still, I'm not letting her go in there without me. The uncle doesn't know everything about this dominatrix chick, does he?" He addressed Paul.

"No. He knows very little, actually. Only that I hired her."

"Good. Then it's settled." Anthony tightened his hold on Sarah.

"What's settled, Mr. de Luca?" Heinz asked.

"I'm the boyfriend of the dominatrix. I'll be coming in with you both, just to make sure she doesn't get hurt. She's safer with the two of us." Anthony looked from Heinz to Paul.

Sarah was caught between feeling angry that Anthony didn't think she could handle herself, and glad he would be there. She settled on being glad because in the end, it was about getting this done quickly and safely. Anno's life depended on everyone working together. Plus, he just said he was her 'boyfriend.' Even if he only meant it as a cover, it still sounded nice to her ears.

"I'm fine with it. What about you guys?" Sarah looked around the room. Touchard's lips twitched. Limmer and Oleson agreed. Paul grudgingly acquiesced.

"Good. Because we need to get a move on, don't we?" Sarah pointed out the obvious, and Touchard and Limmer filled Anthony in on a few details.

Heinz stood by Paul, knowing the man was going to suffer some heartache when it was all said and done. He'd been watching Christiansen's treatment of Miss Brown, and knew a man smitten when he saw one. But after witnessing the gravitational pull between Sarah and De Luca, he knew it was a lost cause. He patted Paul's shoulder in a fatherly manner.

"If we're all ready now, then please follow me." Oleson led the way. Touchard and Limmer followed. Anthony and Sarah were next and bringing up the rear were Paul and Heinz.

"Detective, you'll ride with me," said Touchard. Heinz fell in with the agent.

"Oleson and I will join up with our unit. Christiansen, Miss Brown, and Mr. De Luca, a car has been provided for you. It's a rental so as not to raise any alarm bells with your uncle should he happen to see you drive up. We'll be about two blocks down until you're inside, then we'll move into position." Limmer rattled off the logistics.

Everyone had their orders. All got into their assigned vehicles parked outside in the security parking lot on Schiphol Airport property. The sun began to set, and the wind whipped up. The scent of rain grew strong as clouds thickened overhead. In the distance, windmills spun furiously in fields as they passed on their way into the heart of Amsterdam, and further into the Red-Light District where Peter Knudson kept his office from which he ran his various illicit businesses.

Paul drove them expertly through the traffic while Sarah and Anthony sat in the back together. He kept his arm around her and occasionally brought her hand up to kiss her fingers. He was worried. He didn't like this new development; didn't understand why the hell the police couldn't just use a female undercover officer to play the role of dominatrix. He didn't like Sarah being in danger. And he really didn't like the way Christiansen kept sneaking peeks at her through the rearview mirror. *How the hell did she know this character, anyway?* When this little operation was over, he intended to grill her for details. She had some explaining to do as far as he was concerned. He reached over and tugged her shirt together over her cleavage. Sarah swatted at his hands even as she gazed at him adoringly.

They pulled up to the large, gray three-story building on Oudezijds Voorburgwal. Paul parked the Audi rental and came around to open the door for Sarah. He offered his hand as Anthony jumped out the other side and rushed around the car only to find that Paul already helped his lady exit the backseat. His hand lingered a little too long on her arm, and Anthony began seeing red. Sarah automatically reached out to take Anthony's hand and he instantly cooled down. She stood at his side, waiting. Anthony gave Paul a look that said, *'Mine!'*

Paul was frustrated, but now wasn't the time. "Shall we?" He indicated the door which opened to steep stairs inside. He led the way. The building smelled old and moldy to Sarah's nose. The crumbling plaster inside was chipping off the walls. She could hear sounds from the first floor as they ascended, letting anyone passing through know that the prostitutes were hard at work. Ignoring the moans and shouts, she hurried up the stairs. Anno needed her.

They reached the third-floor landing and Paul headed for the first door. He opened it and stepped through. Sarah and Anthony followed. Inside there were three desks arranged along the far, exposed-brick wall with a wide window overlooking the street below. One was empty, but a young man sat at the second, and an older woman sat typing at the third. She looked up and a smile broke across her stern face. "Paul! Hallo, darling!" She got up and greeted Paul warmly, hugging him like the prodigal son returned.

"Greta, my only love. How are you?" Paul lifted the older woman off the ground and swung her around. She giggled like a young girl and then swatted his arm.

"Put me down, you fool." He gently lowered her, kissing her powdered cheek. He looked over at the other desk.

"Hallo, Daniel." Daniel smiled, blushing.

"Hallo, Paul. Long time, yes?"

Paul ignored the question and turned back to Greta. "This is Nadia, a new hire for Club Tiberius, and her...*boyfriend*, Antonio." Paul sneered slightly over the word, but he maintained the ruse. "So, where's the old man?" He waited to find out if Peter was in.

"He's in there. Go on in. I'm sure he'll be pleased you're back." Greta eyed the blonde woman, miffed that she knew nothing about this new hire. She handled all new hires. It was her job and Knudson knew this. She wondered what the old bastard was up to. They had no need for any new talent at this time.

"Can I get you all something? Coffee? Water?" Ever the good hostess, Greta asked.

Paul, remembering his role, said, "I need some water."

Outside on the opposite side of the street, Oleson pulled the ear-piece out of his left ear, and gave Limmer the thumbs-up. Limmer spoke into his two-way receiver and gave the order for the tactical unit to move in closer but stay out of sight. Now, they must wait until the trio exited the building.

Chapter 25

Paul gave "Nadia" and "Antonio" a look that asked *ready?* They returned his look with imperceptible nods. Anthony held tightly to Sarah's hand. He had no intention of letting it go. The sooner they got out of here, the better. He had a bad feeling about it in the pit of his stomach. Again, Paul took the lead and walked to the wooden door that led into his uncle's office. He knocked twice and waited. His uncle was anal about people just walking in without an invitation.

"Enter," a gruff voice barked from inside.

Paul walked in and Sarah and Anthony followed. As they turned right beyond the door, Paul began to speak but was instantly cut off by his uncle.

"You!" Peter Knudson's face turned thunderous as his eyes settled on Anthony.

Anthony took one look at the dark eyebrows, white goatee, and broad shoulders and instantly recognized Paul's uncle as the same man he stared down at the dock—the same man who he had photographic evidence of beating a young male hustler in Berlin. The same man who now had a fourteen-year-old boy that he kidnapped out of his own home.

"Fuck me! You?" Anthony moved to stand in front of Sarah quickly. Paul looked back and forth between his uncle and Anthony, clearly confused, and alarmed.

"What is the meaning of this, nephew? Who is this, and why have you brought him into my office?" Knudson turned his ominous visage upon Paul, all traces of the charm he could exude when he so wished vanished from his countenance.

Paul, thinking quickly to salvage some of their cover story, launched into his explanation. "This is Antonio. He's Nadia's man." He waited for his uncle to offer his own explanation as to how he seemed to know Anthony.

Peter's eyebrows lowered further over his ice-gray eyes, indicating the answer did not please him. He spoke low and slowly. "And who is Nadia, Paul?" He waited for his nephew to continue as he deliberately walked back behind his desk where he pulled a drawer open and reached inside.

Paul watched his uncle, feeling nauseated and realizing this was all falling apart fast. "That's Nadia." He tossed a glance over at Sarah, who was standing behind Anthony. "She's your new hire." He placed his hands on his hips and tried for casual sarcasm. "Remember? I texted you about her."

Knudson had yet to take his hand out of the drawer and straighten up. He stood with one palm flat on the desk and the other hand out of sight, menacing and coiled like a snake about to strike. A slow smirk spread across his lips. "Is that so?" He turned to Sarah. "You're the Italian, yes? Si sculacciare gli uomini per vivere, vero?" (*You spank men for a living, do you?*) He waited.

Sarah, knowing she hadn't understood a word he just said, went with a shrug. Her heart was racing. Anthony, who did understand Italian since it was spoken still in his parents' home, answered for her.

"No. Fa niente del genere. Ma tu...tu sei un vigliacco, un bastardo che ama i ragazzini." (*No. She does no such thing. But you...you are a coward, a bastard who likes little boys.*) The expression on Anthony's face warned of murderous intent. He knew the jig was up, and was going south fast.

"A bastard, am I? A *coward*!" Peter stood up raising a Luger in his right hand and aimed it at Anthony.

"Uncle, no!" Paul spoke up, trying to distract and diffuse the situation. "What is this? How is it you two seem to know each other?"

"I caught your uncle eyeing two little boys just a couple of days ago down on the dock." Anthony spat out the words. Knudson, if at all possible, looked even more evil as his smirk turned to a full-fledged smile that was at odds with the hateful look in his eyes. That look quickly turned to surprise and stunning outrage as Anthony made another revelation. "I also caught him on camera beating a young male hooker nearly to death with his cane in Berlin about six months ago."

"That was you?" Knudson's voice was almost too soft to hear, but the sinister tone didn't escape anyone's notice.

He worked to compose himself. His nephew had brought this man into his office under false pretenses. He didn't know what Paul was up to, but he knew there was one more lie to expose, and then he had a decision to make about this monumental betrayal.

Peter turned his malevolent gaze upon "Nadia." "And what, exactly, is your purpose here...Miss Sarah Brown?" Paul's mouth fell open. He knew then they were fucked. His uncle must've had him followed. Gruber had obviously been in Berlin doing more than just planning a kidnapping. Peter continued. "Just last night you were on a romantic date with my dear, pathetic nephew, and now I see you hiding behind this man who seems ready to defend you to the death? You do get around, don't you? Perhaps you would make a decent hoeren for my brothel."

Outside, Limmer, Oleson, and Touchard scrambled to come up with a plan B as they listened to what was going down three floors up. They were found out, and now Christiansen, Sarah, and De Luca were in real danger. Heinz stepped outside the vehicle while Touchard spoke rapidly on the two-way with Limmer. He pulled out his last cigarette and lit it. Inhaling deeply, he blew out the smoke and stared up at the three-story structure.

Inside, Anthony saw red. Hearing that Sarah had been on a date with the pretty-boy next to him had him ready to rip Paul's head off. Seeing Knudson pointing a gun at Sarah and calling her a whore had him mentally fantasizing about bashing the old bastard's face in until only a bloody pulp remained. Knowing the evil fuck still had the kid lit the fuse, and Anthony roared as he ran straight at the man intent on disarming him, then pounding him into the floor.

Caught off guard, Peter stepped back, stumbling a bit. He raised his arm to aim at the enraged bull of a man charging him and fired. POP! The Lugar fired poorly afield and the bullet slammed into Anthony's left shoulder. He went down just short of reaching the old man.

"Anthony!" Sarah screamed and ran to his side, trying to staunch the flow of blood oozing from the bullet wound. Peter reached down and grabbed a fistful of Sarah's hair, yanking her up. She screamed in pain. "Let me go!" She began to kick, then stopped when she felt the hot tip of the gun burn against her temple.

"You'd be wise to settle down, Miss Brown." Peter looked to Paul and barked, "Help that one up. We're getting out of here. If you make one single wrong move, I'll put a bullet through her head."

"Uncle, please. She's innocent. Let her go and take me." Paul looked at Sarah and cringed at the fear in her eyes.

"Care about her, do you?" Peter asked.

"Yes. Yes, I care. Please, just let her go." Paul pleaded for Sarah's release.

"I don't think so, nephew. You see, you've let me down. Betrayed me. You deprived me of something I cared about long ago, and again, recently when you fucked up a simple recruiting mission, tearing another angel away from me. I can't let that pass." The maniacal look in Peter's eyes told Paul he would have to tread carefully. On the floor, Anthony clutched his shoulder, trying to stem the bleeding and alleviate the pain. He watched as nephew and uncle circled each other verbally. He kept his eyes on Sarah too. He knew the moment he had a chance, he was going to kill that miserable bastard.

"You can't just take a boy away from his family, Uncle. You can't do that. Please, just tell us where Anno is, and then I'll come with you anywhere you want to go. I'll protect you. Just let everyone else go. Please. I love you, Uncle." Paul added the last as his voice broke, and the child inside him, the one trapped forever within a nightmare came to the fore.

"I love you, too, but it's too late, Paul. You're all grown up now, and you know how much I despise that. But you will come with me. All of you will, now get moving!" He jerked Sarah's hair, eliciting a loud yelp of pain from her.

"I'm going to kill you, you motherfucker!" Anthony rose unsteadily to his knees as Paul leaned down on his right side to help him stand.

"You can try, '*Antonio*,' but she'll be dead before you get within ten feet of me. Tut, tut. Don't want that now, do you?"

Knudson waved Paul and Anthony ahead of him and followed, forcing Sarah along with her neck cocked at a difficult and painful angle. The gun remained pointed at her head. As they entered the outer office, Paul noticed that Daniel and Greta had fled. *Fuck! Does no one think to call the police? And where the hell are they? Didn't they hear all that downstairs? Where's the fucking cavalry?* Paul looked down at his shirt, thinking of the wire beneath. He hoped it was still on. He looked back at Anthony, who was bleeding steadily. He reached for a handkerchief in his jacket pocket and handed it to the man, not that it would do much good, but he didn't want him to die. Sarah would never forgive him if he let the American bleed out.

"Thanks." Anthony snatched at the cloth and wadded it up, shoving it onto the wound. It hurt like hell, but seemed to be slowing down. He glanced back at Sarah, wanting desperately to take her into his arms and protect her. The sight of the gun pressed to her head kept him conscious and walking. He prayed an opportunity would present itself so he could get her safely away.

Sarah caught Anthony's eye through the blur of tears in her own. The pain she felt in her scalp was nothing to the pain in her heart seeing Anthony go down when the bullet hit him. She thought for a moment he was dead. When she realized he'd been shot in the shoulder, a portion of her terror subsided to be replaced with sickening concern and a driving need to help him.

"Down the back stairs, Paul." Peter pointed toward an alternate stairwell used only by the staff.

Paul had reached a point where he would no longer beg, whine, or allow fear to rule him. He was through. His uncle was obviously out of his mind. His only concern now was to save both Sarah and Anno.

"Where are we going, Uncle?" Paul began descending the back steps.

"To my car. You'll drive." Peter quickly reached into his pocket where he grabbed his keys and tossed them at Paul's head. Sarah experienced a momentary relief before that large hand was back pulling her hair.

Not expecting this, the keys flew past him, and landed a few steps below. Paul leaned down as he approached and picked them up.

"I want to see Anno. I need to know he's okay." Sarah, feeling some fight return to her, spoke up.

Peter yanked her hair harshly. "Shut up, bitch. You'll be seeing him soon." They reached the ground floor landing and exited out the back.

Sarah now had an idea of where they were going. She hoped Touchard and Limmer heard all that through Paul's wire. It was their only hope. With any luck, they would follow. If they didn't, if for any reason the wire wasn't strong enough to transmit outside of the building or across whatever distance they happened to be apart, then any chance of being rescued was out the door, and Anthony could die. They all could, because Peter Knudson had crossed the line from vicious pedophile to desperate criminal intent on murder; at least that seemed his intent when he shot Anthony.

Rain that threatened earlier began to fall in earnest as Knudson forced everyone into his vehicle. Paul was to drive with Anthony sharing the front seat, and Sarah was shoved in the back where Peter climbed in next to her, never once lowering the Luger. As Paul started the car and put it in gear, a man with graying hair at his temples strolled past on the sidewalk smoking a cigarette. He barely glanced in their direction seeming to be lost in thought.

Paul looked over at Anthony who kept his eyes forward. Sweat trickled down the side of his face from the exertion of trying to remain conscious and focused while fighting through the pain in his shoulder. Paul hesitated a moment longer and then pulled onto the road. Behind them, a car drove up and pulled over to the curb. The gentleman tossed his cigarette down and climbed into the passenger seat.

"Well?" Touchard asked as he rejoined the traffic.

"De Luca's been shot. Looks like an arm or shoulder wound. Christiansen is driving, and Knudson has Miss Brown in the back seat...at gun point."

"Shit!" Touchard grabbed his two-way and relayed the information to Limmer. An electronic sound beeped at regular intervals as they drove. Heinz looked down at the screen sitting on the console between them.

"Signal's strong. How far back can we remain without losing it?" He glanced at the side view mirror and saw Limmer's car come up behind them, then pass and take the lead. It was unmarked, which helped keep them from being spotted.

"Usually, it matters not, but in this weather…" Touchard looked up at the dark, cloudy skies releasing a torrent of rain that had him upping the speed of his windshield wipers. "…in this weather, it could be a problem. Those bugs depend upon 3D triangulation from satellites, and you know what happens to anything receiving a signal from a satellite during a downpour."

Heinz blew out a frustrated breath. "Can Oleson still hear anything coming from the wire? Maybe he can at least get some idea where they're headed just in case." A detective was always thinking ahead.

"Good thought." Touchard radioed Oleson. "Timon, come in. Over."

"Oleson here. Go ahead. Over." Static crackled through the speaker.

"Timon, are you still able to pick up any conversation inside the car? Over." Touchard opened the vent to let in the air as the window fogged up.

"We're monitoring. Over." Static.

"Listen for any clues as to where they might be going in the event we lose satelite connection from the storm. Over."

"We're on it. Over and out." Oleson signed off to get back to monitoring the inside of Knudson's car.

Ahead, Paul drove not knowing where he was supposed to be heading. "Where are we going, Uncle?"

"Turn right at the next corner and then take the first left." Peter kept his eyes on all three, but he knew he had only to control the one to keep them all in line—the girl. Both his nephew and this 'Antonio' or Anthony cared for her, cared about what happened to her. He'd keep the immediate threat on her until they got to their destination. She would get to see young Anno one last time.

Paul followed the directions. They were in an industrial neighborhood near the wharf. "Now what?"

"The red brick warehouse on the right. Pull into the side alley, and then stop the car."

Paul did as bid, then turned off the engine. The sound of the rain grew louder without the car running. "What is this place," he asked as he eyed the building. He knew nothing about this, and he knew all of his uncle's buildings; at least, so he thought.

"It's one of my businesses. A sort of studio, if you will. Now, get out, everyone, and no nonsense." He yanked Sarah from the backseat into the rain, causing her to scream and then curse.

Anthony grew weaker on the ride over and had trouble standing. Paul came around to offer his arm to lean on. Everyone quickly became soaked as Knudson indicated they should enter through the side door.

A spark burned Paul's chest and he grabbed at the wire, trying to rip it away without being noticed. It had gotten wet and electronics never behave when wet. Anthony saw this and deliberately stumbled, reaching out to wrap his good arm around Paul's waist.

"Get up, and walk!" Peter barked out the order. Sarah noticed something was going on, so she tried to distract the man. "He's hurt, you bastard! Can't you see that? You shot him. You shot him!" She let herself get a little hysterical and then began to cry loudly. Knudson hated crying women, and turned his attention to her.

"Shut your gaping hole, woman, or I'll shut it for you with this!" He slid the gun from her temple until the tip forced its way into her open mouth. Sarah stopped immediately, knowing he had not seen Anthony remove the wire from under Paul's shirt and stuff it into his pocket where it wouldn't be exposed to wet skin.

"Now walk! Go straight down the corridor and turn left." They entered into a large, open space filled with massive metal equipment. The high ceiling was mostly scaffolding overhead, and the floor, concrete. As they approached the far side, their ears picked up the tones of soft music. Childish music, like the kind one hears in fairytale movies.

Around the back of a rusted vat sat a stuffed chair, a side table, a bed, and a video camera on a tripod. In the chair, Aleks Gruber lounged, leafing through an old magazine on mechanics. On the bed lay Anno, turned on his side. As they approached, he rolled over to see who was coming in. He sat up slowly, fearfully. Then he saw her.

"Sarah! Sarah, you're here!" Anno started to get up, and Gruber jumped up and pushed him back onto the bed.

"Sit your ass down!" Gruber pulled out his handgun from his backside where it was holstered in the waistband of his jeans. He aimed it at Paul and Anthony.

Anno's face was a mess of tears and misery. Sarah's heart broke and she tugged and pulled until Peter let go. She ran to the boy and wrapped her arms around him.

Peter looked at the boy and was moved by the child's tears. He was mesmerized by his angelic looks, and wanted to be the one he clung to, not the damn woman!

"What's this, boss?" Gruber asked Knudson as he looked from him to the two men and the woman.

"Change of plans. Still, it could all work out rather well." Peter stood watching the boy as if hypnotized.

"It's okay, Anno. We'll figure something out. Please don't cry. I need you to be strong. Be strong for me, and for your sister. We promised we'd bring you back home to her." Sarah whispered these words to him as she rocked him like a baby in her embrace. "Have they hurt you?"

"Not really. But that man scares me, Sarah. He's always staring at me and touching me." He spoke the words into the crook of her neck and shoulder.

Anthony came and sat on the other side of Anno, and Paul stood in front of them all, determined to provide a wall of protection. He couldn't believe what his eyes were seeing. It became clear that his uncle was making the most evil, most disgusting form of illegal films in this space. *He's fucking filth! If he hurt Anno...so help me, God, I am going to kill him!*

❧ ☙

Outside, the rain continued to fall. It drowned out the sounds of a tactical unit entering the building and gaining positions from which to make their move.

Limmer nodded at Oleson, who sank down as he climbed in through an upstairs window from the fire escape onto the scaffolding. Touchard and Heinz stood behind their vehicle under the only awning in the alleyway.

Limmer's two-way radio crackled. "We're in position." Oleson's voice spoke low. The decision was made quickly. There was no more time to wait. One civilian was injured with a gun shot wound, and the boy was inside. Touchard could see exactly where Sarah was sitting in the building on the screen of his portable GPS from the tracing device she still carried. It pulsed a bright red beacon, an SOS. The officers within would notify them of everyone else's whereabouts, and then Limmer was prepared to make the call as soon as he was informed of a clear opportunity to take Knudson down.

❧ ☙

Inside, Peter Knudson watched as the boy clung to Sarah Brown. His expression could not hide his longing, but there was no time for that. He needed to confer with Gruber. It was time to make good on his promise to make Paul suffer. He spoke low to his henchman as the other three formed a protective barrier around Anno.

Gruber recognized an opportunity to take advantage of his boss's change of plans. "This wasn't what we discussed. If you want me to do this, it will cost you, old man." He had no desire to end up back in jail for any period of time. If he was to expand his criminal rap sheet to include murder, it was going to come at a hefty price, one which he would need in order to leave the country.

"That's extortion!" Knudson did not like being in a position where he did not have the upper hand, but he needed the thug.

Gruber sneered, and spat on the floor. He hooked his thumbs into the belt loops of his ripped and dirty jeans, waiting.

A vein throbbed in Peter's forehead as he stared back at his hired man. He blew out a breath, reluctantly giving in. "I'll pay your price, damn you. Just do it."

He stepped aside and Gruber approached the trio with gun drawn. "Move!" He pointed the weapon at Paul, who turned to face him, shielding the others. "I said move it, pretty boy!"

Gruber waited, but Paul wouldn't budge. "No way in hell." Paul squared himself, determined not to let the low-life get his hands on the boy. Gruber swung the gun at Paul, catching him on the side of his face with the force of the hit. Paul went over sideways, knocked to the ground. Ears ringing, he steadied himself, and reached up, feeling his temple. His head bled from the gash created by the blunt force of the metal.

Gruber ignored Paul and reached over him. Anthony swung out his good right arm, punching the man in the jaw. Gruber reacted quickly, swinging out to pistol-whip Anthony. In his weakened state, he fell over sideways on the bed. The thug grabbed Sarah and pulled her to her feet away from Anno and the others. She was dragged to the open space nearest the vat where Gruber pushed her to her knees on the concrete. He pointed the gun at the back of her head.

Anthony struggled back up into a sitting position. "Let her go, you dirty motherfucker!" He started to rise, but Knudson stepped forward shoving his Luger, point blank, in his face.

"Stand down!" Peter shouted the words and brought Anthony's attention away from the gun at Sarah's head to the one pointed at his own.

Paul sat up, holding his wound and appearing too disoriented to stand. "What the hell are you doing, Uncle?" He looked to where Sarah trembled on her knees, terror in her eyes.

Anno moved closer to Anthony and climbed up further on the bed behind his back, prepared to bolt. Anthony reached his good arm around to shield him. Peter offered a self-satisfied smirk to Paul. "It's time for you to understand just how disappointed I truly am in you, nephew. You were my first love. Did you know that? It was all so perfect, and then you had to grow up. You left me, Paul. After all I did for you, you left me." Peter shook his head sadly as he rattled on.

"You're crazy, Uncle! All you ever did for me, you did *to* me! You abused me. You hurt me! You sick fuck! And I hated you for it. I still hate you for it." His eyes squinted to slits as his anger and years upon years of fear and torment came to a boiling point.

"I know." Knudson's simple reply was completely without remorse. "And then you tried taking away my Berlin angel." He turned to gaze at Anno. "My angel."

Anno ducked down behind Anthony's back, refusing to look at the monstrous man. Anthony sat up straighter offering more protection, and helping to keep the boy hidden behind him.

"Well, you can't think I would let your betrayal slide, did you? Of course I knew all along who Miss Brown was. That's one of the reasons why I had Gruber follow you. To find out what, if anything, you care about. I have to admit, I was surprised. You formed such an attachment to this women here while fucking the real Nadia. That takes balls, boy." Peter kept up the conversation as if they were simply talking over coffee.

Sarah looked at Paul with raised eyebrows. He hung his head in shame. Anthony smirked.

"Still..." he continued. "Still, I'm happy that you did because had I not discovered a way to hurt you as you have hurt me, I would simply have had to kill you. And that just wouldn't do. Don't know how I would explain it to my dear sister, your mother." Knudson's insanity lit his eyes with self-righteous zeal.

"What are you talking about, you mad old man? What are you going to do?" Paul's eyes grew wide as understanding slowly dawned on him.

"Why, I'm going to kill your woman, of course!" Peter watched as horror dawned on his nephew's face. He began to laugh. It was a maniacal sound straight out of a nightmare that seemed never-ending. Paul, Anthony, and Sarah all stared, horrified.

Zing!

The laughter stopped abruptly as Peter Knudson's eyes grew wide and then fixed. A small trickle of blood oozed out, then ran in rivulets down his face from a single hole in his forehead. He fell forward, landing hard. His gun flew from his hand and skittered across the floor. Paul lunged quickly, grabbing the Luger as Gruber looked up in surprise.

Thinking fast, he ducked and ran as a second shot rang out. Sarah was suddenly free, and Anthony reached out for her as she stumbled forward into his arms. He held her tight as she cried. Looking over his shoulder, she spied Anno sitting in the middle of the bed, shocked. She broke free of Anthony's embrace and climbed up, enfolding the boy protectively in her arms. Anthony leaned in, holding them both. Paul stood with the Luger in hand, looking at his uncle's body lying, unmoving, on the cold concrete floor. The back of his head was blown out and bits of brain, blood, and bone covered the floor behind him.

Oleson and four officers in full tactical gear came running from overhead, while Limmer ran up from the corridor by which they'd entered almost twenty minutes before.

"He's getting away!" Paul spoke out, informing Oleson and Limmer of Gruber's escape.

"Stay here." They turned to run out the direction Paul indicated. Time passed, and Limmer returned empty-handed. No one had moved.

"We lost him, but we'll get him. He has nowhere to run. We know his aliases and we have an all-points out on him. He won't get out of the country."

Touchard and Heinz approached. The expression on the detective's face was one of gratitude, and of personal redemption. Despite everything going wrong, they saved the boy. Heinz pulled a cigarette out of his pocket and started to light it up, then stopped. "Fuck it." He flicked it away. *Time to quit.*

Oleson leaned down and rolled Knudson's body over. Lifeless eyes stared back at him. Paul stood two feet away still holding the gun, still not believing it was over. The monster of his nightmares lay dead before him. Tears welled in his blue eyes, spilling over. Something broke inside him. He ran up and began furiously kicking his uncle.

"You miserable fuck! You bastard! You stole my life. You stole my childhood. I hope you rot in hell, you sick fucker!" He kicked the body in the ribs, arms, head, and legs as he ranted, releasing his inner demons.

Everyone stood back, refusing to interfere. If anyone deserved to defile the dead, it was Paul Christiansen. Finally exhausted, Paul stopped. Heinz put his arm around the man to lead him away. They walked outside together into the rain-soaked air. The night was quiet and oddly peaceful.

Anthony, Sarah, and Anno followed. Sarah kept Anno's face tucked into her shoulder as she led him out so he wouldn't see the dead man on the floor. Touchard brought up the rear while Limmer and Oleson stayed behind to confer with the investigative unit that had been called in.

An ambulance pulled up behind the police vehicles. Anthony was escorted to a gurney where they laid him out and buckled a safety strap around his chest. The gurney was lifted inside and locked into place. Sarah and Anno climbed into the back to ride to the hospital with him. No one spoke. No one had the energy. Anno leaned on Sarah as she sat holding Anthony's hand. The paramedic started an IV as the ambulance pulled away, the siren blaring into the humid, silent night.

Chapter 26

Nearly a month later, Sarah and Anthony boarded a Eurostar train bound for Berlin. He'd spent a week in the hospital after having the bullet removed. With a possible risk of sepsis from the wound, doctors erred on the side of caution, pumping him full of antibiotics and making sure he received plenty of rest. The local newspaper ran a feature on the American travel photographer who helped save a young boy from a vile pedophile. The mention of Amsterdam Canal Cruises as his current employer created such good advertising for the company that they paid Anthony's medical bills and gave him an extension on completing the last three cruises, which he shared with Sarah during the past week. She made for a pretty good assistant, helping him carry his camera equipment and to set up shots using the tripod.

Heinz escorted Anno home to a grateful and tearful sister. Elsa smothered the boy in hugs and kisses, causing her brother no end of grumbling although he didn't seem in any hurry for her to stop fussing over him. For her part, Elsa vowed to find a more stable career, one that would have her home every night. She would not let Anno out of her sight ever again, or at least, not until he was grown and off to university.

Kriminalkommissar Joseph Heinz regained his purpose. For the grizzled detective, it felt good to be fully alive again. He returned to duty feeling that all was right in the world...for now.

On the Eurostar, the conductor gave the all-clear sign to the engineer and hopped up the steps behind them as the doors closed.

"I think it's up here." Sarah walked ahead of Anthony, reading the doors of the private cars as they passed looking for theirs.

"Should be the next one, right?" Anthony pointed with his left hand only recently free of the sling he'd had to wear for two weeks. It was still a bit stiff. He hefted his bag on his right shoulder. Sarah dragged her suitcase and then stopped in front of their car.

"Oh, look. It just slides," she said as she moved the door to the right. A huge smile decorated her face as her excitement bubbled over.

Anthony was again struck by how much he loved that smile. "How about that, princess?" He followed her inside. Dove gray upholstered benches faced opposite each other. They stored their bags overhead, then closed the door. Sarah sat down and looked out the window as the train slowly pulled out of the station. He sat next to her, stretching out his legs. Her phone rang.

"It's Elsa." She laughed as she answered. "Yes, ma'am!" Anthony watched as his girl talked to her friend. She was so animated and happy, nothing like the young woman he met almost two months ago in Barcelona. Then, she'd been sad, unsure of herself, and alone. Now, she was happy, confident, and had not only accumulated good friends, but gained a boyfriend. *Yeah, a boyfriend. How about that?*

Although the word 'love' bounced around in his head, he was reluctant to say it out loud. He had no problem telling her he 'loved' her laugh, 'loved' her body, 'loved' how she took such good care of him. He even told her he 'loved' how she made him feel his world was complete, because for him, when he was with her, it was. He wanted to say it in that way all women want to hear, but he admitted to himself that he was afraid. Anthony wasn't quite sure of what, but the thought of putting it completely out there terrified him. He knew it would leave him fully vulnerable, and the real fear was that somehow, he wouldn't be good enough for her. What if she met someone else? Someone younger and less jaded. Someone like Paul Christiansen.

Just the thought of Christiansen made the line between his eyebrows deepen. He didn't hate the guy. It would be difficult to hate someone who'd gone through what he had and still found it within himself to risk his life to save others. Still, he was a good-looking fuck who'd taken his girl on a romantic date. Sure, Sarah explained it was *only* a date, and that she'd thought about him during most of it, but that didn't ease all his anger and frustration.

"We'll be there in less than seven hours, Elsa. Tell Anno I miss him and can't wait to see you both again. Love you guys!" She ended the call.

She looked over at her Anthony. That was how she thought of him now—as *her* Anthony. It was his own fault because he literally told her he was hers just the other night after they made passionate love. Right in the middle of orgasm, he'd held her face, kissed her, and said, "You're mine. And I'm all yours, baby." The emotions combined with the physical connection and her world exploded. For Sarah, being with Anthony was the best thing in the wide world. She was blissfully happy.

A knock at the door interrupted her introspection. They looked up as a waiter slid the portal open.

"Good afternoon. I have a delivery for Miss Sarah Brown and Mister Anthony de Luca." He reached down to the rolling cart and picked up a silver bucket containing a bottle of champagne. He stepped in and lowered the table that came out between the two benches and then sat the bucket down. He reached for two crystal champagne flutes, placing them in front of each on the table and began uncorking the bottle.

"Anthony, how wonderful! You're so thoughtful, sweetie." Sarah grinned and clapped when the cork popped.

"It wasn't me, hon. Much as I'd like to take the credit." They looked at the server.

"Compliments of Mister Paul Christiansen. There's a card and a package. Hold on." He looked behind him and found the card and a small pink and white package sitting on the trolley. He placed them both in Sarah's outstretched hands.

Sarah tore open the pretty pink and white wrapping paper, revealing a book on art. Eyebrow raised, she then opened the envelope as the bubbly liquid was poured into her glass. Anthony eyed the book dubiously looking over her shoulder, but she leaned away, laughing, knowing it would drive him crazy.

"Well? What the hell does it say? What?" *Christiansen! Goddammit.* Anthony didn't like it that the man made such a magnanimous gesture to his woman. He didn't care that it seemed to partially include him. No other man was allowed to put that kind of smile on his woman's face but him.

"He says he's doing well. He's taken over his uncle's businesses and promoted Greta. Together, they're cleaning up the clubs and brothels. All the girls now have their passports back and can come and go as they please. Greta is starting a union for them. Good for her! He's still having difficulty dealing with things, though. Says he's seeing a therapist to try and work through it. That's really good. Oh! He's got an art dealer interested in his paintings. That's fantastic. I can't think of a better way for him to work out his issues. Good for him."

Anthony took a swig of the champagne. "That's nice." His non-committal reply didn't fool her. Feeling cheeky, she kept reading.

"And what's with the book?" He tried to seem only mildly interested, but he was burning to know just what the hell that was all about.

Sarah knew, but telling Anthony would probably set him off. Although, messing with him just a little would be fun. "Well, he's an artist, so I guess that's what that's about. So that I won't forget him, I suppose."

He looked at her askance, trying to keep cool. Then Sarah began reading the card again.

"Oh. Well..." Her voice sounded a little surprised and disturbed.

"What? What is it?" Anthony looked at her. His alarm bell was going off.

"Um, well. He says he really misses me and that he hopes I'll come back and let him paint me...in the nude." She waited.

"What the fuck! I'll kill him first! I'll be goddamned if he's ever going to see you naked. I forbid you to pose for him, to see him for that matter. Promise me, Sarah. Goddammit!" Anthony's outburst had Sarah doubled over laughing. Tears streamed down her cheeks as she watched her man turn red, ranting. She knew she could never, ever tell him the truth; that Paul had already seen her naked, as had Elsa, Nicolette, and Nadia too. Some things were just better left unsaid, although his reaction now was still hilarious.

Anthony saw her laughing. "What? What's so funny? I don't find this funny...wait. You putting me on? Seriously, please tell me you're just joking?" A smile slowly replaced his outraged expression, and he realized his girl was not only the most beautiful woman in the world, but she was a fucking comedian too.

"He didn't say any of that." She laughed more and tried to wipe the tears away and catch her breath. "You're wonderful!" She leaned over and kissed him full on the lips. It went from sweet to sizzling in seconds as he deepened that kiss and took her breath away all over again.

Someone cleared his throat. They broke apart and realized the waiter was still standing at their door, looking discreetly away.

Anthony suddenly came to and reached into his pocket, pulling out his wallet. He handed the guy a ten euro note.

"Will there be anything else, sir," he politely inquired.

"No, it's all good. Thanks." Anthony laughed as the door slid closed. "Now, where were we?" He reached to wrap his arms around Sarah, leaning in to kiss her again, then stopped.

"Wait. What did that fucker actually say, anyway?" He had trouble letting it go. He knew he had a few issues where Christiansen was concerned.

Sarah giggled, then got serious. "He said thank you. He told me to tell you to take good care of me, and Bon Voyage." She traced his lips with her fingertip.

"Well, I guess that's okay, then." He kissed her deeply. Sarah felt her body respond as it always did when Anthony touched her in any way. He pulled back and looked down at her. "And I will, you know."

"Hmm? Will what?" Confused, she whispered the words.

Anthony chuckled at seeing his lady befuddled by his kisses. "Take good care of you, princess."

Another knock interrupted their moment. Anthony blew out a frustrated breath. "Are you kidding me? What the fuck?"

He got up and slid the door open. The car conductor stood there, a stern expression on his thin face.

"Tickets, please." He waited as Anthony handed over his and Sarah's tickets for inspection. The conductor noted the names.

"Miss Brown?" He looked at her.

Sarah was surprised to be singled out. "Yes?"

"One moment, please." The conductor walked down the aisle and then returned two minutes later with a package in his hands. He handed it to her. "I have instructions to deliver this to you."

She looked at the nearly two-foot-long rectangular box. "Who's it from? I don't see any name on it." She flipped it over, and Anthony looked about ready to pop a blood vessel as his first guess was, of course, *Christiansen!*

"I'm not privileged with that information, ma'am. The instruction simply said to deliver it upon your arrival." The conductor turned to leave. "Good day, ma'am. Sir." He moved down to the next car.

Anthony closed the door, finding the lock, and then pulled down the shade. He was tired of being interrupted and wanted some alone time with his woman. She had train fantasies he was ready to fulfill.

"So, what's in it?" He sat down across from her to give her room to open the box while he took a deep breath and counted to ten.

"I have no idea. I can't think of anyone who'd send me something on a train. Paul, maybe? But he didn't mention anything about another present in his card." Sarah began to rip the brown wrapping paper from the box.

"Great. Another present from Paul." Anthony wiped his face with his hand, trying not to overreact. *That prick and I need to have a little talk about boundaries!*

The box inside was plain and unmarked. Sarah popped the tape on the side and lifted the lid. Inside were layers of tissues. She moved the wrapping aside and reached in, locating a handle. She pulled it out.

"What the fuck is that?" Anthony looked at the red leather riding crop. *Christiansen sent his girl a fucking riding crop. What does that mean?*

Sarah turned as red as the leather and sputtered with laughter. The sound grew louder when she looked at Anthony's face.

"Okay, what's funny this time?" He was losing patience with another man trying to impress *his* girl.

"It's not from Paul, Anthony. It's from Elsa. No wonder she was laughing so much when we talked. I just thought she was excited about us coming to visit."

Relief eased the tight lines around his lips. "I don't get it. Why would she send you a riding crop? You ride horses back home in Texas or something?" His confusion was priceless.

The box fell off her lap and as she bent down to pick it up, Sarah saw a card fall out. It was addressed not to her, but to Anthony.

"Hmm. It's for you?" She handed the card over. Anthony opened it and sat back, reading. A slow smile spread across his face, getting bigger and bigger. One eyebrow came up, and then he chuckled.

He tossed the card aside and looked across at his beautiful Sarah. "Well, baby. Some seriously sexy instructions have been delivered and I'm apparently under obligation to carry them out." He slid the table back and dove across the space between the benches, scooping her up, causing her to squeal with delight. "Can't wait to meet your friend now. I like her already!"

She knew what the crop was for, and now, thanks to her very naughty friend, he knew too. At least it didn't appear as if she'd told him the whole tale, and that was good. It would always be their secret—hers and Elsa's. Still, thanks to her wonderful friend, it was going to be a very pleasurable ride to Berlin. *A very pleasurable ride, indeed.*

The Evolution of Elsa Kreiss
Book Two

A Very Familiar Monster

"What are all these red tags?" Elsa reached out to touch one attached to a vertical rectangular canvas featuring a black figure poking a blue-eyed boy in the back with a lion's head cane.

Paul immediately brightened. "Those indicate that the paintings have sold. Looks like not many are left untagged."

"There are numbers on them. What do they mean?"

"They mean that I purchased them. Number twelve is my number."

A tall gentleman with silver hair and pale blue eyes spoke from behind them. Elsa turned and looked at the man whose sharp features and long nose sat on an angular face. His mouth was a thin line, and his eyes emanated both power and cold detachment. His light gray suit had a patina to it, and the only color offsetting the gray palette was a light blue shirt. Even his tie was silvery gray.

Lukas reached out his hand in the age-old gesture of greeting. "Herr Ivchencko. Are you enjoying the evening so far?"

The Russian man refused the handshake and clapped Lukas on the arm, breaking their contact quickly. He was clearly uncomfortable with courtesy. "Yes, Trommler. I am." He eyed the canvas and then turned to Paul. "Truly amazing work, Christiansen. Would that all artists were so blessed with such talent." Again, his gaze returned to the painting completely unaware of the trace of offense that skittered through Paul's eyes. His 'talent' as the man referred to it was really a culmination, and exorcism of very bad experiences that no child should ever have to endure.

Ivchencko backed up from the painting and his glance caught Elsa. He turned to look at her directly. "And what do you think, my dear? Is this imagery not disturbing? Does it impress upon you the deepest horror of a young boy forever lost inside a nightmare?" He waited, his cold blue eyes boring into her.

Elsa didn't understand art, but she understood people, and this man barely hid what she knew was a love of pain. "I think it's sad. While I'm very happy for Paul and his success, to know people are drawn to this kind of thing shows that there is a festering disease of sick minds out there. These paintings weren't meant to be *appreciated*, they were meant as a means to dispel demons." She knew she'd let her mouth fly off without her brain, but something about this Russian struck her all wrong.

Lukas coughed, then interjected quickly. "As you see, the painting has struck quite a chord with our Elsa, a true sign of Christiansen's genius with a brush."

"Indeed." Ivchencko's eyes remained on Elsa longer than she was comfortable with, and she was glad when he turned back to Lukas. "I'll expect delivery to my home by tomorrow afternoon." He turned to Paul. "A pleasure, sir." He nodded his head, then turned to walk away.

"I'm sorry, Paul. I didn't mean to belittle your art." Elsa felt contrite.

Paul began to laugh. "Not at all, Kreiss. I couldn't have said it better myself." He reached out and tugged a lock of her hair in a brotherly manner. "That one there..." he looked at Ivchencko's retreating as he walked out the front door, "is a very familiar monster." His laughter ceased, and his eyes grew serious.

Sneak Peek

Chapter One

*P**skov, Russia*

Present Day

The bells of the church rang informing one and all it was time to begin Supplication. Congregants dropped what they were doing and walked to their rooms. Inside, they were all the same, a palette for a bed, a small table next to it with a lantern sitting on top and a chest of drawers. The walls were cold concrete, and dull, drab gray. One window with a cracked pane faced north over the courtyard below. The chill in the air permeated the thin glass and wind whistled through the crack. Gregor closed his door and went to his pallet. Beneath, he pulled out a length of knotted rope. It was thick and frayed at the ends. The color had turned from white to reddish brown over the years. Oxidation of the blood that covered it created the ghastly stained hue.

He removed his robe and folded it neatly, placing it on his bed. Then, he knelt on the gray stone floor and bowed his head. He began to pray. As he did, he lifted the rope in his hands and flung the knotted end over his shoulders one at a time, flagellating himself. Scars that had built upon themselves over the last ten years stood out stark white against his tanned back. With each prayer, he swung the rope. Skin split, and blood began to run in red rivulets down his backside soaking into his underwear. He knew he was supposed to clear his mind of all thoughts during Supplication. It was one of their rules pounded into his brain since he'd entered the Order of Rasputin at the tender age of sixteen by the will of his parents who could not afford to house and feed him anymore. The Order was an extremist offshoot of the Khlysty, a sect that practiced asceticism, or abstinence from worldly goods. It all bled from the Russian Orthodox Church, becoming more bizarre as it evolved into a close-minded, and sometimes brutal form of conservative Christianity. This Order revered Grigori Rasputin, the Holy man who was a favorite advisor to the Tsar and Tsarina of Russia during World War I. His death at the hands of those who viewed his influence over the Romanov monarchy as destructive was martyred in the inner-most sanctum of the Khlysty. Like Rasputin, all members of the Order were kept illiterate in his honor believing that worldly knowledge corrupted the otherwise sanctified vessels of God, his people. Religious teachings were handed down through verbal instructions and strict rituals. Questioning them was not allowed and doing so could end in a member's death by stoning.

Despite this, Gregor had difficulty clearing his mind and immersing himself in his prayers this day. Images of the young woman recently brought into the compound flooded his thoughts. She was the most beautiful creature he'd ever seen. Her flowing blonde hair and big blue eyes had pleaded with him for help as she was marched past him while he tended the garden. The two elevated members who each had hold of one of her arms barely looked in his direction as they forced the young woman through the doorway into the temple. One of them was Mikael, the guardian appointed by Holy Father Matteus. Mikael was beyond strict and seemed to revel in his role as guardian since it gave him the authority to administer punishment. Something he did on a regular basis and for the most minor of infractions. It boded badly for the lovely girl that she was in his hands.

Out of Gregor's sight, inside the temple, she'd been tied to a cross near the altar and stripped bare. They left her there during morning group prayer for all to see, stating her humiliation would help rid her of her worldly ways. She'd cried, and her tears caused a rush of heat to travel downward and settle into his groin.

Remembering this brought about the same reaction, and as Gregor continued to offer prayer on his lips, his hips bucked with each blow from the heavy rope. His erection strained against his dirty underwear, and the rub from the tightened material stimulated him. He swung harder, trying to clear his mind of his lustful thoughts, but nothing helped, and on his last round of verses, he climaxed. Panting heavily, he bowed his head and cried. Over and over, he begged God to forgive him for being weak. His bloody rope lay on the cold stone floor next to him, and his back bled freely. Rising, he picked up his robe and walked out of his room toward the communal showers. Taking a deep breath, he turned on the cold spray and walked beneath it feeling the sting. He clenched his teeth, and with both palms flat against the tiled wall, he cried once again. He didn't know how he would get her out of his mind, but he knew that after today, he was forever changed. He'd discovered pleasure, and knew that once discovered, he was now a corrupt vessel.

The only other thoughts he could entertain after this experience were how to have more of these feelings.

That night inside the temple, Irina Bromovich hung by her limbs. Pain wracked her entire body as the stress from being stretched and tied pushed her in and out of consciousness. She'd wet herself with no other way to relieve her bladder. She felt water being sponged onto her body and struggled to open her eyes. A young man was cleaning her legs. She could see the top of his dark head kneeling by her feet. His hand shook as he lifted the sponge to her thighs and squeezed the water out allowing it to wash away the urine. She whimpered.

Looking up, the young man caught her eye. He gave her a look of such reverence and apology before dipping the sponge back into the bucket and lifting it once again to her body. This time, he reached between her spread legs and pressed his hand to her privates. He squeezed, and water gushed up and then ran down her legs. The feeling of being cleaner was cancelled out by the fact that a stranger, one who was an accomplice in her kidnapping, was touching her inappropriately.

"Please," she cried. "Please let me go." Her blue eyes pleaded with him.

The young man continued to wash her legs, then his eyes traveled up to her naked belly and breasts. He stood, and ignoring her cries for help, began washing her there, too. Irina struggled with her ropes and cried. The more she struggled, the more he touched her until he finally dropped the sponge and reached out with only his bare hands. Her cries grew louder so he clamped a large hand over her mouth. She couldn't get away. He parted his robe and stepped closer. Fearing the worst, she began to scream into his hand. He pushed harder on her face, covering her nose, too, as he pushed himself on her. Not quite knowing what he was doing, he pushed his groin against hers, remembering a day long ago when he'd woken late in the night and had come upon his father on top of his mother. He didn't know then what was happening, but some part of his uneducated brain told him it was like this because his father seemed to enjoy it greatly. Her screams and struggles spurred him on and lasted only moments longer. Then, she went limp. Still, Gregor bucked until that feeling found him once again. He backed up and gave her a little shake. She didn't respond. He shook her again, then slapped her face, but there were no signs of life. Her lips were blue and hung slack.

Eyes growing large, Gregor backed away looking around the temple. No one was inside at this time. Still, he had to make sure. He searched every corner and once satisfied no one had seen what he'd just done, he snuck quietly out of the side door. He knew he would have to leave. Staying was not an option. Tears stung his eyes as he realized he'd killed her. He'd killed the beautiful woman. He hadn't meant to, but her cries would have woken someone, and he would not have been able to touch her anymore, and he couldn't resist touching her. She was all he'd thought about all day, and the obsession to see her again, to feel her skin, and experience that pleasure was too much to resist, so he'd succumbed to his dark desires. Now, those desires had killed. Strangely, the only thing he was sorry about was that he would not get to touch her again.

He slipped into his room where he packed up the few belongings he owned. He'd have to find his way beyond the walls of the Order somehow. Staying meant certain death. He kept to the shadows until he reached the gate. There, he opened it wide enough only for him to fit through. He closed it behind him so no alarm would be raised. Down the road leading away from the compound, Gregor considered his options. He hadn't been outside in ten years. He didn't know if anything he knew back then might still be as it was. He had a cousin who lived five miles outside of Pskov, the town he grew up in along the river Velikaya in western Russia, and so he made his way in that direction. Ivan would help him. They'd once been close, before Gregor's parents had committed him to the Order. Ivan's parents ran a successful farm so ridding themselves of their child had never crossed their minds. He was lucky, Ivan. His parents loved him enough to keep him. Gregor's parents, however, did not. If they had, then his father would've found a way to earn money, or maybe given Gregor the chance to find a job and help contribute to the family. Why his father and mother had chosen, instead, to hide him away in a religious Order was beyond him. He had little memory of his early years. Those that he did retain were of hardships, no money for food, his father drunk, and his mother taking in washing to try to earn a few coins. They weren't worth recalling.

The night air hung heavily, chilling his bones. It was at least ten miles to Ivan's home. He hoped he remembered how to get there. He kept himself company on his long journey with thoughts of the woman, how it had felt to touch a female for the first time. He knew he liked it and he wanted more. But for now, he needed to secure his most basic needs, lodging, food, and a job. After that, he could figure out how to indulge his growing desire for the female flesh.

Read more (visit my website at micheleegwynnauthor.com) The Evolution of Elsa Kreiss . . . US. UK. CA. AU. DE.

Also By Michele E. Gwynn

Visit my website for these books plus updates on upcoming releases! Oh, and get a FREE book or two! micheleegwynnauthor.com.

Checkpoint Novels

Exposed: The Education of Sarah Brown (novel)
The Evolution of Elsa Kreiss (novel)
The Redemption of Joseph Heinz (novel)
The Making of Herman Faust (prequel novella)

Green Beret Series

Rescuing Emma (18+)
Loving Leisl
Freeing Fatima
Saving Christmas
Loving Freddie
Saving Major Morgan (A Green Beret Series prequel novella)

The Soldiers of PATCH-COM

Secondhand Soldier (18+)
Second Chance Soldier

Second Breath Soldier
Silent Night Soldier
C'est la Vie Soldier

The Harvest Trilogy

Harvest
Hybrids
Census

Section 5 (A Harvest Trilogy Spinoff)

Stand Alones

Darkest Communion (Paranormal Romance, 18+)
Waiting a Lifetime (Contemporary Romance, Mystical)
Hiring John (Romantic Comedy 18+)